Pointless

Pointless

MARISSA HOWARD

Published in the United States of America
ISBN: 978-0-9985935-6-2
Fiction
19.11.15

Love is worth the fight.

1

THEN

It's colder than I thought it would be.

The black is blacker, the silence more hushed, and the motion—my breath, breathing in and out—motionless.

The emptiness fills me up until I can't breathe, punches a hand in my chest and turns, slowly, grinding the air from my lungs into pieces.

Two pieces. Three.

One hundred.

I take a deep breath and look up, and I imagine the ceiling is the sky. The curved walls, the cold rock that I cannot see, is the sky. A black sheet stretched across, pulled taut, with hundreds of burning stars.

I take comfort in that for a moment, and my mind almost believes it. But then the stone comes back into focus, the jagged corners and sloping edges.

It's not the sky. It will never be the sky.

The clock on my wrist ticks silently and I can't see it, but I can feel it. The days slowly becoming hours, the hours becoming minutes, and soon—the minutes becoming seconds.

The timer started at three days. That was 2 days, 23 hours, 54 minutes, and 55 seconds ago.

Five...four...three...two...one.

Make that 2 days, 23 hours, 55 minutes.

It's almost time.

I press my hands to the floor, run my fingers over the surface. Close my eyes, open them again. Silently count the seconds in my mind. My mother always said I was good with numbers. She was wrong. I'm the best.

I reach up, and my fingers feel the neck of my jacket. Thin, so I feel the intense pain of the cold. I shrug it off. Pack it into a ball and tuck it under my arm.

Some of the others have gone crazy wrapped in complete darkness for three days with no food and only the water that drips from the ceiling. Abandoned, alone, so much so that they began to think they weren't. They saw people, shadows in the black, heard laughter bounce off the walls.

They screamed, pounded the walls until their fists were bloody. Red stains that would never be seen.

They asked themselves questions, over and over again.

How am I supposed to live in this darkness for the rest of my life?

That was their first mistake. You never ask questions. It will only make you start to think the question means more than the answer.

Two minutes.

I rock onto my feet and extend my legs, stretch one out, then the other. Put one hand on the wall in front of me. I feel the crack—slender, sloped from the top of the wall to the bottom.

I remember this crack. Three days ago, when the stone door was shut and locked from the outside—I could hear the *click*—this crack held the last bit of light that I saw. It was a small sliver, nothing more than the size of a strand of hair, but it stayed light until it faded with the first night. It never lit up again. They must have shoved something in it so no light would get through.

One minute.

I take a step away from the door and stand there, facing it. My stomach growls but I ignore it. Not now. Not here. I bury the hunger, push it far beneath my thoughts, just like I have done for almost seventy-two hours.

You only need food if your mind thinks you do.

I rub my face with the jacket under my arm, a quick swipe to remove the dirt and the gray. They're coming. Forty-five seconds. Only fifteen seconds more.

I don't move, my arms and legs brace for the door. For the bright, burning light—like the fake stars.

Five...four...three...two.

I hear a *click*, a piece of metal lifting, then falling against the door.

One.

The door shifts, stops for a moment, then opens slowly, slowly. It's stone. It takes four people to open it.

The light is a line at first, dividing the ground in front of me into two separate worlds: dark, and darker. It starts to grow, becomes thicker, makes the dark world smaller and smaller. I blink, and my eyes water from looking at it. The first light I've seen in three days. I don't shield my eyes.

The door is halfway open now, and it stops. I can see the front of the cave, bathed in blue-gray. I slept in the left corner. I can hear the wind, feel the warm air on my skin. A bird chirps from somewhere outside. And then: a voice.

"You may exit."

I stare at the door for a moment, the jacket still balled up in my hand. I drop it. I move to the door, hear the echo of my footsteps on the walls.

I step out.

My eyes fill with color—the golden sun, green trees, a large brown building in the distance. And the wall—redbrick, twenty feet high, stretching from one side of my sight to the other. Surrounding us, like the darkness that surrounded me for three days.

The darkness that I defeated.

A round face with thick, square glasses steps in front of me. "Contender number six of forty-six. You completed your first challenge—well done. State your age and your name."

I stand up straighter, stare past the thick panes of glass and into her eyes.

3

"My name is Jonathan Dabir. I'm sixteen years old." I swallow. I need to give her something more—a reason to remember me. To choose me. I take a breath. "And I'm going to become the leader that saves humanity."

2

NOW

I remember what love was like. It was a thudding chest, sticky palms, a burning heat that seemed to come from my veins. It was the curve of a smile, the length of a laugh.

It was the look in Nash's eyes before I betrayed him.

I wanted to remember, but I wanted to forget. And in this darkness, it wasn't hard. Anything was possible in darkness.

Seconds ticked slowly against the smooth gray walls.

It was cold—so cold. Colder than I remembered it. I missed the air, the way the sun would give you goose bumps even though you were warm. I missed our beds in the branches of the trees. I missed Gavin, and Dalia, and Theodore, and Alese. I wondered if they were okay, locked outside the Dome, in the world. Even though they believed him.

Even though they thought I was a monster.

Memories—they were just memories. And I needed to push them away. The deep hurt on Nash's cheeks. And Branch's eyes. They still filled my mind with the golden color of corn when the sun shines on it from the sky. Those eyes— gentle, understanding, full of laughter. And horrified. Horrified when they provided fake proof that I was the traitor. I didn't want to think about Branch. When I did, the pain I felt was stronger than the bindings on my wrists.

I stared up at the ceiling. Pretended it was the sky. Blue,

cotton clouds, yellowed edges from the sun. But it wasn't the sky. It would never be the sky.

I pushed the thoughts from my mind, then pulled them back again. Pushed, pulled, pushed, pulled. I wanted to forget them, erase them from my memory. But I needed them. Without them, I wouldn't survive.

The door opened with a bang, and I lifted my head from the long, gray cart I was tied to. With wheels, so they could push me from one room to another. I felt a cold sweat form on my neck.

Fearless. I'm fearless.

A person appeared, with hair as black as the air. Mr. Dabir smiled—a thick, superior smile.

"Hello, Laney. I hope I'm not disturbing your...peace and quiet." The corner of his mouth twitched at his joke.

I said nothing.

"Oh, don't be sour, Laney. You have permission to speak now. That should make you"—he paused—"appreciative."

I said nothing again. It had been one week. One week in complete darkness, with food and water shoved under the door. One week without seeing anything or hearing anyone. And here, now, I wished I was back in the darkness again. I couldn't even look at him—the man who had convinced people to pretend to be crazy, who used the notebook of a dead man for the script of his game, and who locked my friends out of the Dome, locked them out of a door that could be opened only from the inside. The man who convinced them I was the bad one. Just so he could be leader again—the leader of a gray people with blank eyes and white skin.

I breathed in, then out, slowly.

The man who had stolen everything from me. Including love.

Mr. Dabir shrugged at my silence. "Your loss. It was going to be a great day."

I watched him—his pale skin, smooth and shining. His gray eyes sweeping over the room. I wondered what had

6

happened in his life that made him want to lock people in rooms of stone.

He stopped suddenly, stepped over to the door, put his hand on the slender knob. He pushed it open, stepped out into the hallway, and let the door go. It bounced a few times, and I heard his footsteps growing softer as he turned the corner and disappeared. But the door didn't click like I had grown used to hearing the thirteen years I had lived in this Dome, before we went to the world above. They always clicked when they closed.

Which meant this one was open.

I pulled one arm, then the other, tried to squeeze my fingers through the knots on my wrists. They were tight, and they pressed against my skin. I bit my lip in pain.

Pain is only in my mind. It's not real.

The door wasn't locked. This was my chance.

I squeezed my fingers in my palms, then stretched them out again, pulling harder each time I did. I put my hand beneath my thigh, pressing on the rope with my leg for support. I pulled, pulled. Just a little harder.

The rope bit through my skin, and I gasped. I rubbed my wrist against my pants, hoped it wasn't bleeding too hard. In the darkness, it was impossible to tell.

Footsteps, outside. I stopped moving and could only hear my breath, hot against the air. The footsteps grew louder, then softer again. I pulled, hard.

The rope twisted and broke under the weight, silent. I only had the feeling of a sudden weightlessness to convince me I was free. Well, half-free.

I tugged at my other hand, pinched the rope, and pulled. The rope broke easily. I reached down, felt for the cords tied around my feet. I untied them clumsily. Then I brought my hands to my head. They had placed something here—wrapped some sort of wire configuration across my forehead and around to the back of my neck. I pinched the sides of the wire, pulled. The pain shot across my skull.

How long had it been? Seconds, hours? The head thing

could wait.

I swung my legs to the side of the cart and touched them to the ground. Gray tunneled into the black, and I put my hand against the wall to steady myself. My eyes cleared, and I stood. Felt along the wall for the door Mr. Dabir had come in through, and the door he had gone out of.

I felt rock, rock, rock—the smooth, slightly sloped surface of the door. Hand down, farther. Cold metal. Grasped it, pushed down.

Click.

I pushed the door forward, blinked from the light—it wasn't much, but it was something. A torch on the wall in front of me, pulsing like a heartbeat. I had never been so grateful for that torch.

I took a step, then another. I shut the door behind me slowly, but in the silence the *click* echoed against the floor.

I froze for a moment. Listened. And then I ran.

I didn't recognize this part of the Dome—no doors, just a long, blank hallway that led to the one I had been in. The stairs. Where were the stairs? I needed to get out. I needed to find Alese, Gavin, Dalia, Theodore, and Branch as much as I needed the sunlight, the air.

My legs were stiff, but I went faster. The hallway stretched farther, longer, with no doors or curves or turns. Where was I?

I sucked in a deep breath, heard my feet pounding the cold floor. A door. I could see a door.

I ran toward it, stretched my fingers to the handle, opened it. And light—bright, blinding light—smashed into me like a wall. I blinked, pressed my hands against my eyes. The light was white, like the sun. But it wasn't warm.

I blinked, opened my eyes. Closed them again. Things started to come into focus. Chairs, with stubby legs pressed against the ground. A platform, wood slapped to its sides and edges so it would be longer, larger. And people. Sitting in the chairs, their heads turned to me.

Mr. Dabir stepped in front of me. Spread his hands out

wide. "Well, what do we have here? An escapee?"

His eyes were wide, but his lips sloped up, into his cheeks. He didn't look surprised—he looked amused. Then, slowly, he started clapping. A girl with short black hair stepped next to him—Blakely—and he smiled. Spoke only so the three of us could hear.

"Mark the results. Contender one of eighty-one. Trial one: the source of hope."

Blakely nodded, opened a notebook in her hand. I swallowed against the liquid in my throat. It was Adrian's. The front of the notebook had been ripped out, so only the last half of it remained. They had removed Adrian's diary entrees. Blakely had some sort of device in her other palm— something digital, with information flashing across a screen. She was copying it over to the white pages.

Mr. Dabir's voice grew louder, and he turned to the people. "Everyone, take a look. This is an example of what will happen if you have hope. It will be destroyed."

I breathed in, took a step back without meaning to. He left the door open on purpose. I should have known. The light around me was softer now, and I realized it was torches— hundreds of them, lining the walls and licking the silent air.

"Do you like them?" Mr. Dabir was watching me. "I figured, why not? We've been in the dark for so long."

He smiled a sick, twisted smile.

I opened my mouth, anger growing inside me, making me hot. And then someone in the audience stood. Graying hair that used to be brown, the sides and ends almost blending into the Dome's walls. Her skin was pulled tight, sucked in like she hadn't eaten in weeks. Delma.

And she had wires wrapped around her head.

I sucked in a breath. My eyes fell to her hands. They were bound tightly with a thick brown rope. I looked across the people, squinting in the light. Hands, more hands, all twisted with rope around the skin. Everyone—all the people in the chairs—had their hands tied and a gray mass of wire around their heads.

9

I looked at Mr. Dabir, and his words flashed in my mind. *Contender one of eighty-one.*

Eighty-one.

Eighty-one people handcuffed, including me. He was—he was doing *trials* on them too?

"Oh, you noticed." Mr. Dabir raised his eyebrows, looked like he was about to share a big secret. "Well, I might as well tell you what the purpose of all of this"—he stretched his arms out toward the people—"is." He stroked his chin. "I'm running trials on all of you. To find the source of love, and all its symptoms. I do this by measuring your brain—which parts of it are affected by which feelings." He leaned forward, tapped my wire with his finger, and didn't step back. His voice was low now—a whisper, angry and short. "And when I do, I'll have the means to destroy it. Again, and again, and again. Every time it pops back up into this world, until love is gone for good."

He took a deep breath, composed himself, and smiled.

I felt dizzy again, my heart pounding in my head. I took another step back. "You're insane."

Mr. Dabir's eyes lit up. "I *knew* you'd talk to me eventually. I told you it was going to be a great day."

He turned to Blakely, then motioned to the people in the chairs. "We're done here. Take them back to their indents."

Blakely nodded and looked past the people. There was movement on the platform in the center of the room, and for the first time that platform came into focus. Eight chairs, with pillows on each seat. And seven people sitting in each, with confidence on their faces and light in their eyes. Arms free and heads without wires.

The seven Mr. Dabir had convinced to pretend to be crazy in the world above. Blakely, Arsen, Brooke, Emily, and three others I recognized but didn't know. The new teachers and leaders of humanity.

My eyes stopped on the eighth chair. Nash was sitting there, feet stretched out in front of him and arms crossed. His eyes were on mine, watching me. I felt a rope wrap around my wrists, my arms being pulled back to the hallway. A white-hot ache shot up to my shoulders and my face scrunched in pain. As I walked through the door, I looked back at him, one more time.

He didn't blink.

3

THEN

I remember the day they told my mother I had potential to be one of the leaders of humanity when the world is destroyed.

It was cloudy, gray, and when they knocked on the door, my mother dropped a plate. It was any day now. Any day that the hate—the men with black eyes—would take over our town, just like they had with so many others.

We never knew they had a plan—a go-to if the world really was destroyed. We never knew until that day.

"We've been watching him in school," the woman with glasses as thick as a window said. "We have…an opportunity for him."

It was a formality, really. They could take me even if she said no. They were our leaders, and they could do anything they wanted. My mother didn't love me, anyway. No one loved since they'd banned it decades ago. So she didn't care when they told me to pack up the few things I had, get in their black car, and drive to a big brown building in the middle of a huge red wall.

Here. Where I am right now.

I peel off my shirt and gray cotton pants and let them fall to the floor. My eyes rest on the pile of gray stained with black and brown. Things get dirty when you're in a cave for three days straight. I would have to wash them later.

I step into the small stone shower in the corner of the

room. The hot water runs over my skin and I do everything I can to keep from thanking it out loud.

The glass is clear, and I look out at the room as I scrub shampoo into my hair. A small bed against the wall. A simple wooden nightstand, straight edges with a circle on top. And this shower.

They told us this is what the rooms in the Dome look like. They created this large brown building to be an exact replica of the inside of the Dome. So we could get used to it, they said. Be as ready as possible.

If we're chosen, one day, we'll see the real Dome—an old, underground war bunker the leaders of society found and are completely transforming as we speak. Well, as much as you can transform something super old and underground. Splendid, they call it.

Only eleven of us will be chosen, will get to have a place in the Dome, as leaders, when the world is on the brink of destruction. The rest of us will die. There are forty-six of us.

I shut off the water abruptly.

I'll be one of the eleven. I'll do whatever it takes.

I run a towel over my hair and drop it to the floor. Three minutes, thirteen seconds. That's how long I have before the next challenge.

I pick up my shirt from the ground and shake it out once, then pull it over my head. I do the same with my pants, and then shoes. And when I flick the switch that opens the door to my "indent"—what they call it—I don't look back. There are no mirrors here, and I don't need one. It's all in your head. If you look your best in your mind, you'll look your best in body too.

The others are leaving their indents and I fall into step beside them. We don't look at each other, don't speak. The leaders of society have done intense studies over the past year about peace, and they came to the conclusion that silence is the way to peace. Gray is the color of peace, which is why everything is gray. And—unrelated, but relevant— competitors are much more likely to try their hardest when

13

they don't know who they're competing against.

I imagine those next to me are people with black eyes—people I need to beat at all costs. And maybe even destroy.

"Challenge two." The woman with glasses claps her hands together as we close in on her in the center of the building, all forty-six of us. Her voice echoes—it's a huge room, with all of us standing around a large, wooden platform. She's on the wood next to a man with a receding hairline and a square jaw, and he's next to another man, smaller, with black hair and red dots on his face. Pimples spread across his forehead and chin. I can't help but wonder who chose these people to lead society. Maybe they chose themselves.

"You all know that the Dome will be dark—it's underground, of course. This was the purpose of the first challenge, a challenge that four people failed. We began with fifty, as you all know." She brings one hand up to her short, curly hair and smooths it down. It's orange, like the sun when it's at the edge of the sky, before it disappears into blackness.

Her hand gets caught in the curls, and someone in the audience snickers. Glasses Lady looks up. Her eyes snap to the person, a girl with red hair, like the leaves during fall, and she raises one finger, points to the door.

"Out."

The girl immediately looks like she regrets it. Her eyes widen, her face pales. She takes a breath, and then another. The air is silent, and she finally opens her mouth. "Excuse me?"

"I said, out." Glasses Lady doesn't look away.

"I didn't—I didn't mean it." The girl is fumbling her words, wringing her hands like they're filled with water and she needs to squeeze it all out. Glasses Lady doesn't move.

"If you don't leave right this moment, I will deliver you personally to someone with black eyes."

The girl sucks in her breath. She looks around, at all of us. Then she turns quickly, on her heel, and I hear footsteps echo on the walls as she walks out of the room. The door shuts loudly behind her.

Forty-five.

Glasses Lady looks at all of us, smooths her shirt, and smiles. "Now, where was I? Oh, yes. Challenge two." She folds her hands and rests them carefully on the podium in the middle of the platform. "This one is hypothetical. You choose the best answer, you win. But there is purpose behind it, I assure you. Listen closely."

I don't move, my feet rooted to the ground beneath me. I clench my fists. Glasses Lady's eyes meet mine for a moment as she sweeps the room, back and forth.

"Put yourself in this situation: The world is at the peak of destruction. You are running to the Dome with only a few minutes until the destruction is unavoidable. You may choose one animal to bring with you down into the Dome. Just one. You will need this animal—it will be imperative to the survival of the people in the Dome. Which one is it?"

Glasses Lady pauses for a few seconds. She lets her words hang in the air.

"We have released a few animals into the Oval. The first person to capture the correct animal and bring it back to me will win the challenge. And as you know, when you win"— she smiles—"you are one step closer to being chosen as one of the eleven leaders of the Dome."

My heart starts to beat, slowly, and I push the sound of it out of my head. One animal. Just one. Which animal is imperative to human survival?

"You have ten minutes. Starting now." Glasses Lady brings her wrist in front of her and presses a button on her watch. Even though I know it's impossible, I swear I can hear the beeping of seconds as they tick down, one by one.

I turn to the door half a second before everyone else. I'm in the lead already.

I jog out the door that leads into the hallway instead of sprinting, so I look like I'm confident. Like I have much more time than I need. But my mind is spinning.

I'm the third person to reach the door to the outside, and I push it open with my palms. The warm air fills my chest and

I take a deep breath. This is the difference between the real Dome and our replica: once we're in the real one, we won't be able to go outside.

I stop for a second and take in my surroundings. All the land in between the redbrick wall is the Oval—green grass, trees, the caves. The wall stretches around it all at a slope, like an egg. It makes a perfect oval shape, which is where it got its name.

I see a person next to me, short blond hair and too-white skin, trying to coax a squirrel out of a tree. Someone in front of me is running toward a horse grazing on some grass a few hundred feet away. The rest are still piling out the door.

One animal. One. An animal that humans need to survive.

I squint into the sun and look around me. A large black bird shrieks as it passes by, and I can see that one wing is bent—secured with some sort of pin—probably put there by the leaders so it can't fly away. An animal three times my height, cream-colored with brown spots, chomps on leaves in a tree to my left, not even noticing the chaos around it. A giraffe, I recognize it from school. I almost laugh. Good luck getting *that* back inside. A yellow-and-black snake hisses from beside a bush to my right. I frown. Definitely not that.

Almost all the other contenders are staying next to the building, grabbing the animals closest to them. At least if they get an animal, they have a chance at being right—I can guess that's what they're telling themselves. You come back empty-handed, you're screwed.

Seven minutes, fifteen seconds left.

I see a clump of tall, leafy trees in the distance moving slightly, and an animal darts inside. The leaders would make sure the correct animal wasn't easy to find, to catch. I run toward it.

When I reach the trees, another minute has passed. I have to make this fast.

I step inside and immediately feel ten degrees cooler. The leaves form a ceiling overhead and because of it, the grass looks blue instead of green.

A stick snaps to my left, and I turn toward it. Nothing. I follow the sound, pushing back clusters of leaves and invisible spiderwebs that I can feel on my face and arms. A spider isn't considered an animal, is it?

I hear my feet crunching the leaves on the ground and push past a bush, the branches stinging my arms and leaving a few red scrapes.

Four minutes left. I don't have time for this. Maybe everyone else is right—there are dozens of animals out there in the open. All for the taking.

I turn around and alter my path back slightly so I don't have to step through the bush again. Or the spiderwebs, hopefully. But before I push through the last tree, I see movement. I turn and it's there, just past a gnarled tree trunk on my right. A gray-brown ball of fur, no bigger than a dog, with pointed ears and a black nose. A coyote.

I stand there for a moment, watching it. It doesn't even notice me. Its head is moving up and down, up and down, and its mouth is opening and closing. It's eating something. Something—black. With feathers?

I swallow as I realize what it is. The bird I saw. The bird with one good wing. Well, at least their theory of making sure it couldn't fly worked. A little too well, to say the least.

I start to turn, in no mood to stay here and waste time when it's almost up. And then I stop. I look back at the coyote, mouth turned to the sky like it's chomping the air. And I have the answer.

There's no time to pretend like the challenge will be easy anymore. This time, I sprint.

I make it back to the center of the brown building with forty-five seconds to spare. Almost everyone is back already, and it's chaos. A squirrel leaps from the grip of a person next to me and she shrieks, lunges toward it. A boy with red-brown hair holds a bird tightly, hands cupped over it, and I wonder if it can breathe. Another boy, a few years older, is pulling a large pig across the floor. He tied a rope around its neck.

17

Glasses Lady is still on the podium, surveying it all with no emotion on her face. She looks at her watch, but I don't need to. Seven seconds.

She clasps her hands together again, smooths her hair, and looks at her watch one more time.

Two. One.

"Time is up." Her voice is sharp, and it causes even the pig to jump. "You will each come up to me, one by one, and tell me your answer."

She nods at the person closest to her, and we all form a line behind him. I'm near the back, and I silently curse myself. So much for being memorable.

I count twenty-three minutes before I reach the front of the line. By now, the girl with the squirrel and the boy with the bird have left, taken their animals back outside. They were wrong. I can tell by the looks on their faces as they walk out.

"Well?" Glasses Lady looks at me as the most recent failure heads to the door. "You brought me nothing. Do you have anything to say for yourself?"

I just stand there. I'm trying to think of words, trying to form a sentence, but I can't. The animals around me are too loud, and the people trying to make them be quiet are louder.

"You failed the second challenge." Glasses Lady looks past me, like I'm wasting her time. "Next."

"Wait."

Her eyes flit back to mine.

"Yes, I brought you nothing. On purpose. I have your answer."

Her eyebrows raise, just barely. But she's interested now. I look back at her.

"The answer is myself. *I'm* imperative to the survival of the people in the Dome. The animal is a human. It's me."

I can feel my chest breathing, in and out. It's right. I can tell by the sudden shift in her eyes.

She looks down at a paper in front of her, then back at me. "Jonathan Dabir, is it?"

I nod. "You can call me Jonathan."

18

"Well, Jonathan." She places her folded hands directly in front of her. "You're wrong. Next."

I blink. I can't be wrong. That has to be the answer. Just like the coyote ate the fluffy black bird. You can trust only yourself.

I take a step to the side, only because I don't want Glasses Lady to get mad and kick me out like she did that other girl.

"Jonathan. Let's tell her our real answer."

I look beside me, jolted from my thoughts. There's only one more person in line. A girl, with long blond hair that falls in curls around her shoulders. It's so blond, so deeply yellow, that it almost looks dark—is dark blond a thing? Her face is turned to me—sharp chin, round nose—and her eyes meet mine. They're green, like the trees. And it takes me a second to realize she has just spoken to me.

"Um...what?"

Her eyes are wide, like they're trying to tell me something. She motions me toward her, and my feet clumsily move. When I'm next to her, she turns to Glasses Lady, spreads her hands out, and smiles.

"The answer is each other." Her cheeks are pink, her voice breathless, like she had just been running. "None of us can survive without other humans around us, to help us and to keep us on track. So when we only have a few minutes to get to the Dome, we take as many people as we can with us. Not animals." She pauses, takes a breath. "People."

Glasses Lady is watching her closely, and her eyes move to me, then back to the girl again. The girl looks at me.

"So I brought Jonathan. And he brought me."

Glasses Lady doesn't move. Her face is motionless, her nose pointed to the sky, like the coyote's was. And then she unclasps her hands, spreads them wide, and starts clapping. The two other men on the podium join her, the sound echoing through the large room. She stops, her eyes bright.

"Contenders four and six of forty-five. You completed the second challenge. Well done, Jonathan and..." She trails off, and her eyes fall to the list in front of her.

19

"Hope." The girl next to me speaks.

Glasses Lady looks up, nods. "Hope." She writes something on the sheet of paper, then stands and walks over to the man with pimples.

Hope looks at me quickly and mouths *thank you*, and it takes me the fourteen seconds she turns, steps past the animals, and walks out the door, her blond hair falling behind her shoulders, to realize what has just happened.

I hear a sound, and above the door, on a torch nailed high up on the wall, I see a bird perched, broken free from its restraints. I wonder how they'll ever catch it.

4

NOW

The sun was shining so bright I could almost feel it, a hazy piece of yellow in a blue cotton sky. I was on a rock in the middle of the water where I had convinced the people to hold hands and step from rock to rock, to make it across. And they had made it. They had made it because of me. But I didn't see any people this time.

The water was rushing beneath me like fire. Blues, purples, reds, greens, all swirling under me, spreading onto the stones and soaking my feet.

I took a deep breath, looked forward. The water tunneled downhill, past rocks and dirt, and then stopped abruptly. Just stopped, like it was cut in half and the rest of it was thrown into the fire. I could hear water pounding the ground somewhere far below.

A waterfall. That wasn't here before.

I felt something grip my hand, and warmth spread through my fingertips up to my neck. I looked over, to my side.

Branch.

He was holding my hand, his blond hair blowing in the wind and his golden eyes on mine. Relief flooded through me.

"Branch, you're okay." My voice was breathless, and the spray of the water all but drowned it out. He smiled.

"You need to jump, Laney!"

I gripped his hand, planted my feet on the rocks as a wave rushed over my feet. This time, it reached my ankles. I nodded, braced myself to leap from my rock to his. He shook his head.

"Not here."

I looked around me. There were no other rocks. The only pathway was his, the one he was standing on. I looked at him again, and his eyes were on mine. Then they moved slowly to the water.

"There."

In the water? I was confused. Branch would never want me to jump to my death. He had saved me.

I shook my head, the spray stinging my eyes.

Branch said nothing for a moment. Then he spoke. "You have to. There is no other way."

I looked down, at the smooth gray rock he was standing on, square-shaped, just big enough for the two of us.

"There's room on your rock, Branch. Please—help me."

Branch looked at me, his eyes on mine, like he was studying me. His face was a mix of sympathy and...amusement. Why was he amused?

"You always take the easy way, don't you?"

His words caught me off guard. I tried to keep my balance, but I felt my foot slipping.

"Branch, I don't have time—"

Hands. I felt hands pushing against my back, taking away any sort of balance I had left. And I realized my hand was cold. Branch wasn't holding it anymore.

I sucked in my breath, looked back as I plunged in the bitter water, pulled under and over and under again. I screamed, but water filled my throat instead of air. I pushed past the waves, tumbled to the top of the water, and my head surfaced.

I could see his face. Dark blond hair, eyes the color of the canyon walls. Not golden. Not Branch.

It was Nash.

His head was cocked, and his mouth was in a crooked

grin. The waves lapped at his ankles, but he didn't seem to notice. He raised his hand and waved.

And then I felt air. I was free-falling, tumbling down, my heart in my throat.

I heaved in a breath and opened my eyes. I pushed myself to a seated position and saw a room. Gray walls, a gray door. A cold silver cart underneath my skin. Rough rope tied to my hands and feet. My chest was moving, in and out, and I could feel my heart beating.

It was just a dream. Laney, it was just a dream.

When they had pushed me back in the room at the end of the long hallway and tied me to the cart again, I had suddenly felt very tired. I had fallen asleep, with the wires pressing against the back of my neck.

The light was on.

A small, round light in the middle of the ceiling. It was flickering in and out, like the bulb was about to die. But it was light. I had been drowning in darkness for days.

Drowning. Like my dream. Drowning, because of Nash.

I pushed the image of his face from my mind and tried to cling to the image of Branch's. Tried to remember the feeling of his hand holding tightly to mine.

I took a deep breath, then another. My heartbeat was slowing, and the air was silent. I couldn't hear anyone walking in the hallway outside.

All at once the morning came back to me. The fake escape, how it had only been a trial in Mr. Dabir's sick love experiment. I sucked in my breath. *The trials.* He had tied up everyone, was holding them and doing experiments on them, not just me. How long had I been asleep? I needed to get out, now more than ever.

I gripped my hands into balls and pulled, twisted them left and right, but this time the ropes didn't budge. They must have tied them tighter, or maybe they had used a stronger rope.

Delma's eyes filled my mind. When she had looked at me, they had almost looked like just another feelingless person's eyes. The color, draining like the air from the Dome. A face that was losing hope.

Then Mr. Dabir's words, eating at my skin: *Everyone, take a look. This is an example of what will happen if you have hope. It will be destroyed.*

If he was tying me up, playing games with me so I confused his experiment with reality, then what was he doing to them? I needed out. Now.

I pulled again and again, until I could feel my wrists start to bleed. They felt raw, like the way ice-cold water feels when it touches your skin.

Voices. I could hear them in the hallways, bouncing off the echoes of footsteps. I turned my head to the door.

"...isn't the same. They're scared, and that's altering the results of the trials. Their fear is getting in the way."

"We can fix that, you know." Another voice, a man's. The first voice was Mr. Dabir. I think the second was—I strained my neck. Was it Arsen?

"What do you have in mind?"

Pause. Then the second voice again.

"Follow me. I'll show you."

This time, it was unmistakable. The second voice was Nash's. So he was really helping Mr. Dabir. He was one of them now. It was true.

I blinked, lay frozen there for a moment. I clenched my fingers in and out, pushed back hot tears from my eyes. And then, in the flickering of the light, I saw something. A thin carpet of yellows and whites and greens was scattered across the floor.

Flowers. There were flowers covering my floor. How had I not noticed that before?

Many of them were wilted, barely flowers anymore. Most of them had only one or two petals clinging to their stems. They were the same colors that Branch had brought to the clearing in his arms, the same colors we had handed out to the people, one by one, to give them courage.

It had to be those flowers. I had seen them on the ground

when Mr. Dabir pushed me to the center of the Dome and blamed the paper book on me. I wondered when the people had dropped them—before or after Theodore provided the "proof," the false paper book that was actually Adrian's?

When had the flowers been brought to this room? And why were they here?

Even wilting, almost dead, they made my heart beat faster. They made me think of the time Theodore had planted flowers around my tree in the world above, just because he wanted to make me smile. The time Branch had held one out to me in his fingers. Golden, like my flowers. Like the flowers from my childhood.

I swallowed. A game. The flowers had to be part of the game—the trials, the experiment, whatever he called it. The game to find the source of love. I couldn't let it get to me.

I lay back on the cold surface of the cart and planted my hands by my sides. I lifted my fingers, one by one, and listened to the tapping sound as they hit the surface of gray lightly. *Tap. Tap. Tap.* I could only hit so hard because of the pressure on my wrists. But I would keep going. I would keep tapping until someone came in and took the flowers away. I wouldn't let him get to me. It was all part of the game. It was all part of the—

"Laney?"

I lifted my head. Stopped tapping. Red hair like Theodore's except long, past her shoulders. Emily. The girl who had let go of my hand so I fell in the water. The girl who had almost killed me.

She held the door open halfway, with one foot in the room and the other in the hallway. Her eyes were wide.

"I'm supposed to..." Her voice trailed off, and she stopped for a second. Her eyes were on me, and she couldn't look away. Then she blinked, stood up straighter, gained confidence in her voice. "I'm supposed to bring you food."

I didn't feel like talking to her. I was getting tired again. And she almost killed me, there was that.

"Most people just set it next to me." My voice came out

25

louder than I thought it would, but it was strained. I set my head back down on the cart.

I heard Emily's breath, and then her footsteps, walking toward me.

I jerked my neck up again. "The flowers."

Emily stopped in the middle of the room. "What?"

"The flowers." My heart was beating fast, but I forced it to slow. "You're stepping on the flowers."

I didn't want to care, didn't want to feel every petal that was crushed beneath Emily's shoes. But I did.

Emily looked down at the ground, then back at me. "That's not funny, Laney. I was trying to be nice, you know."

What? I wasn't trying to be funny. I lifted my neck higher, strained my eyes to the floor. The flowers were still there, scattered on the ground in a lumpy square. Emily was standing in the middle of them.

I looked up, my heart beating faster. She was staring at me. Her eyebrows were raised, expecting something. An apology, maybe. I didn't understand.

"Okay, then." She set the plate of gray mush on a table by the wall. "I was going to apologize. Say I was sorry for—you know." Her eyes locked on mine. "But apparently you're not ready for that."

She turned, started walking back to the door again. On the flowers. I looked down at the ground, then up at her. A cold sweat formed on my back, my neck. She opened the door. She was almost gone.

"Emily!"

The girl with red hair spun around, waited. I licked my lips.

"You really—you really don't see the flowers?"

Emily let out a breath, put her hands on her hips. She looked at the floor, then back at me. "*What* flowers, Laney? There's nothing in here. Mr. Dabir burned all the flowers the first day. You know—the ones you and Branch gave to everyone?" She let out another breath. "I'm leaving."

The door clicked behind her, and I heard her footsteps

fade down the hall.

My breaths came faster now, my chest moving against the cart beneath me. I lay back on it, tried to press against the cold metal. I was sweating.

A game. It had to be part of the game. Emily was pretending the flowers weren't really there. But they were. They were as real as the food on the plate. I could *see* them.

I heard my breath, the only sound in the room. The ceiling was grayer than I remembered, and the light was flickering more slowly now. I started tapping again. One finger. The other. I could feel the smooth surface of the cart.

Feel.

I needed to *feel* them! Then I would know that they were real.

My head jolted forward and I strained against the ropes with all the strength I had left. Nothing. I lunged to the left, pulled against the ropes. Then to the right. And back again, and again, and again.

The cart was rocking. If it fell over, I would be on the ground. I would be able to feel the flowers.

I lunged to the left. I heard the wheels bounce slightly on the ground. Right. The other wheels bounced. Back, and forth, and back again.

If I couldn't break free from the ropes, I would break free from being right-side up, on the cart.

The next time, on the left, the cart paused on its side in the air. And when I lunged to the other side, it hesitated again like it was thinking, deciding whether it wanted to give in to me.

And then I felt air. And I saw black.

My arms and chest ached, and I couldn't breathe. My face was smashed against the ground, and I tried to open my eyes, but I couldn't. The fall—it had made me black out. For how long—seconds? Minutes?

I lifted my neck and heaved in a breath. My forearms were

pinned against the ground, and I moved them slightly, pressed on the floor so I could lift myself up a few inches. The cart was still attached to me, up in the air at an angle, and it was lighter than I thought it would be. Still, I felt it. Hard.

I opened my eyes, and little white dots flashed against my vision. White. Like—like the flowers.

I spread my fingers against the ground, as much as I could. Clutched the ground, felt it. Reached farther, as far as I could with the ropes biting against me.

Nothing.

I felt the cold floor.

I blinked, blinked again. My eyes cleared slowly, the white dots fading like stars in the morning.

I saw the floor, a stretch of gray that smelled like sulfur. Not even a petal lay on its surface.

5

THEN

It's day two of the challenges. Day two of all of us competing to be leader when the world is destroyed.

Ten people were eliminated during the last challenge—I recognized one as the boy with the pig. There are thirty-five of us now.

"You have exactly thirty minutes until our next gathering," Glasses Lady said as we ate breakfast—warm oatmeal drenched with milk—in the mess hall earlier this morning.

I noticed her word choice and wondered if it was deliberate. She said gathering instead of challenge. It took me four seconds to decide that it had to be. These people were deliberate with everything. Every nod, every raise of an eyebrow or switch of a word was on purpose.

Now, as I watch Glasses Lady hand over the podium to Pimples in the large room at the center of the building, I wonder what is deliberate about that.

"Good morning, everyone."

His voice is loud, louder than I thought it would be. But it has a nasally edge to it, like he has asthma or something. That second observation is what I expected.

"I have a question for you." His chest moves faster than it should. "Should we serve dessert tonight, or should we not?"

The room is silent for a second. Is this why we gathered here? I press my hands against my thighs. Pimples opens his mouth again.

"You will stand for the vote. All in favor of us not serving dessert tonight?"

Pause. Three people in front of me stand. Suck-ups. I haven't had dessert in years. My mother never bought sweets. I am all for this.

Slowly, Pimples moves to the middle of the platform, followed by Glasses Lady and the other man. They stand there, heads lifted tall. They're voting for no desserts. Pimples moves back to the podium, and the people in front of me sit down again.

"All in favor of us serving dessert tonight?"

I hear bodies shifting from chairs, feet planting on the ground as the rest of us stand. I see a few people's eyes brighten. Pimples just watches us. Seconds tick by. Then he nods, points to the chairs again. I sit down, content that we got the majority vote. But for some reason, I don't feel like we won anything just yet.

"We would like to begin by showing you a short video." Pimples rubs his eyes and looks out at all of us. He's short—about as short as Glasses Lady.

The other man—the hairless one—pushes a large whiteboard in front of the platform, then walks to the back of the room again and brings a small gray projector in front of it. Glasses Lady is just standing to the side.

Quickly, Hairless presses a button on the side of the machine and I can hear a soft whirring sound as a picture appears on the white surface. The audio is on loud, and I almost clutch my chair as another man's voice fills the air and echoes off the walls.

"This world is quickly coming to an end. Jan knows this, and she needs to make a decision."

A woman pops up on the screen, thin, with her brown hair chopped short around her shoulders. The man's voice continues.

"Jan is running to the Dome, a large underground living facility created by the leaders of society, and on her way she sees seven people in a field."

The woman on the screen is running and something black falls from the sky all around her. Ash, maybe? I hear a few people screaming in the background. The woman's eyes open wide, too wide, like she knows this is fake.

"Six people in the field are women, and the other is a man."

The camera zooms in on the man—big, with broad shoulders and a thick beard on his face. Typical of the movie to choose a man who looks like that. My eyes fall from the screen onto Pimples. Why not someone like him? Much more realistic.

"The six women in the field have their hair tied up, and the man thinks Jan should tie her hair up too. The other women agree."

The video pans to the group: Jan, the man, and six women with hair gathered in buns, so tight it pulls at the skin on their foreheads. The world is literally falling apart around them, and this man cares about Jan's hair?

The camera zooms in on Jan's face. She looks perplexed, and she puts one finger to her chin, like she's thinking. The voice cuts in again.

"What should Jan do?"

The video wobbles, like it was knocked off-balance. It's paused on Jan's face, and she looks like she's being jerked up and down. Then it goes black.

No one in the room moves. Pimples's eyes are darting across all of us seated in the chairs.

"Well?"

Maybe I was wrong. Maybe this is a challenge.

Someone in a chair a few rows ahead of me shifts. Raises his hand.

"Do not raise your hand." Pimples's eyes lock on the boy. "We vote by standing. No one will have time for individual opinions in the Dome, unless you're called up to the platform by one of the leaders. Otherwise, you stand. Silently."

The boy puts his hand down as quickly as he raised it.

31

Pimples nods. "You have two options—two different ways to vote here." He sniffs loudly. "Should Jan leave her hair down, or should she tie it up?"

That's it. That's all he says. If this is a challenge, it's ridiculous. Who in their right mind would vote for Jan to tie up her hair when the world is being destroyed? There are more important things for her to worry about.

"All in favor of Jan tying up her hair?"

This time, I count seven people who stand. I don't understand. Why would they vote that way? I cross my hands on my lap. Well, their loss.

"And all in favor of Jan leaving her hair down?"

I stand immediately. Fourteen seconds pass before everyone else in the chairs—minus the seven—is standing too.

Pimples's eyes dart across the rows in front of me and then meet mine. "I see."

We all sit down again, and I can feel the cool metal of the chair through the thin fabric of my pants. Pimples looks at Glasses Lady, then back at us.

"You're all wrong."

The air around me seems to get colder. How are we all wrong? There were only two options to begin with. Pimples points to the projector at the back of the room.

"You see, it's not about the answer. There are no right or wrong answers—whether Jan ties her hair up or leaves it down. It's about whether they all agree." He takes a breath, silent this time. "The *only* thing that matters—that should matter in the Dome—is getting a unanimous vote."

He can't be serious. I turn my neck slightly, see a few people looking exactly like I feel right now.

"Think about this." Pimples's eyebrows raise. "If Jan disagrees with the man's request and says she's going to leave her hair down, the man and the six women will likely protest. Seconds will pass—precious seconds that they do not have. And then, because of their disagreement, it will be too late. They will all die."

He pauses. He said that so matter-of-fact, it was like he was giving us a history lesson or something.

"But let's see what happens if Jan ties her hair up."

Pimples nods at Hairless, who walks to the projector and presses the button again. The whiteboard comes to life. The bearded man and the six women point at Jan's hair, and she doesn't hesitate. She ties it up quickly, a brown ball on the top of her head. The man nods. And then they all run, with ashes and fire popping in and out from the sides of the screen. I see a large stone door appear in the middle of a canyon, getting closer, closer. The Dome? The screen fizzes out again.

Pimples nods. Hairless wheels the projector to the back of the room again, and then the whiteboard, slowly. I can hear the scrape of the wheels as they move across the floor.

"Peace is more important than differences of opinion." Pimples's voice echoes against the walls, like the voice from the video did. "So you change your answers until they match. Unless it is a unanimous vote, it does not matter."

He stares at all of us again. I see Glasses Lady shift from one foot to the other. The boy next to me has wide eyes.

"So." Pimples walks a few feet away from the podium, then walks back, each step tapping the flat pieces of wood nailed tightly together. "Should we serve dessert tonight, or should we not?"

He unfolds his hands. Brushes the platform, like he's cleaning off dust.

"All in favor of us not serving dessert tonight?"

Then he lifts his hands, folds them again, and steps slowly to the middle of the platform. Glasses Lady and Hairless follow, again. Their eyes are on us.

This time, everyone stands.

Thanks a lot, Jan. You cost us dessert.

6

NOW

I couldn't see anything.

The air around me was so gray it was almost black, the light having flickered out hours ago. I was still pressed to the ground, cold cheek against hard floor. My back ached. The bindings held, so the cart was still attached to me. It was like thirty extra pounds had grown on me and were pushing me deeper, deeper.

I couldn't breathe.

I pressed my fingers out slowly, once more. Nothing. No crushed petals, no long stems. No flowers. Had I really just imagined them? Or was this all part of Mr. Dabir's game?

I closed my eyes, tried to take a deep breath. And then I opened them. I never thought I would be so glad to hear footsteps.

The door clicked open and there was a pause. Light from the hallway left a watery square on the floor. I heard someone let out a breath. The door clicked shut, and I heard steps getting closer, felt hands press against my wrists. Something slid between the bindings and I heard a slicing sound, quick, like air. My hands were free. I felt myself sinking into the ground, grateful. I stretched out my fingers and closed them again, shutting my eyes when I felt the raw, red circles I assumed were growing by the day around my wrists.

My legs fell free, and I felt the cart being lifted off me.

There was the sound of metal hitting against the wall as I assumed the cart was righted and pushed back into position. And then, hands again. Grabbing my arm, lifting me up. Pulling me to the door.

It took me a moment to realize there was no rope this time. The person was touching me. Mr. Dabir never touched me.

The door opened and the light pressed into my eyes. I blinked, looked to my left. Dirty-blond hair. His face forward, brown eyes on the door at end of the hall.

It was Nash.

I felt my heart pause when I saw his face, felt my palms grow wet. My breathing quickened. The anger flooded back—anger at him for making a deal with Mr. Dabir, for letting it all happen. For locking our friends out of the Dome. And most of all, for not trusting me with any of it. He knew Mr. Dabir was alive all this time, and he didn't tell me. Every time he took my hand, every kiss we shared, he knew. And I had been next to him, blind.

I stood there for a moment, paralyzed. Nash reached behind him and took something out of the black pack he was wearing. Rope. He tied it around my hands without even looking at me. Mr. Dabir still forbid touch, he knew that. But Nash had touched me in the room. Hypocrite.

I knew I had betrayed Nash, if that was what it was called. I didn't mean to have feelings for Branch, didn't even know if that's what they were. But here, now, ever since Nash had agreed to be a leader in the Dome and walked out that door, he had betrayed me more. And so I would walk away from him. Forever.

I breathed deeply, never knew I could feel this way about someone before.

Never knew I could feel this way about Nash.

"Mr. Dabir asked me to get you. He wants you to see something."

Two sentences. Two sentences, and the blood rushed to my veins. Those were really the first words he said to me?

I said nothing. *Only talk if it is absolutely necessary*, they always told us. This wasn't one of those moments.

I followed Nash to the door, through it, and into another hallway. When we were halfway down it, he took out a key.

My heart was pounding, and I didn't know why. I had shared so much with this boy, and he had ripped it all away. Tore it from the ground like the wildflowers the men with black eyes had ripped from the ground and tossed into the air when the world was being destroyed.

Nash led me into a dark hallway, one I had never seen before. It smelled old—musty, like water had dripped from the walls and the air had never been dry enough to suck it back up again.

"Where are you taking me?" The words came from my lips before I knew I was thinking them. They were cold, like ice.

Nash stopped for a second. He hadn't expected me to speak.

"We're almost there." His eyes were on the end of the hallway again. He hadn't looked at me once.

Cold. Dead. I had never felt this way when I was with him before. I swallowed, tried to push the thoughts away. Whatever Mr. Dabir had planned, I needed to be focused. But as hard as I tried, I couldn't stop the trembling in my hands.

The boy next to me pressed his hand against the gray knob at the end of the hall and the door opened. I had to blink to see what was inside—torches were burning on the walls. The whole room was bathed in gray. Gray walls, gray ceiling, at least a dozen gray carts pushed up against the walls. Gray—bodies, on the carts?

I took a step back, felt my heart beating against my chest.

"Laney." A voice filled the air and was such a contrast to all the gray that I put my hand against the wall. "So nice of you to join us."

I felt a push on my back—not hard, but not soft either—and stumbled into the room. The door closed behind me, and

I looked back, suddenly wanting to be anywhere but here. Nash was gone.

The body that had spoken moved from beside one of the carts and over to me.

"What do you think?" Mr. Dabir spread his arms wide, a sickening smile filling his face.

I heard thick breathing coming from almost all the carts in the room, and my eyes darted back and forth. Legs were stretched to the end of each one, arms bound by their heads. There was a loud groan, and the pain behind the voice made me want to shut my eyes again.

People. At least a dozen people were bound tightly to the carts in the room, with devices fitted to their heads like the one on mine.

"What are you doing?" I was breathless all over again. My mind was filling with emotions—shock, disgust, regret. Fear. I pressed my hands against the wall behind me, tried to clear my head. I wondered if a person could experience *too* much emotion—if it could kill them, like too much of anything else in this gray world would.

Mr. Dabir just looked at me. "Attention, everyone." His eyes didn't move from mine. "We have a visitor."

A head lifted on a cart to my right. Gray hair. Pale, wrinkled skin. I swallowed. Alfred. The man Delma had grown fond of. The man who had been the first to stand up for love so long ago.

"Laney?" He blinked once, twice, like he was trying to decide if this was real or not.

Emotion. I felt so much emotion.

"Alfred?" I rushed over to him, the end of the rope Nash dropped dragging on the floor behind me.

"Laney." He coughed, and I watched his chest rise and fall. He was struggling to breathe. His eyes met mine, and they were wet pools of confusion. Maybe he didn't believe what Mr. Dabir said, that I was the traitor. Maybe he knew it couldn't be true.

"You're killing him." I whipped around and faced Mr.

Dabir. "Can't you see that? Take these off of him."

"Take?" A voice came from the cart next to Alfred's. A woman was lying there, short brown hair tangled behind her head and arms bound to the wall. Her eyes snapped to mine. "You. It was you." Suddenly, her eyes were round. White, like the moon. "You took them, one by one."

"No." I tried to breathe, shook my head quickly. I looked at Alfred again, and his eyes were still on me. I couldn't tell what he was thinking. "It wasn't me. I was never the one who—"

"It's her!" The woman's arms were moving now, pulling against the bindings like she suddenly had a new strength inside of her. She was shrieking the words, and she said them again, and again, and again.

All in a moment, heads turned from the resting places on their carts. Gray eyes fell on me, and bodies started thrashing, pulling against the ropes on their arms and feet. Eyes, once gray and dull a moment ago, were now white, wide. Full of fear.

"No. He's lying to you! It wasn't me. I would never—" My heartbeat was thudding, my chest pulling in breaths like I was underwater.

More of them started shrieking, and their words cut me like knives. *Traitor. Liar. Monster.* I took a step back and pressed up against the wall, my hands to my ears. Emotion, so much emotion. Filling the walls, the air, my lungs. And for the second time that day, I couldn't breathe.

All my life, the air in the Dome had been silent. A world without wind and movement and sound. Now, the sound crushed me, struck me in the ribs over and over. All because of a lie. It wasn't me. It wasn't me. It wasn't—

"Silence." Mr. Dabir held up his hand, and the sound was sucked out of the room almost immediately.

I could hear my breath, and I slowly took my hands from my ears. They were ringing. I had never felt so cold.

"Blakely." Mr. Dabir said her name loudly, and she opened the door, stepped in the room. She had the paper book in her hands again. Mr. Dabir nodded at her. "Mark the results. Trial three: the source of hate."

I looked up. "Hate?"

Mr. Dabir's eyes snapped to mine, his mouth painted in a line but satisfaction in his beady eyes. "Yes. Hate."

Brooke closed the door, and he just stood there, watching me. "I'm finding the source of love, so why not find the source of hate too? And what more do these people hate"— he spread his arms wide—"than you, Laney? And with good reason."

He said nothing more, and an amused smile spread across his filthy lips.

"All of this is because of a lie." I felt my heart beating faster, faster. "They need to know it wasn't me." I whirled around, stepped over to Alfred, breathless. "It wasn't me! I would never hurt you, any of you. Tell them, Mr. Dabir. Tell them what you did."

"What *I* did?" Mr. Dabir spun toward me. "I gave them peace, Laney. I gave them safety, and order, and knowledge. And then you had to come and take it all away." His voice was rising, and the air felt hot. I clenched my fists. He had taken everything. He had made them hate me. And here they were, just lying there, silent. Watching the world go by without blinking. Gray eyes. I was *so* done with gray.

I took a step forward, felt the words form in my throat, but they stopped before they reached my lips.

A sound. Suddenly, slowly, a sound came from the corner of the room. It was small at first, a breath of the nonexistent wind. Words, rising and falling like water. Long tones reaching into the silence, wrapping around it, and squeezing.

Someone—someone was singing.

Theodore? The thought of his voice, his tones that filled the air, made me want to cry. But it couldn't be. He was locked out, in the world above.

Mr. Dabir blinked and turned, looked behind him to the sound. He always tried to hide it when he was surprised, but I could see it. I could see it in the corners of his eyes.

39

I took a step forward, then another. Before I knew it, I was standing in the middle of the room, staring at the corner. It was a girl. She was a few years younger than me, with long black hair that was drenched in sweat, plastered behind her head on the cart she was bound to. I couldn't see her face. Her hands were pressed to her eyes, her cheeks scrunched at the edges. Her shoulders were shaking, moving forward and then back, like the pulsing of the torches on the walls.

She was terrified. And she was singing.

"Hush, little baby, don't say a word. Papa's gonna buy you a mockingbird. And if that mockingbird won't sing—"

I had never heard anything like it before. When Theodore sang, he never had words. His voice would just rise and fall, over and over again. But not this. The girl's voice was small, breaking every few words, like she was trying not to cry.

"—Papa's gonna buy you a diamond ring. And if that diamond ring turns brass, Papa's gonna buy you a looking glass."

Papa. That used to be a name for a father, didn't it? We were forbidden to say that word—we always had been. Where did she hear this? My feet were frozen to the floor now, my palms wet and cold, so cold. There was no sound except for her soft, shaky singing.

Mr. Dabir moved suddenly, like he realized what was happening. Like he realized so much of what she was singing had been forbidden decades ago. So how did she know the words?

"Shhh." He stopped at her cart, said the word softly. "Everything is going to be okay."

"—and if that looking glass gets broke—" The girl stopped suddenly. She moved her hand from her face, looked at Mr. Dabir. Her cheeks were wet with moisture, her eyes wide.

Mr. Dabir nodded once. Then, slowly, he reached behind his back. Took something out of his pocket.

"Close your eyes."

The girl looked at him, and she seemed to believe his

words. She nodded, took in a shaky deep breath. Closed them.

And then it was too late. I didn't realize what he held in his fingers until there was blood dripping from the cart to the floor.

I sank to the ground, shouting words I couldn't hear. Arms grabbed me from behind, pulled me up, out the door and down the hallway. The last word she sang was ringing in my ears.

Broke.

She didn't know how true that word really was. He broke everything he touched.

7

THEN

"Don't break them!" Glasses Lady holds out her hands as we fasten the devices onto our heads.

It's cold, made of some plastic gray material that winds around wires in a complete circle. And it looks morbid, like something one of the men with black eyes would have made.

I grip a strap behind my head and tighten it, fastening it to the side of the plastic. One knot. Two knots. Done. They told us to do two, no more, no less—said it would be impossible to get it back off with more than two knots tied to the side. It was designed that way. And suddenly I want nothing more than it *not* to be on my head anymore.

"Well done, everyone." Glasses Lady looks nervous, like her precious headbands cost a lot of money. She folds her hands when our fingers stop fastening and the plastic spheres are all still intact. "Today, you will complete challenge three. These devices are crucial to the results."

Devices. Does she even know what these are called? Torture circles. Headbands of death. I wonder if I'm close.

"We'll each take one of you down the hallway, one after the other." Her eyes dart across the rows of chairs in the largest room in the building, the room where pigs and deer and birds were running rampant not long ago. It doesn't even smell in here. I'm almost impressed.

"For your knowledge—" Glasses Lady pauses, and her

42

eyes snap to someone a few seats down from me. "People will be eliminated today. I guarantee it."

The room gets quiet then. We all sit, chests moving in and out and hands folded in our laps, as Glasses Lady takes the first person down the hall. Hairless and Pimples each take someone from the group of people too. At least it's three at a time—there are still thirty-five of us. This one will go faster.

I hear bodies shifting, feet tapping as people wait to be taken to wherever they're taking us. I still can't shake the quietness of it all. Out there, in the world, it's so *not quiet*. There are horns honking and birds chirping and a mother scolding a child as he runs down the street. There are phones ringing and feet scuffing the ground and hammers pounding signs onto cement walls. But not here. Here, we're encouraged to be silent. Told that it will keep the peace. I shift in my chair, listen to my breath as I push it from my lungs. I don't know if I'll ever get used to it. But then again, if the choice is a silent Dome or death, well, I know my answer.

My eyes shift slightly as Pimples steps into the room and beckons to the girl with blond hair. She stands quickly, like she was caught off guard. Her hands are clasped, and she rings them out, then follows, her steps echoing on the cold floor. She may have successfully completed challenge two, may have made it so it looked like *I* successfully completed challenge two, but she's weak. I can tell by the way she glances back at the room before she steps into the hall. Hope, was her name? I can't help but wonder if her parents were delusional.

The door opens again. It's Glasses Lady. Her eyes search the room, flicker back and forth like a torch starved from air, and then stop on me. Of course. It's always Glasses Lady and me, like two peas in an unconventional pod.

I stand, not too slow, not too fast, much better than Hope had. I set my eyes forward and stroll to the door, knowing the rest of the thirty-five are watching me. What they see is a boy, dark hair and dark eyes, determined. Confident. A boy who will soon be the leader of them all. I'm as sure about that as I

43

am about the thickness of this woman's glasses—they're much too thick, and I'm much too smart for this.

"This way." Glasses Lady leads me down a short hallway and holds a gray door open as I walk inside. The room is small, a little dark. A light buzzes on the ceiling, and I have to stop myself from mentioning that they need to fix it. It's annoying, and it distracts me for a second. I push the sound deep in the edges of my mind, at the corners, where it can buzz all it wants. Just not here. Not while I'm trying to win.

"Have a seat, please." Glasses Lady is holding her chart, clenching it with her thin, white fingers. I wonder if this is all she has to hold on to in life now. Her chart, and the idea that one of us might save humanity. It probably helps her sleep at night.

I sit in a gray, sloped chair in the middle of the otherwise empty room and turn toward her. Why do I feel like I'm about to get interrogated?

"Challenge number three." Glasses Lady opens her lips wide as she speaks.

So that last one, the video about Jan, *was* just a gathering. I was right—every word they say has a purpose.

"I am going to show you three pictures. They are all different people, each with their own strengths and weaknesses. This is a hypothetical situation again, and you will choose the best answer."

I don't swallow, don't move. I don't have time for that. I watch Glasses Lady's eyes, hold her gaze. Take in every word. Slowly, but deliberately, she reaches into her pocket and takes out a thin stack of three pictures. I can tell by the way the last two are slightly off-center from the first, their corners a little higher and a little more to the right.

She pauses for a second, then grasps the edge of the picture on top and flips it, the thin edge making a small *pop* sound as she does. And I stop, but so briefly that it's not noticeable. She didn't even say what the question was. I take in a breath, put myself back on course. Everything has a purpose. Maybe she'll say the question after she shows me the pictures.

I focus on the first small gray square, just larger than the size of her hand. The picture is faded, from the looks of it taken long before I was born, but then again maybe it was just left out in the sun too long. It's of a person. A man. He's old—forties maybe. And he's a doctor. I can tell by the uniform he's wearing—deep blue, blank except for a small rectangle name tag on his left breast and a stethoscope around his neck.

Glasses Lady flips to the next picture. It's a girl, young, much younger than me. Six or seven maybe? She has light brown hair and deep blue eyes set high on her face. She's standing, and the background is faded out, so she looks like she's in the middle of nowhere. Or everywhere, depending on how you look at it. The picture is black and white, and her dress is ripped on the left side, up to her knee. Her eyes are wide, her face white, like she's looking at something behind the camera that I can't see.

That picture disappears and the final one is held in front of me. It's another girl, but this time older. Only her face and arms are visible as she's staring out the window of a building that's burning. Flames are reaching up to the sky, like her arms. Her hair whips out behind her back, like some invisible wind is pushing it. Blond hair—deep blond—and curly. Her eyes are open wide, her lips painted red. In fact, now that I think about it, she looks a lot like—

"Time is up."

My eyes flick from the picture to Glasses Lady. She places the pictures back in her pocket again, gently.

"The world is ending, and you have ten seconds in which you will only have time to save one of these three people. Who will you choose to bring with you to the Dome?"

My mind immediately sets a timer. I can't take too long to answer—then it will look like I'm not competent, can't make decisions quickly enough.

I run the pictures through my mind again, like flashes of a camera. The doctor. I remember briefly from a "welcome

45

card" they gave us—more like an information card, with two short paragraphs sharing about the wonders of this Dome they were creating—that no one will ever get sick. The Dome will be sealed off the moment the door is shut, and as long as we don't bring in any sickness, the people will remain safe. So, I wouldn't bring the doctor. He's irrelevant.

The two faces of the girls fill my thoughts. The girl standing in the middle of nowhere, and the other, older girl caught in a burning building. I lick my lips. The girl in the burning building would take too long to be saved. We would both die if I picked her. At least the other girl was standing there, easy to call to, someone who could follow quickly.

Fifteen seconds had passed, and that was all I needed.

"The second picture. The young girl in the dress."

Glasses Lady nods, acknowledging my answer, and scribbles a few words on her chart. "You may exit."

So that was it. That was challenge three. It was easy. I stand and walk back to the other room, open the door, and sit back in my seat. Some of the other kids look nervous. I almost feel bad for them. Almost.

I watch the final few people leave the room and return. The whole challenge, everyone combined, has taken less than an hour. I'm watching the door when Glasses Lady walks in one final time, Pimples and Hairless by her side. Their faces are all in a line. I can't tell what they're thinking.

"Everyone, please untie the devices on your heads and place them in this bin next to me. You may return to your rooms for fifteen minutes, and then please direct yourselves to the center of the building."

The headband of death. How did I forget that? I panic for less than a second, wondering what they could have possibly used this for during the challenge and why Glasses Lady hadn't mentioned what it was doing here, on my head. My hands go to my hair and I grip the tie on the side, untangling it with my fingers. As I stand, I see one of the boys a few feet from me, yanking at the thing like it's hurting him—like it's slowly squeezing his head, more and more, pressing against his brain. He finally gets it off, ripping several hairs off his head in the process. He stares at it in his hands for a second, and my eyes drop to it too. Thin, black-gray, twisted into a circle. It looks kind of like the horns on one of the animals I saw in the challenge before this one. A moose, maybe?

The boy looks up, and his eyes meet mine for a second. He looks angry, but his face shifts almost immediately and becomes emotionless again. White, blank. Never let your opponent see how you really feel. I pause, watch him step to the front of the room, drop the headpiece in, and walk out the door.

It's a piece of plastic. It couldn't have affected the challenge that much, right? I step to the bin and lay the device inside on top of the others. As I walk away, my hands are cold.

8

NOW

It's colder in here than I remembered.

For a brief moment I wondered if they made it that way, turned off all the heat in my room so I would be uncomfortable, shiver uncontrollably. Maybe it was another part of his game, the tests.

Or maybe I was shivering because I had just seen Mr. Dabir kill a little girl.

I was in and out of sleep, my mind and body exhausted but never able to rest. When had it come to this? What had happened to our world above—our own little slice of earth where Alese had taught the people to laugh, to smile, to touch, and the gray from their eyes lifted a little more each day? We were so close. And now it was all back to the way it was before. But even worse than that.

The door opened and closed a few times, but I kept my eyes shut. Without warning, a memory came back to me. I don't know why I thought of it, because it wasn't important at the time. Maybe it was the door—when it shut with a small scrape and a click. Like the first day I ever walked into this place, the Dome. The place that would ruin us all.

But that was now. Then, I was hopeful. Then, I was grateful. That first day I walked through the Dome's door, I was chosen to be one of the few people who survived.

Getting to the Dome was a blur—a rush of hazy houses

and streets and grass and people that I can never piece apart. But after I stepped into the Dome for the first time, it's like my memory sharpens. I remembered that part vividly, though I've tried to push it to the corners of my mind over and over again. It was the first day of my new life, a life of gray eyes and stone walls and cold skin.

And it was the first day I saw Nash.

I don't know why I remembered him. The world was ending, and I had just seen the men with black eyes ripping up what was left of it. I don't remember who brought me to the Dome, just their fingers, soft to the touch, and the whisper that I would be okay. That everything would be okay.

But when I stood in the center of the Dome for the very first time, watching the people around me—faces stretched in worry and wide, white eyes—I held the flower I had brought with me in two hands. I clutched it tighter and tighter, breaths heavy, trying to wrap my mind around what was happening. I was just a child. And then, without meaning to, I dropped it. The flower sank slowly to the ground and I stood, blinking, the breath all but gone from my chest. And that's when I saw him. Our eyes met, I thought he would look away, and he did. But his eyes fell to the ground in front of me, on the flower.

He stepped forward slowly, carefully. He bent, and when he stood again, the flower was in his hand. He paused for a second, hesitated like the world wasn't just going to ashes above us. And then he held it out, and I breathed in, and I took it.

I remembered wondering why he did that. No one ever helped anyone; there was no reason to. But he did. Nash did, that very first day. I kept the flower for months, until it was a pile of dust, like the world above us.

The door opened and closed again, and I pushed the memory away. Nash's face appeared, and for a second I wondered if it was fake. If I was still thinking about the memory. But then it moved, like it was hovering over me with no body attached. And his face was stone. Definitely not fake.

I closed my eyes again, quickly, hoping he wouldn't bother me if I were sleeping. I tried to stay still, peaceful, but I accidentally shivered.

"I know you're awake, Laney." Nash spoke. There were no footsteps on the ground, so he must be standing there now. I didn't move. Nash sighed.

"You're wasting time. Mr. Dabir needs you."

I kept breathing slowly, in and out. *Go away. I don't want you here.*

I felt Nash's touch on my arms as he untied the ropes. I hated that his touch still had an effect on me—it burst through my skin like heat, though it was dulled slightly now. I heard the ropes drop to the ground.

"Laney, get up. This isn't a game."

At the sound of my name, I flinched. Something about his words made a different heat flush through my veins. I opened my eyes. "This isn't a game? That's exactly what it is. All of it. Some sick, twisted, deranged game."

Nash's face didn't move. My words hadn't affected him at all, and suddenly I couldn't hold it in any longer. The words rushed out of me like fire.

"Have you even thought about Dalia? Theodore, Alese, Gavin?" I paused. "Branch?"

His mouth twitched at that last name. Finally, I had gotten a reaction.

"You shut them out. *You* did, Nash. They could die out there. And Mr. Dabir is killing everyone in here. *Please*, just don't do this anymore. Do you really want to be Mr. Dabir's callboy? Stop this and help them. It's not you." *At least I hope it's not you.*

The air was silent for a few seconds. Then Nash bent, grabbed one of the ropes from the ground, and stood. The memory flashed in my mind again. His face—wide, innocent as he held the flower out to me and almost smiled. I blinked back hot tears from my eyes. He tied the rope around my wrists quickly and pulled.

50

"Let's go."

There was nothing I could do but follow.

This time it was a different door, a different room. Smaller than the last—I could tell by the way the doors were closer together. I said nothing else on the way, and neither did Nash. Maybe I was wrong. Maybe he really had changed, and this wasn't just a way of getting me back for betraying him. I took in a deep breath. I still wasn't completely used to *feeling*—love, like the exhilarating feeling in your chest when you soar through the trees. And anger, like the feeling you'd get if hands kept pressing you underwater just until you almost drowned, and then pulled you back up again. Down, up, down, up. It was tiring. And infuriating.

Nash opened the door, spoke some words I couldn't hear, nodded, and then pushed me in without a word. But right before he did, I caught his eye. There was something different—a flicker of a feeling that broke through the stone. Like he saw something in there, something he didn't want to see.

I blinked and my eyes slowly adjusted to the dim light. A few desks were propped up against the walls, useless. A larger desk stood at the end of the room, still in its place. This was an old classroom. I swallowed. Wait. *End of the fourth hall, just past the two doors without windows.* That's what I used to tell myself, so I could find it without getting lost. It was my old classroom.

"Ah, splendid to be back in here, isn't it?" Mr. Dabir stood from his place at the larger desk. He used to be my teacher here. That was *his* desk.

"So many years of teaching, and teaching, and teaching." He rolled his eyes dramatically and put his hand to his heart. Then he looked at me and smiled. "I personally think studies are a waste of time. Too much thinking, not enough doing."

I didn't respond. The face of the girl, singing in the corner, was still in my mind. The blood.

"What, did you not see the gift I left you?" Mr. Dabir's face changed to a mock pout. He gestured to one of the desks shoved up against the wall next to me, but I kept my eyes on Mr. Dabir. I didn't break his gaze. He needed to know how horrible he was, how it wasn't okay that he killed that girl.

"Okay, okay, I get it. The girl. Maybe if you look at what I brought you, all will be forgiven?"

I looked at him for a few more long seconds, making sure he knew that would never happen. Then I turned, bracing myself for whatever ridiculous or horrific or devastating thing this man had brought me.

I froze. I tried to move, tried to take a breath, but it was like something had squeezed the air from my lungs. How was it possible? I thought I'd lost it when we all went to live in the world above.

All at once the memories came back to me—the journey, the house. The books and the sweet, soft music that seemed to spiral through the air with the smoke from the fire. The tiny twirling figures with painted smiles. Theodore's face when he found—

"The black box."

The words escaped my lips, a whisper in the dark room. Mr. Dabir took a few steps toward me.

"Yes, that's what Nash said all of you called it. *The black box*. Apparently, it used to sing? That is, I'm sure, before it became this charred mess."

"Yes." I didn't move. Couldn't. My words were nothing but puffs in the silent air. I couldn't seem to get my breath back.

"I have to say, I'm curious." Mr. Dabir moved closer to me again, slowly. "What is it about this black box that is so incredible?"

I swallowed hard, looked up. But he wasn't being sarcastic. He was looking at me with pure, innocent curiosity. I shook my head. Pure and innocent. Those words and Mr. Dabir should never be used in the same sentence.

"If you tell me, I'll let you keep it." His words hung in the air.

I looked at the black box, then at him, debating. Even if it was burnt, just a shell of what it used to be, it was a piece of my journey, my memories. A piece of the life when I was happy and I had everything. And as much as I hated it, I needed it. I needed something to hold on to when I was lying in a dark room, chained to a cart, day after day.

"Why?" The word came out like an accusation, and I meant it to. There was no reason for Mr. Dabir to give me this. Mr. Dabir never gave anyone anything. It was against his nature.

The man smiled again, and I hated the look of it. That wasn't what smiles were supposed to look like—stretched out, thin, ominous. I realized in that moment that eyes have so much to do with a smile—whether it's full of joy, or full of manipulation.

"As an apology. For killing the girl in front of you. I should have waited until you were gone."

Heat rose in my chest, and I clenched my fists.

"You have fifteen seconds."

I opened my mouth and closed it. I would give in, just this once. But with nothing else.

"Theodore dug it out of the house we found in the world above." I spoke louder than before, and I think it surprised him. Good. "It was something different, something we had never seen before, so I carried it back with us."

There was a pause in the room. Mr. Dabir blinked once. "Is that it?"

I hesitated, nodded. He sighed.

"Ten seconds, Laney. To give me the *real* reason why this little object means so much to you all."

I clenched my fists again, unclenched them. I felt hot. The blood was draining from my head. He didn't deserve to know this. Didn't deserve to hear our secrets.

"It's exactly as I said. Theodore found it under the porch of the house in the world above."

Mr. Dabir looked at an invisible watch on his wrist. "Five seconds."

I took a deep breath, wrung my hands together. My palms were wet.

"Four...three...two—"

"When he found the black box, he brought it in the house." I forced the words out. Mr. Dabir stopped counting. "We were all amazed. It was this thing—this small, little piece of the world in the past—that none of us had ever seen before. It was beautiful. And then"—I paused, took in a deep, shaky breath, the memory flooding my thoughts— "And then Theodore opened it. And the air, once silent except for the rustle of trees brushing against each other, was filled with sound. That sound, small and soft and simple, seemed to stretch around the room, to take everything and everyone with it, up into the sky."

"And then Theodore—" My voice broke. "Theodore started singing. His voice reached up for the song from the black box, met it in the air. And he just sang. He sang until the black box wasn't singing anymore. And then he cried for his mother. We brought it with us for the rest of the journey, even after Arsen tried to destroy it."

I swallowed back the emotion, let the silence in the room hover for just a moment.

"That black box is more than just something Theodore found in a house in the world." I shook my head. "It was hope."

I stilled my breathing and looked Mr. Dabir directly in the eyes. He didn't say anything for a second. He seemed to be looking at me—no, *through* me. Maybe I had cracked that gray wall inside his chest. He nodded.

After a few moments, I nodded back. This was the only agreement I would ever make with him.

"I'm taking the black box, and I'm leav—"

Something crashed behind me. I turned, confused. Arsen was there, standing next to the desk against the wall with a grin on his face. And he was holding a hammer. I let out all my breath.

"*What did you do?*"

The black box was gone—no, shattered. Pieces of it were scattered on the desk and the floor. I couldn't tell what went where, which part connected to which. It was only pieces now, parts of a whole that would never be seen again. And it felt like a part of my heart was ripped from my chest.

"You—" I whipped around, and Mr. Dabir was smiling again. "You promised me! Why? Why would you do that?" My breaths were shallow, and my head felt light.

"Mark the results. Trial four: the source of joy." His eyes flicked on me again before he walked to the door. "We're done here."

I was so stupid. I shouldn't have trusted him, should've known it was another part of his game. I gasped for air, looked from Mr. Dabir to the black box. But this wasn't a game to me. He used me. He knew that memory would make me feel things again, if even for a moment.

But it was gone—shattered into a thousand pieces. Theodore's face filled my mind, his green eyes wet as he looked down at the black box, touched the tiny plastic girl in the pink dress on top of her head lightly. *I'm sorry.* He had said those words, over and over again. *I'm sorry.*

Arsen grabbed the end of the rope, twisted around my wrists, and pulled. "It's about time I destroyed that the right way. Apparently, fire isn't strong enough." He winked.

55

9

THEN

When I was younger, maybe seven or eight, I loved going swimming at a pond outside my house. Well, not *loved*. I've never loved anything or anyone—humanity made sure of that when they voted it from existence decades ago. As far as I know, love doesn't even exist anymore, and I honestly couldn't care less. But, back to the story.

Our house was brown, about as big as my bedroom in this Dome replica, times two, which was big compared to a lot of the world at the time. I grew up lucky, my mother always told me, but I guess I didn't see it. The only times I ever felt lucky were when I was in the pond.

It wasn't ours specifically—the pond sat in the middle of the neighborhood like a big, watery eye. But our neighbors were old, or scared. Either way, they didn't come out much, so the pond was mine.

From what I knew about water, the pond was strange to me the first time I saw it. The water that came out of our faucets and drinking fountains and sat at the bottoms of toilets was clear. This water, though, was a deep blue that purpled at the edges as it spread out to the tall grasses and trees surrounding it. And what was even stranger was that the water was dark. Even when it reflected the sun, you couldn't see the bottom.

It was this fact alone that made me call it mine.

One night, I snuck out to the pond while my mother was cooking in the kitchen. The law obviously stated that we weren't allowed outside after dark, and she wouldn't have liked it had she ever found out. Aside from having a persistent and accurate clock in my mind, I was excellent at being silent. Ever since I was a child I constantly had words in my mind instead of my mouth, and I had respect for silence. How could something be nothing and so powerful at the same time? People were afraid of silence, at the secrets it hid beneath its blank surface. I wanted to be just like silence—seemingly small, inconspicuous, easily overlooked. But terrifying, and powerful, and everywhere. Silence was my idol.

That night, after making my way to the pond so quietly the grass disturbed the air more than I did, I slipped off my shirt and dove into the water. It surrounded me, pulled me in like a hand. It felt warm against the cool air, and when I pushed off from the bottom and my head surfaced, I slicked back my short hair as water ran down my face. I couldn't help but notice it was darker tonight than usual; the moon must have finally realized its job of lighting up a black sky when it was one billionth of the size was pointless. Poor moon. The sun had it so much better, was actually appreciated.

I could see the silhouette of my mother in the kitchen, she was cutting something. She always cut things last—bread, or spinach, or strawberries for the salad. I had maybe three minutes left until she walked to my room, rapped on the door once, and called my name, *Jonathan Dabir*, like she always did in that monotone way, like I was a set of instructions she listed off.

Side note: most people have one name, but I have two. Apparently, there was some mistake when they created my birth certificate, and someone forgot to grab a new one when the boy next to me, Dabir, was born. So the idiot wrote Dabir on my certificate, next to Jonathan, without even realizing it. Long day? I still don't understand how that could have happened, but my mom accepted it like I was meant to have two names all along. So here I am, the only boy in the world *lucky* enough to have two names. I think people mistake change for luck. But, back to the pond.

One more, I thought.

I took a deep breath, appreciating the smell of damp earth and something slightly sweet, maybe the tips of grass or something hidden in the water below me. I would never know what was in this pond, what secrets it held below the surface. It was a lot like silence, in a way. It just sat there, pretending it was less than it really was.

I took a deep breath and went under, deeper into the water, the silence. I felt my feet hit the bottom, and I stopped, just stayed there for a moment. I could hear nothing, see nothing. I *was* nothing, floating at the bottom of a nothing pond. And I had never felt so alive. My senses suddenly pricked up, my heart started beating faster. My throat tightened and my lungs burned. This was why I came here, snuck out of that house at least once a week. To be nothing and yet be powerful. This is what it felt like.

Fifty-seven seconds until my mother would be at my door.

I opened and closed my fists once, lowered my feet so they touched the bottom of the pond again. But they didn't. I must have floated farther up than I'd hoped. I let out even more air and sank deeper. I wanted the momentum of that extra push-off when I swam to the surface; it would get me there faster. I only had forty-three seconds left.

Finally, my feet hit the bottom, hard. I swallowed and felt the shock start to run through my legs, but there was no time for that. I pushed, reached for the surface, and was jerked back to the bottom. My foot was wedged between something, and I couldn't move it.

Thirty-two seconds.

I reached down to my leg, felt my foot and the jagged rock it was jammed into. I pulled, and my lungs burned even more from the use of energy when I had no air. I opened my eyes, but it was blacker than the night had been with no moon. I pulled my leg again, pounded the rock with my hand like I

58

could move it out of the way.

Twenty-seven seconds.

I swallowed, felt along the rest of the bottom for something I could use to wedge my foot out. My hand hit something smaller, and I hoped it wasn't a snail or something living. I hit the side of my foot once, twice, three times, closing my eyes again and pushing the pain to the back of my mind.

Nineteen seconds.

I hit it again, and again. Hit, pull, hit, pull. Finally, like the pond suddenly remembered I was something living and not dead, my foot broke free. I pushed, hard, and felt hot tears burn my eyes as I broke the surface, gasping for air.

Suddenly I remembered dinner, my mother. Seven seconds.

I whipped around in the water so I could see the window. Nothing but a warm, yellowish light. If she was at my door already…

A figure appeared in the window, and I let out a breath. She was waving something in the air—a towel maybe? Her hand pushed the window open a crack, and gray smoke wafted out the opening and toward the sky. She had burned something in the oven. She never burned anything. I stared at her for a few seconds longer. That mistake had just added at least four more minutes to my time.

I pushed back my hair, swam silent strokes to the side. When I reached it, water still up to my neck, I pushed myself up into the grass and rose, grabbing my shirt as I did. My lungs still felt like they were squeezing my insides, and I took a deep breath. Then I walked to the house, stepping over the gravel driveway and the short grass in our lawn, to the door on the side.

When I put my hand on the knob, I stopped for a moment. I looked back at where I had just come from. The pond looked almost gray under the black sky, plain. It was calm, unmoving, like it hadn't just tried to kill me. If it had succeeded, and I was stuck on the bottom of that pond forever, no one would know the difference. It would still look the same—gray, unmoving, nothing worth paying attention to.

And what I realized in that moment was this: nothing is so much more than nothing. And silence is just a way to hide all the screaming.

So, what is the point of this story? Fast forward to right now. In this big, brown building in the middle of the brick-wall circle, I'm standing here, in the bottom of an old cellar, and water is rushing in so fast my feet are already covered and my skin is soaked. Challenge number four: what to do if the Dome floods.

And for some reason, that memory just happened to cross my mind.

10

NOW

Tonight I imagined I was flying.

White wisps of clouds clutched the air next to me, holding it as tightly as the air held me. Tips of trees spread out below me and sky reached above me—or was it the other way around? The world upside-down and right-side up all at the same time. Bright eyes, red cheeks, white fingers. Hot bursts of breath, my heart pounding in my head, my arms and legs losing all feeling because they were just there—with nothing to lean against or step on or touch.

I was nothing, a breeze, a tremble in the wind, and yet—I felt everything. I *was* everything. To be nothing, and everything, is a breathless and wonderful thing.

Sitting in the sky.

That's what Theodore called it as we had rushed by the little peach blur that was him below us. I felt a hand clutching mine, flying with me. Branch. He had told me he would be there, had held my hand the entire time we were flying on the rope in the trees. *Lesson number two about love: trust. Without it, you're nothing.* His words had rung in my ears as I watched him, his blond hair ruffled from the flight. And then he had stepped close to me, to brush my hair off my forehead. His eyes were on mine, focused, as golden as the sun. I could feel his fingers sliding, slowly, from my hair to my cheek. Could see his chest breathing, in and out. He had almost kissed me, that day in the clouds. And I had stopped it.

The door opened, pulling me back to reality. I squeezed my fists together, almost cried out at the way things were now. The constant cold in the walls and the air and the eyes and the people. The room as dark as a moonless night. Someone set a plate by my cart, and I heard the door close again.

What was Branch doing right now? Was he trying to save me, dreaming up a plan with Alese and Gavin and Dalia and Theodore? The thought took the pain away for a moment. But they weren't stupid. If they knew what was good for them, they would run from this Dome and never turn back. I couldn't hope for their return when it would only put them in danger. I couldn't.

Those words shouldn't exist.

Branch had said that too, just before we stepped off the platform and into the air.

You can, Laney. You always can.

I allowed myself to believe it, just for tonight. I allowed myself to believe people still cared, and made sacrifices, and that love was still out there.

But it had been weeks. And the way Branch had looked at me before I lost him was enough to squeeze my heart in my chest, over and over again, until I couldn't breathe. I missed him. But he probably hated me. He thought I was the traitor, the one who had taken people, one by one, from our little slice of earth above.

I pushed the thought from my mind. For now, I would just keep flying, laughter at the edge of my lips and Branch's hand pressed tightly to mine.

The door opened again, but this time, it didn't close.

"Laney?"

I opened my eyes, partly thinking I was imagining it. It was only a few hours after they put me in here for the evening. It was still night in the Dome. I knew it like I knew the bell, the walls, and the pulsing lights. I knew the difference between night and day like the back of my hand after thirteen years of living in this place.

"Are you awake?"

Nash's voice. Even though it was dark, I knew it just as well as the rest.

I heard something scrape the ground, and the room lit up in shadows and oranges. Nash held a torch in his hand, his hair slightly messier than it usually was. He set the torch on the ground against the wall in the corner, but he didn't move. He was standing away from me, by the door.

I stared at him, waiting for him to say Mr. Dabir needed to take me to another room, with another thing placed inside that would rip off a piece of my heart.

But he stood there, and he rubbed his hands together once, like he was cold. Then, after letting out a breath, he walked over to me and untied my hands and my legs. He wouldn't look at me as he did, and he stepped back again after that, to the other side of the room.

The silence in the room was heavy, thick. But for some reason, it was different than the other times. Before, Nash never looked at me for more than a glance. He talked in low, flat tones, like I was wasting his time. And he didn't blink— didn't show even a flicker of emotion.

He rubbed his hands together again, and I tried to decide if I was imagining that he looked flustered.

"I didn't..." He spoke and then trailed off. I was lying on the cart still, though the ropes were on the ground, and I sat up slowly. It felt good to move, felt good to stretch my arms and my neck.

Nash was looking everywhere but at me—the corner of the ceiling, the wheels on the cart, the cold food on the plate beside me. I swallowed. What was he doing here? Suddenly, his eyes snapped to mine.

"I didn't know." He breathed in and out once, ran a hand through his hair, like he had just said the hardest sentence in the human language.

I just stared at him, wanting to know what was going on before I said anything. I didn't want to waste my words on

63

one of the leaders of the Dome if I didn't have to. But after a few minutes of Nash saying nothing else, I let out a breath.

"Didn't know what?"

He had been staring at the ground again, and he looked up sharply at the sound of my voice. He opened his mouth again, his eyes on mine.

"I didn't know he was going to destroy it."

The black box. He was talking about the black box. And all at once, the emotion flooded back. I was trying to push it, to bury it, because I didn't know if I could take much more of something good being destroyed at the hands of Mr. Dabir. But here it was again, in front of me, words falling from Nash's lips and shattering on the floor. Just like the black box.

I opened my mouth and closed it, blinked back the tears because Nash would *not* see me cry. Why was he even here? He was the one who had brought me to that room, pushed me in, and left without a word. Even after he saw the black box on the desk by the wall.

"I would have stopped it if I had known." The words seemed to come slow and fast at once, like they had been waiting to burst from his lips.

I still said nothing. The greatest betrayal of all is silence— something that seems so small but eats away at you, slowly, until you're nothing. He had given me silence, from the moment he looked into my eyes and became a leader of the Dome to the weeks he left me in this room, hours of cold and walls and me. And that silence had eaten at the piece of my heart that once belonged to him.

"Laney, you have to believe me." Nash took a step forward, and he spoke louder than he should have if he was trying to keep this meeting a secret. As if he read my thoughts, he glanced at the door.

"I know what that box meant to you, to all of you, and that—that was crossing a line."

I noticed the way he said *you*, like he wasn't a part of us anymore. Like he wasn't a part of me, Theodore, Alese, Dalia,

Gavin, and Branch.

I clenched and unclenched my fingers, looked away. I could see the corner of the wall, and there was a piece of rock that was darker than the rest. It was blue-gray instead of gray, a puzzle piece that didn't belong, and I wondered if it had been intentional. But this place was built over a decade ago, and none of the builders were still alive, so I guessed I would never know.

"Laney, are you listening to me? I'm sorry. I'm sorry you had to go through that, to get your hopes up just to see it destroyed."

I couldn't help but turn when he said those words. Had he really just apologized? Said he regretted something? But I had learned, from every room that I was brought to and every "test" that Mr. Dabir did. Never trust anyone. Hadn't Nash said that to me once, when we were trying to figure out our lives in the world above? *Rule number one in this new world, Laney: don't trust anyone.* Nash had devoted himself to the Dome, become one of the leaders. How could I know he wasn't just being a pawn in one of Mr. Dabir's games? No, I was done being fooled, over and over again. Trial five: the source of forgiveness, maybe? Nice try, Mr. Dabir. I'm done being your test subject.

"Laney. Look at me."

I looked at Nash, really looked at him. His chest was moving in and out, faster than usual. His gray shirt was wrinkled, like he had been too busy to hang it dry. His dark blond hair, almost brown in the lack of light, was tousled on his head, and his eyes were—I stopped.

His brown eyes were soft, sad, like he was wondering what had happened to all of this. To us. He took another step forward.

"Do you remember that time in the forest, a few weeks ago, when I took that lady's flower, tried to get her to say something nice about me? Tried to remind her what caring about someone was like? And she just ended up crying, saying I stole her flower…" His voice trailed off. "I only did that because I was worried that I would—" He took a breath. "That I would lose everything. The world we had built for ourselves. The people. Love."

I watched his eyes search the room and then land on mine. "You."

This wasn't real. I couldn't believe a word he was saying.

Nash ran a hand through his hair again, his words coming out fast.

"You were the reason I smiled for the first time, Laney. The reason I was one of the eight chosen to go back to the world above in the first place. My first friend. My first kiss." He paused, his eyes lost in thought, like he was reliving the warm cabin, the cool air, his hand in mine, and the echo of the tinkling music from the black box as our lips touched.

I closed my eyes. *It's not real. It's part of the game.* After a few moments, Nash spoke again, his voice soft.

"I can't just forget about all of that because of some rumor that you like Branch instead of me."

My eyes flicked open. Nash was right in front of me now, his hand inches from my own. I could see the worry in his eyes, the sweat on his forehead. His eyes were on mine now, and they didn't move.

"So is it true? I never asked you, and I owe you that much." Pain touched his eyes, but he blinked it away. "After everything we've been through."

I didn't move. Couldn't. What was happening? My heart was pounding, and I hated myself for that. I swallowed, and without meaning to, shifted my hand slightly. It brushed against his, and I pulled it away.

"I— This isn't—" I took a breath. Remembered the way he brought his face close to mine in the cabin in the woods, the way I saw a field of bright yellow flowers, breathless, when he touched his lips to mine. I remembered the way his eyes twinkled when he gripped my hand in his and held it up in front of the people, before we were chosen, for everyone to see. I remembered his look of concern after I had jumped in the lake, how he had placed his only blanket over me. And

I remembered the triumph in his eyes, the exhilaration when we walked up the steps in the Dome and led everyone outside for the first time in thirteen years. But most of all, I remembered how much I had hurt him these past few weeks. And how much he had hurt me. The feelings, hundreds of them, pulled at my chest, twisted my insides. And I couldn't breathe.

He reached his hand up, slowly, and touched my cheek. His eyes were still on mine, and I felt a stab of some emotion I couldn't name in my chest.

It's all a game. It's not real. I told myself that over and over again as he stood there, his chest moving in and out, waiting for me to say something.

But what could I say? If it was all just part of Mr. Dabir's game, I would be humiliated. But if it was real... *It's not*, I scolded myself.

And I had never been so upset at being right.

The door opened, a little more light filling the shadows of the slowly burning torch. But Nash didn't move, wasn't nervous about being discovered inches away from my lips. It was like he had known this was going to happen from the very start.

"Well?" Mr. Dabir's voice stabbed the silence, and Nash's face changed, slowly. Like he was seeing something for the very first time.

The silence was screaming.

"I can't help you." Nash was still looking at me, in my eyes. And I knew I should be furious that I was right all along, that he was playing with my emotions, trying to get the results for another test. But for some reason, I couldn't tear my eyes away.

"Nonsense." Mr. Dabir waved Nash's words away. "Did you actually try? Did you—"

"I told you." Nash's voice came out sharp this time, and he finally pulled his eyes from mine. "I can't give you the results you need. Get someone else for this one."

Mr. Dabir's face turned slightly red, and he watched as

Nash straightened and stepped away, to the door.

"There *is* no one else." Mr. Dabir watched as Nash walked by him through the opening. "Nash, did you hear me? There is no one else!"

I saw Nash whirl around in the hallway. "She doesn't love me anymore." The words cut through the air, and for a second I forgot where I was, what was happening. "I would say get Branch, but you banished him to the world above. So good luck with this one."

Mr. Dabir's face was white, but he quickly regained his composure. He looked at me once, blinking faster than usual. Then he stepped out the door, the lock clicking behind him.

I sat there for a second, and I sucked in a breath. I had been right—it was part of his game, another test. But for some reason, this one felt less like a test than anything else.

I blinked, trying to bring myself back, to pull my mind into the protection of the dark corners and thick walls. The plate of food caught my eye, a lighter gray than the surroundings, and it annoyed me. I leaned forward and shoved the plate to the ground, watched it shatter and the food bounce across the floor, then come to a stop.

I squinted. There was something that hadn't been there before. Something white—beneath the pieces of the broken plate.

With the ropes still on the ground, I stood. I walked across the floor to a white, thin corner that was sticking out under a jagged piece of the gray plate. I bent down and touched it with two fingers. A jolt ran through me. Paper. Just like in Adrian's notebook.

I pulled, and the piece of plate clattered to the side. It was small, about the size of a petal, but it had layers. I unfolded it. And when it was open, papery and soft with words scratched across the surface, I stared.

Hang on, Laney. Just a little longer.

-B

Tonight, I imagined I was flying.

11

THEN

Fifteen people were eliminated in the photograph challenge with the headband of death.

Fifteen.

We went from thirty-five to twenty, just like that. And Glasses Lady never told us what the "device," as she called it, was used for. It made me wonder more than I wished I would. Did fifteen people really answer with the wrong photograph—the doctor or the girl in the burning building? It seemed unrealistic. The head device must have played a big part, something none of us could see. And I feel like I should thank it, for pushing me even closer to leader. At the same time, I wonder just how powerful that piece of plastic really is.

But there's no time to think about that now.

Water rushes in like the way that coyote pounced on the black bird—fast, and unforgiving.

At least half the group is yelping from the pain of the spray, whimpering from its cold touch. But not me. Pain and cold are only in the mind.

I sweep my eyes around the small cellar, only about twenty feet by twenty feet. We're all pressed in here tight, like cattle in a pen. I see a wet arm inches from mine, and I pull away.

Four walls made of stone, at least a few feet thick, by the looks of it. One ceiling that sits on top of us like a lid, except for the small square-shaped door that Pimples is pointing the hose in, big enough to fit a body through, but I know it will be locked from the outside once this place is filled. The ceiling is normal height, maybe double the height of me, so this room will fill up fast. One ax, one bucket, and one small, padlocked box in the center of the room. Nineteen other people. And me.

The water is up to my knees now. Some girl is already shrieking, pleading for Pimples not to let us drown. I feel my lips curve slightly. They wouldn't let us drown; they need us.

Or at least they need me.

Seven people, four boys and three girls, are in the center of the room. One of them holds the lock in his hands, and the others shout out possible combinations that might open it. What do they think is in there, something that will save us all? I'm sure it's a distraction, only meant to divert our minds from what really matters.

I'm drenched by a splash of water, and I whirl around. A small boy with hair so red it's almost orange is tossing bucketful after bucketful of water to the corner of the cellar. Really?

I run an arm across my eyes and survey the space again. The water is up to my chest now.

"Not much for us to go off, huh?" A voice comes from my right, and I turn to it. A tall boy who looks about my age, with bright blond hair and a scar across his left cheek, is watching the room as well. I nod. Other than having us all climb in here and saying, *Challenge number four: the Dome is flooding. What will you do?*, Glasses Lady had given us nothing.

The blond boy is watching a slightly chubby, redheaded girl who just picked up the ax and is hitting the stone wall with it violently. He keeps his eyes on her, amused. "It's like they want to show off our stupidity or something."

I acknowledge I heard him but turn away. The water is up to my shoulders now, and this boy is acting like we're all about to go for a pleasant swim.

Everything is a puzzle, so this has to be too. A bucket, an

ax, and a box. I tense as the water reaches my neck. My clothes feel heavy, and the constant spray is like ice, but all I see is a challenge that I need to solve.

The bucket seemed useless from the start—the boy finally stopped tossing water to the corner of the room, hopeless thing. He should be eliminated just for thinking that action had a purpose in any way. I check the bucket off the list of things that have no benefit to the challenge whatsoever.

The ax—now that might come in handy. In a room made of wood instead of stone. I check that off the list as well.

The box is last. Five more people have joined in on trying to crack the code. The same guy, short but thick, muscular, holds it in his hands, and he tries combination after combination. From the shouts around him, I guess the lock has a word combination with four letters. *Dome, gray, deep, four* (for challenge number four, I assume), and *dead* are some of the words I hear yelled out, followed by him scrambling the letters afterward and then lowering his head, saying "What else?" as the water pours in next to him. I have to shake my head at that last guess. If the correct combination is *dead*, I would actually be worried.

So far it seems like the box is just a waste of time. If the actual Dome floods someday, we're not going to have to figure out a combination on a box anyway.

I push off from the ground and start treading water as it reaches my chin, and I see the boy with the box hold it high over his head and do the same. Everyone crowds around him now except three of us—me, the boy who has stopped using the bucket but is still holding on to it for some reason I will never know, and that girl. Hope. She's treading water in the corner opposite from me, and her hair is soaked. Her eyes, though, are what make me stop thinking for three seconds. They're nothing like they were when she walked into the photograph challenge, nervous. They're determined, strong. And I wonder why I thought she looked like the girl who was in the photograph—wide eyes, white skin, as she stared out the window of a building that was about to collapse around her. For some reason, I have a feeling that even if Hope is faced with death, she'll stare at it like she is now. She doesn't look afraid, like everyone else, and it catches me off guard.

I blink. The water is rising quickly now—they must have increased the flow. We only have a few feet of air left.

"Give it to me! You have no idea what you're doing!" A girl reaches for the boy with the box, but he pulls it away, hugging it to his chest underwater.

"You idiot!" Someone else gasps. "You got it wet!"

Water pours in, higher, faster. I look down, and I see my feet hovering almost ten feet above the ground. The ax is almost directly below me, stuck to the bottom.

The redhead I saw swinging it just minutes ago suddenly shrieks, lunging for the box and pushing the boy underwater in the process. The boy comes up gasping, choking, and the girl holds up the box in triumph. A few people around her reach for it, but she splashes her way to the wall and starts pounding the lock on the stone.

"Why—" pound, "Won't—" pound, "You—" pound, "Open?"

A dozen people yell at her to stop, and a few others are encouraging her. I watch it all like I'm watching a game, a trick. This can't be real. These people are falling apart. And for what? I hope there's a secret camera hidden in here somewhere, and Glasses Lady, Pimples, and Hairless are watching every second.

There is half a foot of air left. I hear people shrieking, gasping, breathing deep breaths like they're already drowning. And suddenly, above the voices and deafening sound of the last bit of water pouring through, I see the bucket the small orange-haired boy is still holding finally fill with water, not big enough for the small space of air left, and sink to the ground. And I hear his voice, above all the others.

"I can't swim!"

And I finally realize why he was holding on to that thing, clutching it like it was his very life and breath: it was holding him up. Like a switch has been flipped, he's heaving in breaths, flailing his arms wildly as the last bit of water splashes in. I move away, annoyed that his flailing arms are causing the water to toss violently, taking away a few extra seconds of air. If he isn't eliminated for this, I'll lose faith in the entire system altogether.

I tilt my head sideways to breathe in the last few inches of air. And while I do, I notice the water calms and the boy's screaming gets quieter, turns into a whimper. I turn, my eyes just above the surface of the water, and I see her.

Hope.

While everyone else is as far away from the lunatic as possible, she has moved closer to him. Her hair floats in waves around her, just inches from the orange-haired boy, and her lips are moving. She's saying something to him. And he's nodding. He's shivering, and gasping, and whimpering— but he's nodding. We have a challenge to accomplish, and she's talking to the boy? Calming him? What is she doing?

The second I ask that last question in my mind, I breathe in one last, long, full breath. And there is only water.

I blink as silence surrounds me. I realize how loud it was just moments ago. But not here. Here, if someone shrieks or gasps or sobs, no one will hear them. It will be like it never existed, because the water will suck it away, pull it into the blue, silent world like it doesn't belong. *Silence is just a way to hide all the screaming.*

I wonder how long the leaders will wait until they start draining this room—I guess I have a minute, maybe less. Most people can't even hold their breath for forty-five seconds. I, on the other hand, can hold it for much longer than that. The pond taught me two things: silence, and survival.

I watch the people around me, wide eyes, tight skin. I watch the redheaded girl still pounding the wall with the box, though slower now, like she finally realizes she might need to save her energy.

The ax is still plastered to the ground, useless. The bucket has joined it, floating a few inches from the bottom of the cellar. And the box won't open, no matter how many codes—or stone walls—are put into it.

I only have a few seconds.

It's a puzzle. It's always a puzzle. I close my eyes. And for some reason, the boy with blond hair, the one with the scar on his cheek, fills my mind.

"It's like they want to show off our stupidity or something."

My eyes snap open. It's always a puzzle. Unless it's not.

I'm on the wrong side of the room. People—there are too many people in the way. I push off from the wall and swim around a girl, eyes closed, mouth open, and it's debatable whether she's still alive. Another boy is on my right, and his eyes lock mine as I pass. He's shaking his head frantically, like this is it. Like we're all going to die.

I pass two more people on my right, one on my left, lift my legs so I don't hit someone below me. I'm almost there. Only one more person between me and the— I stop.

It's her again. Hope is watching me, her hair floating above her head, reaching to the ceiling. And she's—she's touching him. She's holding the boy's arm, the one who can't swim. Something squeezes my lungs, and I back up without meaning to. Touch is illegal, forbidden. And here, in this watery world inside a cellar without sound or gravity or air, she's breaking that law. Like it's nothing.

I shake my head, realize I have no breath left. I move past her, my heart beating in my chest, my lungs burning. And I'm there. The door that was opened before, to let the hose in, is tightly closed now.

I reach my arm up, send all my remaining strength to that door. I push it. It falls open, and in the silence of the water, I can't hear the crash. I pull myself through, and the light and sound and air hit me like a wall.

I slide away from the opening and fill my lungs, breathing deep. And while person after person climbs through the place where the door had been, gasping and choking, water spreading across the ground like blood, I see Glasses Lady nod at me once.

All that time, while people pounded the ax and filled the bucket and shouted out answers to a code, the panel in the ceiling had been unlocked.

What do you do if the Dome floods?

You walk out the door.

12

NOW

There was a time, years ago, when Mr. Dabir made us pretend we were swimming.

It was in our classroom, the six of us that I had studies with since day one in the Dome—Alese, Dalia, Gavin, Nash, Theodore, and me.

That day, Mr. Dabir looked at us all from the front of the room, his long fingers tapping his desk, and said, "Have any of you seen water?"

We all stood, the Dome's way of saying yes. I saw it every day—trickling from the faucets, filling our water glasses, sitting in the toilets.

Mr. Dabir shook his head. "No, no—have any of you seen *water*? Out there, in the world above. A deep blue that purples at the edges as it spreads out to the tall grasses and trees surrounding it."

I was confused. He seemed frustrated, and I didn't know why. We all sat down after that, except for Alese. Mr. Dabir nodded for her to speak.

"My town was by water like that. Before it…" She trailed off and looked at the ground.

Mr. Dabir watched her for a moment. And then his eyes looked past her, focused on something at the back of the room. I turned, slightly. There were only walls, a door.

"Let's pretend this room is filling with water. What would

77

you do?"

Gavin had stood next. "Drink it?"

Mr. Dabir's face turned red. "You cannot drink an entire room full of water, Gavin. It is imposs—" His face straightened. "Stand up, all of you."

I hesitated, but stood. I had never seen Mr. Dabir like this before. Usually it was words and numbers and books.

"Move your arms like this." Mr. Dabir lifted his arms in circles, slowly, pawing at the air. "See? You're swimming."

My eyes were at the front of the room, and I couldn't help but glance at Nash and Dalia, who were in my line of vision. They circled their arms, slowly, like Mr. Dabir was doing. They looked ridiculous.

"A body of water is a splendid thing." Mr. Dabir went on. "Inside, it's silent. Dark. A different world. But I guess"—his lips curled slightly as he remembered the Dome—"not so different from this."

I had pictured it in my mind, then. A large circle of water, black, bottomless. In my mind, it spread wider and wider, deeper and deeper, until it swallowed everything in its path. Like the men with black eyes had done to us.

"Laney! What are you doing? You're drowning!"

I hadn't realized I had stopped moving my arms. And in that moment, Mr. Dabir had seemed so sure of himself, the thought of the water so dead set in his eyes, that I panicked. For a moment, I couldn't tell if reality was the chairs and desks and air in the room, or the one in Mr. Dabir's head.

I felt the same now as I did that day—confused and disoriented, not knowing what was real and what wasn't. In fact, I felt like that almost every day now that Mr. Dabir had started playing these games, these tests, with me as his subject.

But this note.

I held it in my fingers, gripped the soft edges, like it would disappear if I stopped touching it for even a second. Because it might. Things had disappeared in this Dome before.

I thought back to everything that had happened earlier,

when Nash had come in the room. He had looked at me, at the room, at the plate. Did he put the note there when I wasn't paying attention? Was that the reason he came to my room in the first place? But he didn't bring the plate in. I swallowed. Someone had brought the plate in before Nash even came in my room, and I hadn't opened my eyes when they did. Did that person slip the note underneath? I mentally kicked myself for not opening my eyes and seeing who brought the plate. It was either that person who put the note there, or Nash. It had to be.

My heart was beating fast—it hadn't stopped since I first saw the note. And I tried not to think that this piece of paper could just be another one of his tests. That it could be fake.

I shook my head, willing it not to be true.

B.

It had to be Branch. It had to be. I tried not to think of the impossibility of him actually getting a note down here, on the plate of food, and then to my room. Was he down here already? Hiding?

My heartbeat quickened at the thought, and my palms were wet.

The door opened, and I shoved the note in my pocket. Mr. Dabir stood there, his body a shadow in the light from the hallway.

"Come. Since we failed to retie you to the cart last night, it should not be difficult."

I followed him to the center of the Dome, the large room where we used to have Collaboration. When I stepped through the door, the first thing I noticed was that it was dark. The only light was coming from the torches on the walls, and they were burning lower than usual.

The second thing I noticed was the people. Dozens of them, standing in the center of the room where the chairs had been. My heart skipped a beat, and I didn't know whether I should be glad to see them or worried. They were all still wearing those terrible plastic devices on their heads, like mine. And none of them turned when I walked in the room.

79

They all stared at the center, the empty platform. Okay, then. I was worried.

I squinted my eyes and saw Nash standing next to Emily near the front of the group. The words he had spoken last night rushed into my mind. *She doesn't love me anymore.* But did he? Still love *me*? I pressed my fingers to the sides of my head. This Dome was turning everything upside-down, and I didn't know what to think about anything anymore.

"A few of you know I sent a small search party to the world above." Mr. Dabir's voice rang out from the platform in the middle of the room, and I turned my eyes to him.

A search party?

"Now, for reasons I am not going to share, my trials are temporarily halted at the moment. And I am bored. So, thanks to my generous and altruistic nature, I have planned something special for today that I am sure you will all find just splendid."

I narrowed my eyes. I saw Arsen standing a few feet from Nash, and Brooke gave him a look. It seemed like even they didn't know what Mr. Dabir's "special plan" was.

Mr. Dabir raised his eyebrows in anticipation. "I have hidden something in the Dome that doesn't belong. That is the only clue I am going to give you." His cheeks widened, like he was delighted. "The first person who finds it will receive double food rations"—a few people in the audience let out a breath, and Mr. Dabir straightened—"for the next *week*."

I saw the wide eyes, the open mouths, and felt my chest squeeze. Mr. Dabir must feed them next to nothing. Maybe in the future I could sneak a few of them my food somehow. I didn't eat much of it anyway. And I definitely wasn't going to take this win away from them.

"I realize that is more than enough motivation for all of you to try your hardest." Mr. Dabir's voice echoed, hit the walls. "All of you except my fellow leaders."

Arsen looked relieved, like he couldn't possibly be expected to compete for food when he was probably getting all the food he could ever dream of.

"If any of my fellow leaders win, you will receive bragging rights." Mr. Dabir looked Arsen in the eyes directly. "I expect you to try your hardest."

I saw a few of the leaders nod. But not Nash.

"And, of course, there is one other person who needs more motivation." Mr. Dabir's eyes stopped on me. I could feel the silence filling the room like water, sucking out the air. People turned, were looking at me now, and their faces were stone.

"Laney would not compete for food, even if she was starving." Mr. Dabir said these words like they were ridiculous, like I was insane. "My search party in the world above is looking for a young man named Branch. And when they find him, which I expect they will very soon since they have already been there for hours, I give you my word I will not hurt him, Laney. That is, *if* you win the challenge."

I felt dizzy, weak. I couldn't have heard him right. Nash had mentioned finding Branch. Mr. Dabir had actually done it. And now Branch was in danger, all because of me. The world was turning more upside-down than normal. And at the edge of it, like I was hearing through a tube, Mr. Dabir's laughter rang out.

"There it is. Motivation all around!"

It suddenly dawned on me that I would be in the Dome, by myself, free from the cart and the ropes and the room.

I needed to get out.

I would run the moment these doors opened, and I wouldn't stop until I reached the top of the stairs, the door, and the world. I needed to warn him. I needed to find Branch before the others did. And I needed to get out of the Dome, to find my friends again, more than anything I had ever wanted or needed or hoped for.

Right now was my only chance.

Mr. Dabir clapped his hands together once. "Challenge number one: the Dome's hidden prize, the thing that doesn't belong." He shook his head, thinking himself clever, and held up one hand. "The competition begins when I reach one." He lowered his eyes, looked out at all of us. "Five...four."

I saw a man, cheeks sucked in like a deflated lung, push his sleeves up.

"Three."

People—too many of them—turned toward the doors, white eyes, bent knees.

"Two."

I clenched my fists, focused my eyes on the set of doors nearest me, sucked in a breath. I would run. I would run like water was filling this room, like I only had a few seconds left. I would run like I was drowning.

I was drowning.

"One."

13

THEN

I'm not supposed to be here.

It's late, even though I can't tell because there are no windows in this place. Just like the real Dome will have someday, a bell rings in this replica to tell us when it's breakfast time, dinnertime, bedtime. The moon is up somewhere, sitting in the sky next to the stars. At least, that's what we tell ourselves. If they have us sleeping when the sun is out, we would never know.

I stop, tilt my head around the corner before I start walking down the next long, gray hallway. Everyone is in their rooms tonight, as they should be. As *I* should be. I rub my hands on my pants, quickly and silently.

I'm sweating.

But I have to do this. If I don't, it will go against everything I ever knew. Everything I ever was.

I pass a room on my right, the room I recognize as chubby redheaded girl's. I saw her walking out of it one morning, on our way to breakfast. But not anymore. She was eliminated, as well as the short, beefy guy who had clutched the box the entire challenge like it was life, and four others. Six total, gone. Bucket boy was one of them.

The one that Hope girl had touched.

I shake my head, focus on the image of her, eyes bright, hair drenched, fingers wrapped around the boy's arm. How could she? A normal person out there in the world would be seriously punished for breaking the law of forbidden touch. And here, in the replica Dome where *future leaders of humanity* are being trained, she should be punished even more.

And I will see to that. One more person eliminated, my gain.

I whip around another corner this time, angry now. But if I don't do this, I won't be fair. Every future leader needs to be level-headed, smart, and fair. And I am, every day. Why they haven't just chosen me already is beyond me.

I stop. The door to her indent is in front of me, gray and thick and silent. I know it's not locked—though there is a way to lock each room from the inside, they told us to leave them unlocked at all times. We're supposed to trust each other. So much for that, Hope.

I lift my hand and flick the switch next to the door. It slides open, and I see walls and floor bathed in warm yellow light. It takes me a second to realize Hope is sitting on her bed, facing away from me, looking at something. She places whatever it is under her pillow—I'll have to look into that later—and turns. When she sees me, the edges of her lips turn up slightly.

"Jonathan?"

I blink, adjust my eyes to the light. Her hair is down her back, straight. She's wearing the gray pants and shirt we were all issued for pajamas, not vastly unlike our normal day-to-day outfits, but softer, they told us. I can't tell a difference.

She's looking at me, and I can't name the expression that's on her face. Intrigue? She doesn't seem surprised that I'm here, and that annoys me.

"I just came by to tell you I'm turning you in." My voice comes out softer than I mean it to, and I clear my throat. "I saw you touching that boy. You know that's against the law, and *ten times* more against the law in here. So…say your goodbyes."

I don't know why I say that last part. This room is empty except for me and her. She has no one to say goodbye to. But my voice sounded good that time, full of authority. And I warned her of what I was about to do, just like a future leader would. *Punish, but never let the punished be taken by surprise.* And my job here is done. I'll pull Glasses Lady aside and tell her what Hope has done tomorrow.

I'm still standing in the doorway, and I turn around, proud of myself. I'm an even better future leader than I thought I would be. I take a step back into the hallway.

"You chose the young girl in the dress, didn't you?"

I stop. If I expected her to say anything at all after my announcement, it wasn't that.

"What?" I turn toward her, and she's looking at me. She hasn't moved, and her breaths are slow. Calm, even.

"For the photograph challenge. You chose the girl in the dress."

I swallow, unsure what this has to do with anything. "Yes, of course. That was the only answer."

"Was it?" She stands up from the bed now, and I get this weird feeling that she's a ghost or something, and this is all a dream. No normal person would react this way, right? If anything, I imagined she would be begging me not to tell right about now. I swallow again. This is ridiculous. My throat is going to be scratched dry if I don't stop.

"Yes." I can't help the fact that my *yes* came out sounding more like a question. Why is she asking me this?

She stops at the end of the bed, across from me, and her eyes fall on the blanket. About five feet of floor spreads between me and her. "I chose the doctor."

I blink once. "But the doctor is a throw-away. No one gets sick in the Dome."

"The doctor is a *person.*" She says the words like she's correcting me. "Just like the little girl. And the woman in the burning building. You pick a person, I pick a person. We all win." She shrugs her shoulders and smooths out the blanket on her bed.

I take a step in the room, and the door slides shut behind me. I don't have time for this. But at the same time, it's

85

infuriating. She has no idea what she's talking about.

"Fifteen people were eliminated after that challenge. *Fifteen*. If all the answers were right, no one would be gone. Your theory is wrong."

She doesn't look at me, her hands still on the blanket, smoothing every corner and wrinkle and bend. It's like I'm not even here. Weren't we taught to look directly at someone when we talk to them?

"It had nothing to do with which photograph people chose, Jonathan." I cringe when she says my name, like someone so *not smart* can just say it whenever they like. "It had everything to do with this." She taps a finger on the top of her blond head.

Okay, I'll humor her.

"And why did it have everything to do with *this*?" I tap my head as well, mimicking her and wondering why she just doesn't say headband of death. Or device, as she would probably call it, just like Glasses Lady had.

Hope doesn't move, and her lips are a line now. She looks past me once, at the closed door. "Because it's the only thing in the world that can tell if people still have feelings."

I stop, then. Did she really just say that word? We were forbidden to talk about that, just like we were forbidden to love. I should leave, should turn her in for two things now instead of one. But for some reason, my feet won't move. Hope is still watching the door, her eyes not on me but on me at the same time.

"It doesn't matter who you picked, as long as you didn't have any feelings—sympathy or worry or care—for that person. You had to think logically, had to want to save them only because it's your job as leader. If you had any sort of feelings—worry for the woman in the burning building, sympathy for the little girl—the device on your head revealed that, and you were eliminated."

Silence surrounds her words. The headband of death— that's what it was for? But there's no way. There's no way fifteen people had feelings. Feelings were voted out of existence long ago.

Hope nods like she knows what I'm thinking. I take a step behind me, and my back hits the closed door.

"But you weren't eliminated. I guess I shouldn't be surprised." She looks down, like those words mean so much more than just that.

I take a deep breath, bring myself back. "Of course I wasn't. Feelings like that are illegal. It's right they were eliminated. They should be killed."

Her eyes snap back up at those last words. "Killed? You have no idea, do you?"

I look back at her, wondering how me telling her I'm going to turn her in has come to this. I'm confused, and I'm tired. "What are you talking about?"

Her eyes have changed now. They're still green, with gray at the edges, kind of like my pond just when the sun is about to go down. But there's something about the way she's looking at me. She looks—angry, almost. And it's the strangest thing that's happened all night, which is saying a lot.

"I have to show you something."

And again, another sentence from her mouth that I was not expecting. I move away from the door and turn, flip the switch with a flick of my finger. "I need to go."

She moves quickly, and soon she's standing next to me. I step back.

"If you let me show you, I won't deny that I touched the boy. I'll go without a fight, and you'll never have to see me again." Her words are coming out in a rush, and she's so close I can see her chest moving. I take another step back. If she talks any louder, she'll wake the whole building. I close my eyes and wish she would just let me go, that she would stay in her room and be silent, like a normal person. But if this is what it will take to have her eliminated without a fuss… I let out a breath.

"Okay. Show me."

She pauses, and the edges of her lips turn up slowly. She looks around once, her eyes on the long gray walls studded with indents, like a beehive. "Not here."

She takes off, and she's halfway down the hallway before I realize she means somewhere else. As in, not in her room. As in, somewhere else in this building, where people are sleeping and any sound she makes could be heard, and we'll both be eliminated.

I close my eyes again. What am I doing?

"Come on!" Hope whisper-yells, a little too loudly.

I swear, if she makes one more noise. I turn and follow her before she has the chance.

We run down a few hallways, turn next to a few doors, and run down another, longer hallway. It's a miracle we haven't gotten caught yet. Twenty-six seconds later, she stops suddenly. I stop next to her, whirl around and look at our surroundings. This hallway is different. It's darker, grayer, and it takes me a second to realize it's because there are no doors. I blink. I've never seen a hallway with zero doors, just long stone walls and then corners that turn off into other hallways. Still, it's not surprising. This building is huge, and I probably haven't even seen half of it yet.

"Okay, I followed you to who-knows-where for who-knows-what reason." I keep my voice low, and I turn back to her. "I don't get it. What are we looking at?"

I suddenly realize Hope is much closer to me than she was a few seconds ago. She's breathing faster than normal from the run, and she pushes her hair behind her back. Her eyes are brighter than I've seen them, and they're finally on mine.

My skin is cold suddenly. Is there a draft in this building? No, it's impossible.

"I'm not competing to be a leader of the Dome for the reason you think I am." Hope's voice comes out soft, light.

"What are you talking about?" I try to make my voice sound irritated, but for some reason, it comes out sounding like an honest question.

"I'm pretty sure they have cameras in the rooms, for security reasons. But I don't think you came in my room far enough to be in the shot." Hope looks behind me, and her words are still coming fast, bursts of hot air.

Cameras? I feel a pang of something in my chest, but then I remember how she had been. She was sitting on her bed or standing at the end of it, smoothing it, for the majority of our talk. It would have looked like no one else was there. Like she was just going about her night. I blink. She could have turned me in, just as easily as I was going to turn her in. And she would have had more proof. But she hadn't.

Why?

I look back at her, confused. But that was all in the past now. We're here, out in the open, and anyone can walk by at any moment.

"What do you have to show me?"

Hope stops speaking. Her green eyes meet mine, wide and curious, and something else. Like she's trying to read me, to understand me. I don't realize what she's trying to understand until she takes a step forward and reaches her hand up, slowly, inches from my face.

Panic fills my chest. "What are you doing?"

And then her fingers touch my cheek.

Warmth hits me like a wall, fast and hard and unapologetic. Heat rushes through my cheek to my chest, and from my chest to my arms and legs and fingers and toes. It sucks the air out of me like silence, like water. And then, all at once, it gives the air back.

I heave in a breath, back up against the wall, away from her. My heart is pounding, my head is spinning. For a second I can't see if what's in front of me is the wall or the ceiling or the floor, and I blink, desperately wanting the world to be back to what it was. I see her deep green eyes, her pointed chin, her blond hair. Her head is tilted slightly, like she's amused by my reaction. And I want to yell, want to scream at her for breaking a law, not once but twice, and with *me*. But my heart is thrashing, and my breath is gone, and my face feels like rubber.

She watches me curiously, like she didn't just break a law, like she didn't just turn the world upside down.

"If you turn me in, you'll have to turn yourself in too."

Then she steps down the hallway and disappears into the darkness, the trace of a smile on her lips.

14

NOW

My mother told me something once, when the world was falling apart and people hid behind curtains and crooked walls.

I had asked her what love was like, because I knew it was love that was causing the chaos, the destruction. And for some reason, I think to help me understand before the devastation hit our town, she answered me.

I heard that love is like a storm. It starts silently, but then the first raindrop falls and soon the air is full and the world is thunderous. And it doesn't stop. And you don't know whether you are dancing, or drowning.

She said something else once too, when we heard the first reports of a murder in our town. We had been sitting by the windowsill, drinking tea, watching the rain. And someone had died. Just like that. She looked at me, with dark eyes and a firm chin.

When you see a man with black eyes, you need to run. Do not look back. Do not hesitate. Just run. Run like the world is cracking behind you, falling apart bit by bit, and if you stop for even a moment, you'll be pulled in with it. Run, Laney. Promise me you'll run.

I had promised her that day the rain looked so dark it was like blood, pouring from the sky. And I made that same promise to myself now, with the cold floor falling farther and farther away with every step. *Cracking behind me. Falling apart.*

I didn't look at the stone walls and pulsing lights and black air as I sprinted through the Dome. I just ran.

I saw a few people turn down hallways and push into rooms, and others overturning beds and nightstands in the indents. One woman passed in front of me, her red hair sticking up in curls around her face. Her eyes met mine, and I almost stopped for a second.

They were wild, hungry.

It turned my skin cold, like there was suddenly a draft in this place that burst through, strong and unapologetic. I let out a breath, and I pushed on.

I passed person after person, moving through hallways and peeking in doors. In a normal world, a scene like this would be thunderous, chaotic. But not here. Here, no matter how many people ran or how many tore apart rooms or scraped walls, it was completely silent. It was like they weren't real—like they were floating from place to place, and if I accidentally ran into one they would just dissolve, like mist, and I would find myself on the other side. Like that white fog we saw in our journey to the world.

I ran, pulling in breaths so they were as silent as the air. If there was anything I had learned from almost fourteen years of living in the Dome, it was silence. *Silence when you eat, when you sleep, when you speak. Silence is the way to peace.*

I ran down five hallways. Six. That day we went into the world for the first time in so many years will forever be in my mind. And because of that, the way to the Dome's door will be too.

I passed room after room, not looking to see whose they were, or what they were. My lungs started to burn, but I pushed on. I had to warn Branch. I had to get out of here.

I was just about to turn the corner to the last hallway before the stairs when a laugh echoed in the air. I stopped, pushing myself against the wall. A few minutes ago, I blended into the others, was just another person trying to win the competition. Here, I was too far out. Mr. Dabir wouldn't have hidden anything on the outskirts of the Dome, where most people have never even been.

Another laugh burst into the air, followed by a "Shhh!"

I was confused. Who would be out here this far? And…and laughing? Still pressed against the wall, I looked around me. I was in a hallway that was different from the others. No doors, just long gray walls that spread like the edges of a mouth until they sloped into another hallway. I turned back again, to the sound. That hallway was the only way to the stairs. I had to get past whoever was there, somehow.

"Arsen, stop!" Another fit of laughter.

I froze. Arsen?

"Shouldn't we get back?" It was a girl's voice, one that I didn't recognize at first. And it was dripping with feeling. With desire.

My heart stopped beating for a second. It had to be Brooke. Arsen and Brooke. But them, together here, in the Dome, was breaking Mr. Dabir's rules.

"I'm not competing in some stupid challenge for *bragging rights*." Arsen emphasized those last two words a little more than the rest. His voice grew softer. "Besides, this is the perfect excuse to break away from the others. To be alone."

I couldn't believe it. After everything he had done, after pretending to be Mr. Dabir's most loyal subject this entire time, Arsen was breaking his own rules. He was here, alone, with a girl.

The girl giggled again, and then the air grew strangely silent. Something stabbed my chest. I missed him. I missed Branch. I wanted to be in his arms, wanted him to say those words to *me*. I had to get to the stairs.

The hallway was still silent after a few moments. I took a deep breath. It was darker in here, with no doors and fewer lights. They probably wouldn't see me. I held my breath as I leaned just the tip of my face past the corner, so I could see the hallway. And about halfway down, I could just make out two bodies. They were pressed against the wall, and I saw Arsen's hands tangled in a girl's hair, their faces together.

He was kissing her. And she was kissing him back.

My head snapped backward, my heart pounding. If only Mr. Dabir knew. After everything Arsen had done to me, I could finally get him back. I could finally show the world what he really was—a liar. But there was no time to tell him, not now. This might be my only chance.

I shook my head, slowed my breathing.

Getting out of here was more important than anything else. I would have to let Mr. Dabir know some other time.

Heart beating but no time to waste thinking, I stepped around the corner and held my breath. They were still together, arms wrapped around each other. Too focused on each other, I hoped, that they wouldn't notice me.

I walked a few more steps, kept my eyes on them the whole time. So far, so good. I almost went back, almost gave up just before I passed them. But I was too far now. I stayed against the opposite wall and could almost feel the warmth of their bodies as I slid by them. The hallways were large, and there was at least a dozen feet between us. Still, I wondered how they couldn't hear my pounding chest.

This is why love was banned—I couldn't help the thought from clawing into my mind. *Because it distracts you from everything else.*

I was past them now. I was almost to the end of the hallway, and I couldn't believe it had worked. They were still kissing, hadn't even noticed me at all. When I ducked into the landing before the stairs, I let out a breath. I did it. I was here. Only stairs and a doorway between me and Branch.

I hadn't felt so alive in weeks.

I took the stairs two at a time while still staying silent. I couldn't feel my lungs anymore, couldn't feel the pain in my legs. I felt light, like mist. Like the fog.

The stairs seemed to go on forever, as always. Hours passed that I knew were only minutes, but the climb up had never seemed so long.

I rushed up spiral after spiral, scraping the back of my hand on one of the rough patches of the stone wall in the process, and then nearly fell as I hopped the last step and burst into the room at the top. Cold, gray, emotionless. Like the rest of the Dome, and everything in it. I was so ready to get *out*.

My heart pounding in my head now, I rushed to the rounded bar sticking out from the wall next to the door. That door—the entire length of the wall, at least a dozen people wide. It was as big as I remembered. Bigger, even. I put both hands on the bar, grabbed it firmly. And I pulled down sharply, just as Mr. Dabir had done months ago.

There was a long, low creaking sound, and then nothing. Silence. I blinked. Pulled the bar up once, then down again, harder this time. The door groaned and a puff of air swirled dust in the room, like it was breathing. A pause.

And then I saw a sliver of light.

It was thin at first, so thin it barely cut a line across the dark floor. But it did. It cut the floor in half, and I was so happy I almost cried.

I watched the line grow wider—half an inch, an inch. Slowly, slowly, it grew, painting the gray a brilliant, dazzling yellow. I could feel a breeze push through the crack in the wall, making my skin tingle all over. *Come on, come on.* My hand was still on the bar, but I couldn't make it go any faster.

The opening was about half a finger's length wide now, and I saw sky. Soft, blue, buttery sky with clouds—clouds!—placed here and there, white and powdery and perfect.

I whipped my head back, looked at the stairs to make sure no one had followed. It was empty. I smiled. And when I turned my head around, to the glorious ever-widening crack in the door, I realized the warmth was gone. A shadow had fallen just outside, between me and the clouds and the sky. I squinted.

But not before the shadow spoke.

"Laney?"

Between the crack in the gray walls, the space between this world and that, I saw him. Sleeves ripped to his shoulders. Blond hair that was swept back like waves of grass. Eyes like the sun, golden and strong and soft, all at the same time. And that smile that seemed to light up his face, his cheeks, his eyes, even when the entire world was against him.

And I didn't know whether I was dancing, or drowning.

15

THEN

I feel different.

Watered down and lit on fire, all at the same time.

Once, when I was a child, I got sick. My mother insisted I lay in my bed, like all children that were sick did. I lay there, blanket up to my chin, wondering what I had done in life to deserve such a thing. My chest was heavy, head light. And when I stepped out of bed to go to the bathroom, I had fallen over, hit my head on the desk that was pushed into the wall. I didn't know why I had fallen, just that my body wasn't working quite right. Something was off—my balance was un-balanced, my normal functions that helped me walk and talk and stand, un-normal.

That is how I feel right now—un-normal, like my body is trying to walk under water when it should really be walking in air.

I know touch is illegal, but I didn't know it could make you sick. Before last night, I had never been touched before, as it should be.

What has she done?

I shake my head, push the covers back, and stand. I put my hand against the wall as my head clears. Challenge five is in less than ten minutes. I need my un-normal to get back to normal, *now*.

I push my hair back and straighten. One step, two steps,

the door. When I'm in the hallway, I take a deep breath and hold my head high, like I'm not sick or defiled. Like I'm not touched.

She did this to me.

Two can play this game, Hope. I don't think you know who you just messed with.

"Have a seat, please." Glasses Lady gestures to the chairs as the fourteen of us walk into the large room in the center of the Dome replica. Fourteen. Eleven are to be chosen as future leaders of the Dome. There are only three more people to get rid of.

I sit in a chair on the edge of the two rows, taking in five large cardboard boxes in the center of the room next to Glasses Lady, Pimples, and Hairless. I'm not even nervous.

"Thank you, silence please."

No one has said a word since we walked in, and I wonder if Glasses Lady has a script that she has to keep to no matter what. What will she say next, "Everyone please wear gray clothes and live in a Dome replica"?

Glasses Lady folds her hands in front of her and nods to Pimples. He clears his throat before he speaks.

"Well, yes. As I'm sure you have noticed, there are fourteen contenders left."

If anyone hasn't noticed that, they shouldn't be here.

"Eleven leaders are needed for the Dome. After this challenge, three more will be eliminated, and eleven left. Eleven. Our future leaders of humanity." Pimples pauses for effect, and I see a few people fidget nervously. There it is, sitting in front of me. Only one more challenge to go.

"Of course, the chosen eleven will continue to battle for the leader of leaders, the top dog, if you will."

I grimace at his word choice. But still, if being *top dog* means I'm the head leader of the Dome, you can call me top dog all day. Well, maybe not *all* day. I sit back in my seat and cross my arms. Can we just get this over with, already?

"For this challenge, everyone will need to choose two other partners, creating groups of three."

I'm surprised at that. I thought this was about survival of the fittest, one person coming out on top. Pimples straightens his gray shirt.

"As you know, the leaders in the Dome will need to work together to ensure a promising and effective future. It is about getting along with each other as much as it is about being strong enough to survive on your own." Pimples clears his throat, his voice growing louder. "Without unity, the Dome will fail, just as this world has."

Well, then just don't put me in the Dome with Hope.

"You have thirty seconds to choose your partners. One group will only have two, of course, as we have fourteen competitors." Pimples blinks once. "Begin."

No one moves for a moment. Most of us have only ever said a few words to each other before, if that. Everyone seems thrown off, like they walked in here prepared to fight, and instead we have to make friends and sing songs around the campfire.

Twenty seconds.

I look to my right, see the boy with the scar pair up with a boy and a girl who look so alike they could be brother and sister. Great. He was the only semi-promising candidate in the room.

I sweep the rows of chairs, see a girl with straight black hair cut short to her neck, pair up with a thin, gangly boy who hasn't grown into his legs yet. Nope. Don't want to join that team. Come on, come on. There has to be someone who is not completely incompetent. Someone smart enough to just stand there and listen while I do the thinking.

A short girl with choppy brown hair catches my eye. She's sitting alone, her hands crossed on her lap, staring at the floor. She's the one. She won't question me, I can tell by the way she looks: like anything and everything in the world is more superior than she is. I wonder how she got here in the first place, how she even made it this far.

"Hey. Partners?"

She looks up, surprise flashing in her eyes. She glances at

the chair to the left, like there's no way I could be talking to her. Her chin is larger than it looked from where I had been standing a few moments ago. Pudgy, even. She looks back at me, her eyes wide, and nods.

"Geena."

I nod back. "Jonathan Dabir. But call me Jonathan."

If I have any luck at all, everyone else will pair off and we'll be the team of two. Less people to worry about.

"Great, so we have our team."

The voice comes from behind me, and I turn. Hope stares, a hint of a smile in her eyes.

"No, there is no way I'm going to be on a team with you." The words come out fast, but I don't care. "Find someone else."

Hope's expression doesn't change, and it's like my words haven't affected her at all.

"Hi, I'm Hope." She turns to Geena, and Geena's eyes widen even more. For goodness' sake, hasn't the girl talked to anyone before? Then Hope's green eyes lock on mine.

"It's too late." She whispers the words, and I'm light-headed again for a moment. I shake my head, clearing it. This is ridiculous. And I hate so much that she's right.

Two...one.

"Thirty seconds is up. It looks like everyone has a team; well done." Pimples nods his head, satisfied. I don't know why I've started to sweat. "Each team will have one of these boxes for the challenge. And challenge number five is this: What does a leader look like to you?"

I see Glasses Lady's lips tighten, and I wonder what that means. Pimples looks at a watch on his wrist.

"You have ten minutes for this challenge." He clears his throat, presses a button on his watch. I hear a small beeping sound. "Begin."

Hope steps over to the first box in the row, clutches it with both hands. I just won't talk to her. I'll figure it out on my own, do my own thing. I swipe my hands on my pants once.

"Okay." She drops the box in front of me and Geena with a bang.

"Be careful! It might be breakable." The words tear out of my mouth before I can stop them. So much for that plan.

"Like I was saying. Here's the box, you're welcome for getting it." Hope gives me a look. "Let's see what's inside."

She tears the tape off the top and pulls the tabs to the side. I lean forward. It's filled to the brim with odds and ends. Suitcoats, glasses, wide-brimmed hats, starched skirts, polished shoes. Hope pulls something out, and it looks like a dead animal, small and furry and limp.

"Look." Her lips turn up at the edges as she places it on her head. "A wig."

I shake my head. This isn't a joke. It's our lives at stake.

I reach my hand into the box and touch the bottom, the sides. That's it? Costumes?

"A leader should look professional, right?" The mute speaks. Geena peeks over at Hope as she says the words. I can barely hear her, she's so quiet.

"You would think so." Hope is staring at the box, deep in thought. She looks over at a few of the other groups, all pulling out items from their boxes. They're all the same—a bunch of old clothes and shoes.

"Maybe we should look like the president—he's the leader of our people right now," Geena says.

Apparently, this girl talks more than I thought.

"*The president* is currently leading a world that's gone to hell." I say the words sharply, done with stupid ideas. Geena's eyes fall and she looks down again, at her lap. Good. Now I can actually think. We have seven minutes and three seconds left.

Hope frowns at me. "You're on the right track, Geena. Keep thinking."

Really, Hope? I had just gotten her to be quiet. We don't have time for useless ideas that waste precious minutes.

What does a leader look like to me? Confident. Determined. Someone who isn't afraid of anything. So how do some shiny shoes and stringy wigs play into that?

And then, in the middle of Hope's ridiculousness and Geena's self-consciousness, it comes to me.

"It's us. We're the future leaders of the Dome. So it's exactly how we look, right?" I look at the box in front of me. "This is all just a distraction, like the ax and the bucket and the locked box."

Geena says nothing, too scared to speak again. Hope looks up at me. She's silent for a moment.

"We're not leaders yet, though."

"But we will be." My head tilts again, and I close my eyes. Open them. Look back at her, confident and annoyed. "That's the answer. I know it is."

She shakes her head. "If he had said *what does a future leader look like to you,* that would probably be correct. But he didn't."

I shake my head, my palms growing hot. "I've been right about more of these challenges than anyone. You're really going to question me on this?"

Hope looks past me at other groups putting on ironed pants and crisp shirts. Then she looks back at me. I can't help but notice how green her eyes are today. It pulls the air from my lungs for a moment, and I mentally kick myself. *What is happening to you? Get yourself together.*

She doesn't blink. "Yes."

I let out all the air from my lungs. This is impossible. She's going to ruin this for me, for all of us.

Pimples's nasally voice fills my mind. *Without unity, the Dome will fail, just as this world has.* I don't think he's met Hope yet. Three minutes to discover a unity that simply doesn't exist is just not going to happen.

"Okay. I'll do my thing. You guys do yours." I take a step back from them, from the box, and cross my arms. It's a reasonable solution, right? If they're going to fail, might as well be two of them instead of three.

"You haven't even heard my idea yet. Is it impossible for you to trust someone besides yourself?" Hope stands, and her eyes meet mine. Geena sinks even lower in her chair, hoping to disappear, I imagine. I just stand there, unmoving.

"It is if that person is wrong."

"You're ridiculous. You think no one in the world is better than you."

My mouth falls open. No one has ever spoken to me that way before. "This is why I didn't want you in the group. If you would have just gone somewhere else for once instead of bothering me—"

"I'm sorry, I wasn't aware I was *bothering* you." She shakes her head, but her voice remains calm. "After all, if I remember correctly, it was *you* who came to me first."

Really? She's bringing that up now, here? Is she trying to get us killed? My head feels light again, and I place a hand on a chair.

"I only came to you because I was trying to warn you, like any confident and successful leader would." The words come out of me in a fierce whisper.

"You're so kind. I should have thanked you." Hope rolls her eyes, and it just makes me even more infuriated. Who is this girl who talks this way and breaks laws and thinks she knows better than me? No. This ends now.

"You should be gone by now, after everything you've done. In fact, I think I'm going to march over there right now and—"

"Time." Pimples's voice echoes through the air and bounces off the wall behind us.

No. It can't be. I do a quick sweep around the room, see every other team patting their wigs or straightening their button-down shirts one last time. It's true. Time is up, and we have nothing.

I swallow. If Hope doesn't agree with my idea, they'll eliminate us anyway. There's no way out. She finally ruined me. She ruined us all.

I turn to shoot Hope one last, infuriated glare, but she's not looking at me. She bends down and swoops her hand in the box, so quickly that Pimples doesn't notice. Then she places something on her face. Glasses? I say nothing, my face hot. Well, at least we'll go out looking ridiculous too.

I clench my teeth as the other groups share their ideas.

"The president, the vice president, and a member of Cabinet," a small, pimply boy shares as he presents himself and his team members, all wearing professional suits and shirts. I steal a glance at Geena. She's cowering even lower in her chair, and is she shaking?

"A doctor, a nurse, and a nurse's assistant," the girl with short black hair says proudly. She's wearing some sort of dress while a boy next to her has a short, gray wig. "Without the healers of this world, it would be deteriorating even faster than it already is."

I shake my head. The killing is going on anyway, more every day. Stupid answer.

I focus my eyes on the wall as I drown the rest of the groups out. May as well spend my last few moments in the Dome replica in peace. But when the last group goes, the group right before us, I snap back into focus.

"It's us," a tall boy with jet-black hair says. "We're the future leaders of the Dome, so *we're* what leaders look like." His eyes meet mine as he speaks, and he looks down. They're the closest group to us, only a few feet away the entire time. He…he stole my idea? My head pounds even more. I can't believe this.

The room stills. It's our turn, and we have nothing. All eyes fall on us, and I see Glasses Lady watching me, expecting me to speak. Well, sorry to disappoint.

"What does a leader look like to us?" Hope steps forward, her voice filling the room. It's strong. Confident. I look up.

"The answer came to us almost immediately. It's simple."

I narrow my eyes. What is she doing? Making us look even more incompetent than we already are?

"There's only one way to answer, really. The only leaders we see right now are in this very room." She turns suddenly, and her eyes land on the platform. "What does a leader look like to us? The three of you." She gestures to Glasses Lady, Pimples, and Hairless.

I blink. The glasses on Hope's nose are thick and gray, just like the ones Glasses Lady is wearing. And Hairless has a slightly hunched over back, just like the way Geena is sitting. But Pimples? I squint my eyes, trying to see the resemblance. And as much as I hate to compare myself to that pathetic excuse for a man, I do. Dark hair, strong chin. Just like me. And they're all wearing gray clothes, just like us. But it's impossible. It can't be right. There's no way.

Glasses Lady stares at us for a moment, her eyes flicking from me, to Geena, to Hope. Hope stares back. And then, by some miracle, she nods.

"Well done, Hope, Geena, Jonathan." She tilts her head. "You have used teamwork and unity to come to the correct conclusion, as a team."

I do everything I can to keep from falling over. She was right? *Hope* was right? I turn to her in shock, and her eyes meet mine.

It's not so bad when you trust someone, is it?

I can see the question in her face, in her eyes.

"To the team leaving us, thank you for your participation." Pimples sweeps his eyes up—and is that pride in his eyes? "To the rest of you, our final eleven, congratulations. You are our future, the sole thing that will take humanity from the ashes and build a strong, new, flourishing world."

And as Pimples eliminates the team with the worst answer—the president one, of course—I can't help but think about Hope's answer.

It was hasty, and sudden, and not approved by Geena or me, as it should have been.

But it was kind of brilliant.

16

NOW

My breath was gone now, my body suddenly so light I felt like one of them—one of the ghosts running around downstairs, clawing at the walls and floor.

My heart beat outside my chest, my lungs were in my throat. I stared at the shadow, and the shadow stared back at me. And I let the word finally, *finally*, fall from my lips.

"Branch?"

I saw a half smile, the way he looked when he was surprised, but it grew quickly, suddenly, until it lit up his whole face. "Is it really you?"

His voice melted in my ears and hot tears filled my eyes. I had wanted to find him, to warn him. But he was here. I had prepared myself to step out the door and run, to never look back. But he was *here*. And now I would step out the door and run, his hand in mine.

"Yes." My voice came out breathless, barely a word. I would never get used to what it felt like when your heart beat wildly, when your head was light and heavy all at once.

"How did you— I thought they were holding you—"

"They were." My throat was suddenly tight. "I escaped. I came to find you."

The door was only a few inches wider than it had been when I first saw him. It didn't used to open this slowly, and I wondered how long it had been since it had been opened before this. If only it would hurry. I needed it to hurry. He was right *there*. Suddenly the emotions flooded me like water.

"Branch, it wasn't me. I didn't take those people. It was Adrian's journal, not—"

"I know, Laney."

I looked up, and our words, rushed and breathless, stopped. He was staring into my eyes the way he always did. Like he was looking in me, not at me.

"You do?"

He shook his head, concern so deep in his eyes it made my heart skip a beat. "I can't believe he did that to you. Are you okay?"

"Seriously, Laney?"

I blinked, the sentence throwing me off. It had come from behind me, not through the crack in the door. I whirled around.

Arsen was standing at the top of the stairs, staring at me. Brooke was next to him, arms crossed.

No. *No.*

I turned back without thinking, and Branch was watching me, eyes wide. I shook my head quickly, a million thoughts pulsing through my mind but one standing out above all the rest: If they knew Branch was here, they would capture him. And who knows what they would do after that.

Something squeezed my chest, my lungs, and I couldn't swallow. Couldn't breathe.

And as the door slowly creaked open, almost a palm wide now, I shoved my hand through. I had to touch him, had to know he was real and here and waiting for me. I saw him take a breath and reach his fingers to mine, reach in the light, in the air that pulsed between the crack in the stone.

There was a loud *bang* beside me, and I jerked back my arm on impulse.

"I'm almost impressed." Arsen was next to me now, and he had put his hand by mine, pulled up sharply on the lever to the door.

I looked back, pushed my hand through again frantically,

but all I felt was stone.

Branch was gone.

"Are you trying to get your hand taken off too? Be my guest." Arsen watched me, amused. The gap was closing quickly, and the stone scraped my skin as I pulled it free, cold.

Feelings—so many feelings. They were welling up inside me, growing, ready to burst from my chest. Branch was there. He was *right* there. I breathed in deep, then pushed the air out, then breathed in again, like my lungs were broken. Maybe they were.

"Now, Mr. Dabir would *not* be happy with you right now. He trusted you." Arsen said the last words with emphasis, like a parent would to a child. His lips curled into a devilish smile. "You know this was all part of his plan, right? A test?"

I felt like I had been kicked in the chest. No. He was lying. I had almost broken free, and Branch had almost touched his fingers to mine.

"Come on, Arsen. Take her back to her prison indent, and we can get back to what we were doing." Brooke spoke for the first time. She stood in the corner, her arms around herself, like she was afraid to come in the room.

"All right. This is incredibly boring, anyway." I saw his fingers tapping a knife that was sticking out of some belt he configured around his pants. He thought for a moment. Then he put his hand in his pocket and pulled out rope instead. "Would you look at that! How convenient." He winked at me.

I saw Arsen standing there, arms outstretched, rope in his palms. I saw the walls that connected to the other cold stone walls. I saw the edge of gray that connected to the door.

The door.

Branch was behind that door. Only a wall of stone stood between me and Branch, a few impossible feet. The wedge between two worlds.

And the bubble of feelings finally burst.

I lunged at Arsen, slapping the rope from his hands and pushing him against the wall. His eyes widened for a split second, and I could tell I had caught him off guard. For a moment, I had the upper hand. I bent over him, one arm still on his chest, and grabbed the knife from his belt. He was struggling, his face suddenly white. He pushed me with both arms, and I stepped back, held the knife in the air, the blade pointed at him.

I heaved in a breath, two. I would get out. I had to get out.

"Drop the knife, Laney."

I kept the blade high but turned so I saw both Arsen and Brooke in my sight. Brooke held her own knife in the air, turned on me.

And in the brief moment I lost focus, Arsen grabbed my arms, pushed them together so hard I sent the knife clattering to the ground. Funny how he used to cringe at even the thought of touch.

"You think you're clever, don't you?" Arsen was pressed up against my back, my arms against his chest, his mouth by my ear. He pulled on my arms, hard, and I bit my lip, focused on anything but the pain.

"You should have actually tried to win the competition, Laney, instead of your stupid escape plan." His voice was low, breathing heavy. "When they find Branch, after Mr. Dabir performs his experiment, they're going to tear him apart, piece by piece. And you can confidently know you did *nothing* to stop it."

A cry escaped my lips, and I suddenly felt like my limbs were made of lead.

"Are you so delusional that you're still holding on to the hope that love exists?" He let out a short, emotionless laugh. "Give it up already. You're wasting your—"

"Let her go, Arsen."

I struggled to move, to shift my head at the voice. In the black of the room, the door now tightly closed to sunlight and air, I saw Nash. His eyes were on Arsen, and he looked angry.

The room was suddenly silent, and I saw Brooke slip her knife back into her pocket. I waited for Arsen's sarcastic response, for his defiant refusal. A second passed. And then he released my arms.

I stepped away from him quickly, pressed myself to the wall.

Nash didn't move. "Leave."

Arsen stood there for a moment. He looked at Brooke, then back at me. He shook his head, and I could see him bite his lip. Why didn't he say anything? Slowly, he reached down, grabbed his knife from the floor. His eyes were on Nash as he stepped away from me, to the door, nodding once at Brooke while he did.

Right before they reached the top of the stairs, Nash stepped in front of them. In the dim light, I saw him lock eyes with Arsen.

"You touch her again, you won't be walking away next time."

His words were as sharp as the knife had been. Silence. He stepped to the side again, and Arsen looked back at me once more. I had to blink once to see if I had seen right.

There was fear in Arsen's eyes.

And I wondered what had happened in the Dome—in this gray, lifeless place—that had made Arsen do what Nash said. Arsen had ever only respected one man: Mr. Dabir. But now he respected Nash too.

Suddenly the room was much colder than it had been.

Nash turned to me when they were gone. "Are you okay?"

I stared at him, and I had to remember to breathe.

"Laney." Nash took a few steps into the room, but he stopped with a dozen feet left between us.

I forced myself to nod, slowly.

He looked back at me for a moment. And for some reason, it felt different. Off, somehow. I saw his dark blond hair, his tanned skin, even though we were cut off from the sun. It was his eyes. Still gray-brown, strong. But all the laughter in them was gone.

His gaze fell on the thick gray door, and then back at me. Pain flashed across his face as he realized what I had tried to do, but it was gone as quickly as it had come.

He had learned how to turn his emotions off. He had learned how to turn his face to stone.

"Nash?" The word escaped my lips before I realized I had said it.

His face didn't change, eyebrows didn't twitch. It was as if I hadn't even said his name. He just stood there, his eyes on mine.

Then he turned and walked to the stairs, leaving me alone in the dark room next to the world.

17

THEN

For the first time in my life, I don't know where I'm walking.

I don't know why I pushed back my blanket, swung my legs over the side of the bed, and stood. I don't know why I put on my shoes and flicked the switch next to my door. And I don't know why I stepped out, in the middle of the night, with the moon hidden somewhere above the gray ceiling.

Again.

Walk with a purpose, Jonathan Dabir, my mother told me over and over again when I was a child. *Every step you take should be deliberate. Never go anywhere without knowing your destination, or there is only one destination you will end up: failure.*

She told me that when I was walking inside the house, to the store, to the car, across the park. Always have a destination. A purpose. Never go anywhere you haven't already planned in your mind. A successful person doesn't waste his steps.

And I hadn't. Ever since I could walk, I had followed her words. I always had a destination, a plan, a purpose. It was who I was, and it was why I was here today. I had never wasted a single step.

Until now.

I don't know why I'm walking. Just that I needed to get out.

I walk down the hallway, pass a few doors. People are

sleeping behind those doors, names I don't recognize. But maybe I should. After all, they're going to be future leaders of the Dome. They may not be the main leader, but we'll be living together, creating a *strong, new, flourishing world.*

I wonder what Pimples will be doing at that time. Are he, Glasses Lady, and Hairless really handing over the baton? Sentencing themselves to death?

I can't help but think of Pimples, cowering in a corner and begging for mercy while the men with black eyes take over the city. My lips curve slightly at the edges. I'm a terrible person.

But maybe she isn't.

The thought flashes across my mind before I can stop it. The girl with dark blond hair and bright eyes. The girl who argues with me, challenges me, and makes me feel like I'm soaked to the bone and lit on fire, all at the same time. The girl who is like no one I've ever met.

I shake my head.

This is why I stepped out in the first place. That stuffy indent wasn't enough room to think.

I dislike her still, I know I do. She touched me, and that's against everything the world has put into law. It's against everything I've ever known.

But then why does my mind keep coming back to her?

I press my hands to my temples as I walk. That answer she gave...that was almost impressive. And the fact that anyone almost impresses me in general, well, that's saying something.

I round a corner, my breath silent against the cool air. I pass more walls, more doors. I don't know where I'm going, but I don't stop. If I'm going to waste a step, might as well waste them all.

I've just rounded another corner when I hear something. It's quiet, like the light padding of feet on the ground. And for a second, I freeze. I didn't expect to see anyone out here. I imagine Pimples or Glasses Lady or Hairless walking the halls, making sure everyone is in bed. Except I'm not in bed.

I swallow, and my heart beats faster. I look to my right,

my left, and realize I don't know which hallway I'm in. Stupid. Never waste your steps, my mother said. And now going against her very advice is going to get me kicked off the Save the World Squad.

I see a flash of yellow, and I press myself against the wall. Wait. Yellow?

I swear I can hear myself breathing. But I'm ninety-nine percent sure I'm right.

"Hope?"

I say the word quietly, just a whisper in the air. But it's loud enough for her to hear. I know it is.

The footsteps stop. Five seconds pass, and nothing happens. But then, slowly, I see a face peek around the corner. Bright green eyes, squinting, slightly nervous but determined. I let out a breath. And when she sees it's me, she whirls around the corner.

"Shhh! What are you doing?" Hope walks up to me quickly, and I take a step back without realizing it. She looks around, her hair falling behind her shoulders as she does.

I can't help but be amused. "Calm down. It's just us."

She snaps her eyes to mine. "How do you know that? You were walking so loudly the entire building could have heard!"

"I don't *walk loudly*, Hope. If there's anything I know, it's silence. You're the one who—"

A door shuts in the hallway next to us and I cut off my words. My heart starts beating again, this time faster. *What was that?* I know she's thinking the same thing as she whips her head around toward the direction of the sound.

And then I know I'm not mistaken—footsteps. Coming our way. I swallow, my hands suddenly wet. This is it. We're both done for.

Hope turns back to me quickly, and her eyes meet mine. They're wide, green. So green. And without saying a word, she points in the opposite direction. I see one word form on her lips as the footsteps grow louder.

Run.

I hesitate for a second. And then I obey.

I jog down the hall around the opposite corner, pushing my breath to my lungs as I do. *Be silent, be silent.* All my years of practicing, of learning from the pond, have come to this moment. I keep running.

I can't hear Hope behind me, but I know she's there. I can hear the other footsteps still, and I don't know how or why they're moving so fast. But I know Hope wouldn't have gone the direction of that sound in a million years.

I pass doors, walls, flickering lights, small pieces of stone that have chipped from the walls and fallen on the floor. It all goes by in a blur. *Run with a purpose, every step counts.* It takes me a few minutes before I realize I might be going in one large circle. I look back, silently scolding myself as I do. I should be the one leading. But if it's life or death, I guess I can hand the baton over for one minute—just one.

Hope doesn't even look at me as she runs past, turning a corner and then taking a left, leading me down an even smaller hallway. Shouldn't we be going back to our rooms? The thought occurs to me as she leads me around a corner and jogs toward one large, heavy, ash-gray door that dwarfs the wall around it. I recognize it. A twisting pain fills my chest as she presses her hands to the surface and pushes, hard.

We shouldn't be here. In fact, we should be anywhere *but* here.

The footsteps are still behind me, Glasses Lady or a ghost or our shadows, I'll never know. And I don't have time to think as the door cracks open and Hope and I slip through, feel the cold night air against our faces as we step out into the world.

Never waste a step. Right?

18

NOW

Before I was taken to the Dome, in the moments between my mother's death and my descent down the long, gray stairs, I had to walk through a world that was being destroyed right before my eyes.

It was in those moments—those seconds that seemed like hours—that I had seen him. The boy, older than me, with dirty brown hair and eyes that once held the world.

He had made his decision there, in the middle of the streets that were being kicked into dust and the buildings crumbling to piles. He had taken one look at this broken world and fallen onto his knees a horrified, desperate boy. And then he had stood up as a man, black eyes and hands clenched and face turned to stone.

I remembered him more than I remembered anything on that day, the end of the world but the day that started the rest of my life. In less than a minute, he had made his choice.

And now, seeing Nash's muted eyes, his clenched fists and stone face—it was too familiar. It turned my blood cold.

I stood there in the hollow room next to the world, the door just steps behind me. Branch just steps behind me.

I breathed a deep, shaky breath. And then I did everything my mind was screaming not to. I turned, followed the echoes of Nash's steps down the stairs, into the darkness.

Nash was one of the first to laugh, to smile, to discover a

hunger for the world. It had always come so easy to him, like breathing or dancing or dreaming. Or holding my hand up to the ceiling, confident, hopeful. Proud. I shut my eyes.

What had I done?

I couldn't remember ever feeling like my heart was being torn in two jagged pieces. My heart beat for Branch. But it ached for Nash. I couldn't just leave him here, living in gray and darkness. I couldn't let him turn into one of them. And if I left, who knows if I would ever be able to get back in.

I had to right this wrong I had created, and then I would leave forever. I made this promise to myself, quickly, in the gray.

A woman ran past me when I reached the bottom of the stairs. She was silent, but her gaze locked on mine as she passed by. Her eyes were cold, full of fear, and hungry.

I suddenly remembered the competition, Mr. Dabir's words. *I have hidden something in the Dome that doesn't belong.*

Even if I was down here instead of in the world, I could still help Branch. I just hoped I wasn't too late.

I started jogging when I reached the end of the hallway without doors. I ran toward the people, toward the silent sounds of eyes searching and gray clothes swishing as they ran from room to room. The farther I ran, the more people I saw, and I knew: no one had found it yet. Everyone was still searching frantically for the thing that didn't belong.

Arsen's face filled my mind, his words echoed in my ears. *When they find Branch...they're going to tear him apart, piece by piece. And you can confidently know you did nothing to stop it.*

Arsen had never been so wrong.

I jogged past a corner and down another hallway, thinking. In the few times I had left my room in the past weeks, I had seen gray, stone, flickering lights, white people with tight buns and plastic devices strapped to their foreheads. It was all common, normal. Nothing had been off or out of the ordinary. There was nothing that didn't belong.

Maybe it was in a room I hadn't seen? I turned, a boy nearly running into me as he rounded the corner. He turned back, gasping, his eyes wide. We had almost touched, and he was horrified.

I shook my head and saw a door to my right, stopped and put my hand on the knob. It would take a year to check every indent in this Dome, but I might as well start with what was closest. I turned the knob and the door creaked open, but I heard a sound behind me. I froze. It was different from the silent searching, the people floating through the hallways like ghosts. Someone was talking.

I shut the door quietly and walked down the hall. I heard the hushed voices just around the corner, and I blinked through the darkness as I rounded it. There weren't as many lights here, and the hallway seemed smaller, the walls closer together.

In the gray, I saw two people standing in the middle of it, staring at the wall. They were older, their backs stooped with age, and one had a loose, gray bun on the top of her head. I was confused. Why weren't they searching with everyone else? What were they looking at?

I made no noise as I walked up behind them and stopped. The wall was gray and looked damp from the cold air. I squinted, still confused. And then the old man in front of me stepped back, and the world around me seemed to slow.

It was a drawing.

There, in the lack of light, I could barely make out a sketch someone had scraped into the stone wall. It was two people, straight lines for legs and arms and wobbly circles for bodies. And the two tiny people, scratched in the hard gray rock, had their arms outstretched: they were holding hands.

My heart started pounding and I let out a breath without meaning to. The people in front of me turned, and I recognized them at once. It was Delma, the sweet old woman who had helped Theodore and all of us, the woman who had been kind and gentle in the world above. And Alfred, the man who had been the first to stand in the Dome and fight for love at the very beginning because he remembered he once had a family.

"Delma." My word faded off as I stared at the picture on the wall, and back at her. Had they drawn this?

She blinked once, and her eyes didn't register my face. It was like she was looking past me. I swallowed and looked into her eyes, concerned. Maybe she couldn't see me in the dark.

"Delma, it's me. Laney."

She said nothing, her eyes distant and gray. Then she smiled and turned back to the wall, her fingers touching the thin white lines as she did. She was mesmerized, taken by this picture in the stone. And I knew at once the artwork wasn't theirs.

She spoke softly, the words just barely reaching my ears. "It's still here. It didn't leave us yet."

I stepped forward, wanted her to look at me. To see me. "What's still here?"

I heard footsteps down the hallway, and then Mr. Dabir's voice. It was loud against the hushed silence of the rest of the Dome, and I almost jumped.

Alfred's eyes swept past mine toward the sound, his expression suddenly worried. He took Delma's hand in his and they both stepped away, quickly, to the hallway next to us. Delma fell back for a moment, and she turned. I saw her gaze fall on the wall again, on the tiny bodies scratched into the wall. A whisper fell from her lips into the air.

"It didn't leave us yet."

I watched them leave, frozen for a moment. My eyes turned back to the wall. Who drew this? My heart skipped a beat, but there was no time anymore. It was beautiful, a flower in a pile of stones. It didn't belong as much as the grass or the trees or the sky. But this wasn't the answer. Mr. Dabir would never have drawn this.

I tried to remember the oval heads, the tiny dots for fingers, as I rushed down the hallway and turned the corner Alfred and Delma had. I knew Mr. Dabir was coming to scrape it away, to destroy it. But it had been there, as real as Branch was through the space in the door.

119

Theodore drew something like that once. The thought hit me as I walked, my mind in a haze. Branch had been teaching him to write in the world above, and he had drawn three bodies in the dirt, sticks for arms and circles for heads, hands pointed to the sky.

I thought of the note, and now this. The thought made my head light. I didn't know how it got there, or who drew it. But it was there. And it was hope.

I turned another hallway and realized the door to my indent was just a few feet away. I didn't know why I had come this way—habit, I guessed. I stepped closer and saw the door was open, cracked slightly. I touched the note in my pocket, thankful I had kept it on me rather than in my room. But still, I wondered what someone was doing in there.

I pushed open the door and saw someone crouching by the wall behind the cart. A stone lay on the ground—that blue-gray stone that was a different color from the rest of the wall. The one I had noticed when Nash was in my room. I blinked.

The person turned, and her eyes locked on mine.

"I found it."

She stood slowly, her red hair in two messy buns by her ears. She held a small square of paper in her fingers.

"Emily?"

I stood there, and my gaze fell on her hands. The thought that it might have been another note, hidden in the wall, sent a jolt of panic through me. But then she held it up, slowly, and I saw it wasn't. There was a picture on the square—faded, dusty, gray, and I couldn't see what it was from where I was standing. My heart dropped. She had found it before me. The small chance I had to help Branch was gone.

Emily's eyes were wide, her feet frozen to the ground. Then she stepped forward quickly and pushed the piece of paper in my hands.

"What are you—?"

"I get enough to eat. And Branch was always kind to me." She was breathing deep breaths, like she was terrified at what she was doing. "We're even now."

I felt the paper in my fingertips as she looked at me once more and then pushed the door open quickly, left me standing in the room alone. I tried to swallow, but my throat was dry. What had just happened?

Suddenly the door opened and Mr. Dabir crashed through. His face was red, and he was furious.

"Laney, I've had it with you. It is absolutely appalling that you would scratch a picture into the wall with—" He stopped. His eyes fell on my hands. I blinked, suddenly aware of what I was holding.

"The thing that doesn't belong." I pushed the words from my lips, my voice hoarse. "It's this."

Mr. Dabir fell silent, looked at the paper square in my hands for too long. "Where did you get that?"

I closed my mouth, confused. He seemed stunned, at a loss for words. And I didn't know why.

"Where did you get that?!" His voice punched the air, loud this time. I took a step back, my breath all but gone from my lungs. I looked back, at the stone on the floor. The hole in the wall.

"From—from the—"

"Give it to me."

Mr. Dabir was stone again, eyes narrow and skin tight. But he was shaking—I could see his fingers, trembling lightly, as he held them out and demanded it. I didn't know what was happening. Didn't know what I did.

Without thinking, I looked down at the paper square clutched in my fingers.

"Give it to me!"

My eyes snapped up. I held it out, and Mr. Dabir snatched it from my hands. He looked at me, and I looked back at him.

"How dare you." The words came out strong, but his voice was shaking. And his eyes looked strange—while they were usually gray, confident, seething, I saw some emotion in them I had never seen before. Sadness. And it caught me so off guard I didn't notice when he pushed back through the door and clicked the lock shut.

But in the second I had glanced down, I saw it. The paper square—it was a photograph. The dusty picture of a girl with bright green eyes and blond hair curled down her back standing next to an older man with wrinkled hands and a green hat. But what made it different, what made it stunning, was this: the girl had her arms wrapped around the old man in a hug, a smile spread across her face. And the man was a younger, slightly less wrinkled version of Alfred.

19

THEN

The world—the real, outside world—is lighter than I remember.

I've been inside for so long, with dark rooms and stone walls and gray, that I've forgotten what it's like to feel the cool air of night on my face, to see black that isn't black, but gray-white and blue-gray that fades to dark blue at the edges.

For a second my senses seem to tumble back inside my lungs, my nose, my eyes. And I wonder if someday I'll forget what it's like to step into night, to feel the cool air squeeze my chest. I wonder if, after living in the real Dome for so many years, I'll even care.

And then, with my senses, reality tumbles back too.

I want to speak, want to ask Hope *what in the world she's thinking* by breaking the biggest rule and bringing us outside the replica Dome at night. Outside! Two future leaders of humanity, leaving the very building that's supposed to keep us safe.

But it's quiet, and I don't know if there are any guards outside at night. I don't want to risk being heard, and I don't want to turn around and charge toward the footsteps in the hallway and risk being caught by Pimples or Glasses Lady.

I'm trapped. And the only thing I can think to do is run.

The sky is light on one side, and I realize it might not be the middle of the night after all. The colors fade to soft blue and yellow as the sun slides beneath some hills in the distance, behind the redbrick wall. Do they really have us going to bed before the moon is out? I blink. Apparently we're being treated like toddlers and I had no idea.

Hope runs to the bushes and trees I saw the coyote go into, being careful to stay close to the wall, in its shadow, so we're not seen. I swear my heart is ready to plummet out of my chest. I've heard about people having heart attacks before, and I wonder if this is what it feels like. Short of breath, pounding head, the nagging thought that my life is almost over. Yep, I'm gone.

I'm just about to turn around, the thought of facing the footsteps so much more welcoming than venturing out into the cold, forbidden night, when Hope stops just inside the trees.

She's barely panting. It's like she does this for fun.

"Are you insane?" I finally let the words escape in a loud whisper. "We can't be out here! We need to go back!"

Hope just looks at me. She says nothing, just stares, and I wonder if I have something on my face or if my hair looks ridiculous from running. Then, suddenly, her face breaks into a smile. And something bubbles up from her lips—is—is that laughter? I clench up, my blood cold at the sight, the sound.

This—being outside, the smile, the laughter—it's all illegal. What is happening?

"I'm sorry, I—" Hope takes a deep breath and calms down. I'm shaking. Or fuming. I can't tell. She keeps her eyes on mine. "Why did you follow me?"

"Follow you?" She can't be serious. "We were going to get caught!"

Hope's lips are still curved. "Yeah, but you could have gone back to your room. There are other hallways, you know."

I hesitate. Is she right? Could I have simply gone another way? A thousand thoughts cross my mind, one of them being her confident answer for challenge five. Why am I thinking about that right now? This girl—she's messing with my mind, my decision-making, my chance at being a respected leader of the Dome. And to top it all off, she keeps breaking rule after rule. I stare back at her lips, curved like the bottom of a bucket.

"Stop smiling. And if you *ever* laugh again…"

"What, you'll report me?" Hope's smile doesn't move. "We saw how well that worked out last time."

I take a step back, run a hand through my hair in frustration. "This is insane. I'm leaving."

"Jonathan, wait." Hope says the words in a whisper, like how we've been talking the whole time. But something about hearing my name makes me stop, and I don't know why. I turn around one more time and look at her.

Hope nods toward the sky. "Don't you want to see it?"

I narrow my eyes and follow her gaze. She's looking above the wall, at the sliver of sun that's disappearing quickly. And again, I wonder if this girl is crazy. Why on earth would I sit here staring at the sky?

"Nope." I turn again and start walking. I'm almost out of the trees when I feel something in my chest. It's small, like the prick of a needle or a papercut. But it's there. And it makes me stop. Well, I guess *one minute* will ensure the footsteps are long gone. I can spare one minute.

My eyes adjust in the shadows of the trees, and I see Hope. She's sitting cross-legged in the damp grass, her arms out behind her, and she's staring through a hole in the leaves up into the sky. She's not smiling anymore. Instead, she looks lost in the clouds, the air. I wonder why anyone would waste precious moments of life on the ground, their eyes on something unreachable.

She turns suddenly, catches me watching her. I don't move, but I tear my eyes away, hoping she thinks I was watching for guards or something. She speaks.

"You can't even see from there." She beckons to me with one hand, lifts it from the grass. "I promise it's not going to kill you to watch one sunset."

I don't move for a moment. This is crazy. Am I crazy? But

125

before I realize it, I'm walking. It's like my legs have a mind of their own. This has never happened before—my body has always been in sync, has always obeyed my mind. I must be crazy.

I stop next to her, but I don't sit. I shoot a glance at her that says *this is only for a minute*, and then I turn to the sky. After all, it's my duty as leader to make sure all the other leaders are safe, isn't it? She sits back again, satisfied.

I swallow. Then I let out a breath in the cool air. Then I swallow again. The air is getting cooler, and our shirts are made of some thin, cheap material. We're going to catch a cold.

"We should really go."

"Shhh!" Hope's whisper butts in. "You're ruining the moment." She looks at me and sighs. "You're messed up worse than I thought, aren't you? Just look." She commands the words and points to the sky. "*Really* look."

"Messed up? I'm the smartest person in that replica Dome—"

"Jonathan." Hope sighs and falls silent again. And I swallow my words.

"You promise we'll go back if I stand here silent for three minutes?"

Hope turns to me. "Five."

I hesitate. "Four. Four minutes. Not a second more."

Hope nods and turns back to the sky. And I start counting.

Three minutes, fifty-nine seconds...three minutes, fifty-eight seconds...three minutes, fifty-seven seconds.

A squirrel barrels from a tree into a bush, and I almost jump. Stupid animal.

Three minutes, fifty-six seconds...three minutes, fifty-five seconds.

I tap my fingers on my pants and look around the small clearing, bored. My eyes fall on Hope again. She looks so taken, so enthralled by the sky that I can't help but follow her gaze. So I look.

The sky is darkening slowly, like the flickering lights from the Dome replica, except the flame of the sun is slowly going out for good. The sliver of yellow is bright—brighter than Hope's hair—and it fades into a deep orange, and then purple. The colors stretch to the sky, and it makes me remember something I've heard about people painting in the past, using colors to create images on paper. All the colors in the sky blend together, fade at the edges, like water. And I see hot, white dots of light sprinkled in the orange, the blue, the purple-black. Stars. Thousands of them, splashed across the sky like someone tripped while they were carrying a cup of milk.

Then, suddenly, it's like the world pauses. The wind and the leaves and the birds stop moving, and the edge of the sun freezes as if to say, *I know I'm brilliant, and you'll miss me while I'm gone.* And then it un-pauses, and the sun slips under the earth, and everything starts moving again, except slower, to match the pace of the darkening sky.

I don't realize I've stopped counting until I hear movement next to me and I turn, see Hope watching me. I blink. And for some reason I remember the words she said to me in the hallway, right before she touched her fingers to my cheek.

"You said you weren't here for the reason the rest of us are." I pause for a moment, my eyes still on hers. "Why are you here, Hope?"

She hesitates. She didn't expect that question. But I wait. The touch, the laughter, the sunset, everything. There has to be an explanation. And I know, more than I know anything, that I'm not leaving until I have it.

Slowly, Hope stands. She turns to me, her eyes a deep green in the shadow, and she reaches into her pocket. When she holds her hand up in front of me, there's a small square-shaped paper in it. It's the one that she pushed under her pillow the night before—it has to be. I don't move, but she nods. So I lift my arm, take the paper from her fingers, and flip it over.

127

I have to squint to see it in the darkness. But I recognize Hope immediately—her bright eyes and long blond hair that curls around her face.

I swallow, and my eyes flick back to hers. She doesn't move, and I look down at my hands again.

In the photograph, she's touching someone. Her arms are around a man, much older than her, with gray hair and light gray eyes that fade to mint blue at the edges. His wrinkled hands are clasped in front of him. And both are smiling, wider and with more confidence than I have ever seen before.

I look back up at Hope, the photograph still in my fingers. She's watching me, her eyes searching mine. She seems different than normal—less confident, more vulnerable. Like I chipped back a part of her *always prepared, always ready* brick wall.

Then Hope nods at the photograph once. "My grandfather." And those words are enough to leave me speechless.

Grandfathers don't stick around with their own son or daughter, let alone their child's daughter. Males help populate the earth once and then leave, never to be heard from again. The mother raises the child until the child is old enough to go out on his or her own. And the fact that Hope was posing with her grandfather—*knew* her grandfather—was enough to get them both killed, twice. In fact, *grandfather* isn't even a word anymore. I only recognize the word because I know much more than the average person. I start to speak, but she beats me to it.

"My mother died when I was young." Hope looks down at the square in my hands, lost in it for a moment. "My grandfather heard about it and he…he came back. He snuck me food when no one was looking, found me housing. He taught me to live, to survive, all in secret, when no one was looking. I would be dead if it weren't for him."

I open my mouth and close it. Just hearing this could get me jailed for life. I can feel the sky darkening, the air getting colder. But sweat is trickling down my shaking hands. "Why would he do that? He could've been killed."

Hope's eyes snap back to mine, as if the answer should be obvious. "Because, Jonathan. He loves me."

I feel like something slams into me, like the yellow and purple and black all fall from the sky in one giant heap. I heard wrong. I must have.

"I'm here because of him." Hope keeps speaking, like the world isn't suddenly spinning. "I'm here to make sure love is never gone for good."

"What are you talking about?" The words come out of me quickly, in one breath. "Are you crazy? Love *is* gone. Banned. Forbidden. Even if you wanted to, you could never—"

"It's not, though." Her words, quiet but firm, make me stop. "It's in a smile. In a sunset. It's there, I just need to help people find it again."

My throat is suddenly dry, and I hear the leaves shake as the wind picks up. A raindrop lands on my neck.

"You just watched the sunset." Hope's hair is twisting in the wind, like the flames of a fire. She's frustrated—I can hear it in her voice. "Didn't you feel anything?"

Feel. Everything I have ever felt was smart, or angry, or confident, or strong.

Or like I'm soaked to the bone and lit on fire, all at the same time.

And I suddenly wonder what that feeling is. It's not anger, or confidence. It had felt like my world was falling apart and pulling together and falling apart, over and over again. It has to fit into one of the categories, though, doesn't it? There is nothing else. Being infuriated and intrigued, wanting to leave but being pulled to stay, my mind tearing in two around this girl called Hope who breaks laws and turns worlds upside down. There has to be a name for that feeling, a perfectly acceptable, legal category. I just don't know what it is.

Rain is falling now, faster, each drop planting on a leaf or the grass or our skin. The world becomes *un-silent*, alive. And I swallow, suddenly desperate to know what that feeling is called. Everything has a name in this world. Every step has a purpose.

Hope's green eyes leave mine and look at the darkening sky, the trembling leaves. "We should go." She says the words loudly, over the sound of the rain. Then she turns and pushes back some branches, starts to walk out of the trees and bushes in the middle of the field in between the redbrick wall.

"Wait."

I have no idea why that word comes from my mouth. For a second, I think someone else must be in the clearing with us, must have said the word instead. The rain, and the colors of the sky quickly fading to black, and the disappearing stars, and the cold air, and the wind screaming between the trees, and being *outside* and not in the Dome replica must be making me crazy.

Hope turns, and I see her push her hair back as the wind whips it in front of her face. She stands there for a few seconds, her eyes on me.

I take a breath, my mouth suddenly empty. My mind is pulling again, stretching in two different directions. *Wanting to stay but being pulled to leave.* I think of the Dome, the challenges, being named one of the eleven leaders of humanity. I think of laughter, the orange-and-blue sky, the feeling of Hope's touch, like fire on my skin.

And I do everything my mind is screaming not to.

"This way is faster."

I point to the left, slightly off from the place Hope is standing. I look at everything but her—the shaking leaves, my soaked clothes, the large gray door a hundred yards in front of us—as I walk past her and out of the trees.

I'm not crazy. If there's anything I know for sure, it's that.

As I walk through the door and back into our world, I suddenly remember I still have Hope's photograph in my fingers. I turn around, but she's gone, disappeared down the opposite hallway. I put it in my pocket.

20

NOW

Nothing changed while I sat against the wall in my indent, the door tightly locked and seconds slowly ticking by.

The walls were still gray, the air still dark, the piece of blue-gray wall still lying on the ground next to the cold metal cart. Nothing had changed since Mr. Dabir had come into the room, eyes burning and face white.

But it felt like everything had changed.

My fingers still felt the trace of the small piece of paper I held minutes, or hours ago, I wasn't sure. The image of the blond girl with Alfred—Alfred!—still clear as the sky in my mind. Who was that girl that Alfred was with? And why was Mr. Dabir so shaken by the photograph?

I pushed back a few strands of hair that had fallen out of my bun, and my hands brushed the plastic device still fastened tightly to my skull.

Why had Emily given the photograph to me? Did she really think it was the prize, really want to help me win? Or was it all part of the endless tests?

I hugged myself, the cold air even colder down by the floor. I never thought I would miss those thin, scratchy blankets from our journey in the world above.

I heard footsteps in the hall and a key turning in the lock. The door opened, and Nash walked in. He stopped just inside the door, held it open with one of his hands.

"Mr. Dabir is calling everyone to the center of the Dome."

He looked at me, and his eyes were unreadable. Emotionless. The event with Arsen in the room next to the door flashed through my mind, and I swallowed, my throat tight.

"Hey, thank you. For saving me from Arsen earlier."

Nash blinked once, but his expression didn't change. "I was just doing my job."

His answer surprised me. Blunt, not harsh, but matter-of-fact. It was too much like the people who buried themselves from the world, hid all their emotions so deeply within themselves that the only thing left was gray eyes and silence.

It wasn't Nash.

The panic surfaced again, like a dull punch to my gut.

"He wants everyone to come to the center of the Dome. Now." Nash spoke the words again, without moving. His hand still hovered on the door.

The emotions flooded me then, quickly.

"Do you remember when we saw water for the first time?" I stood slowly, my words coming in a rush. "You took one look at it and you ran—dropped your backpack on the grass and threw your hands up in the air. I thought you were crazy." I almost laughed at the memory of Nash, sprinting across the grass and then jumping into the pool of blue.

Nash was staring at me, and the expression on his face didn't change.

"Or when you found the trees when we were climbing up the mountain—you found them, Nash! And it made Alese smile for the first time."

Nash just looked at me. "We need to go."

My expression fell. No, it should be easy. He should remember. He should be Nash again.

"What about the time we found the house in the woods? Or when you found the books, and you were mesmerized? Or when I had to jump into the water because I lost that challenge, and you gave me your blanket—"

"Laney." The sound made me stop. I looked at him, and

he turned to the hall. "You can come on your own, or I can get the rope."

I opened my mouth, closed it. Looked back at him in silence, stunned. He stood there, his gray-brown eyes on mine. Not angry. Not anything.

Of all the people who would change, it would never be Nash. He would never give up the world, the chance to live and breathe and *be*, for a pile of stones and darkness. He wouldn't. He of all people knew how priceless it was.

I took a step forward, and then another. Followed him out of the room and down the hall, my heart beating faster than it had in weeks.

He couldn't.

No heads turned when we stepped through one of the pairs of doors that lead to the room where we used to hold Collaboration. The air was quiet, and it felt heavy. Everyone was sitting in chairs, and Nash nodded to an empty seat on the last row as we passed. I looked at him, but his eyes faced forward, and he kept walking to the front of the room, sat next to the other leaders of the Dome on the platform, facing us. Emily was next to him, and her eyes flicked to mine for a moment, but then turned to the back of the room. I sat in the chair just as Mr. Dabir took the stage.

"Splendid, we're all here." His hands were clasped together, and he looked pleased. The trembling fingers, the shocked face, gone.

"I brought you all here for a little celebration." Mr. Dabir's eyes fell on the back of the room, like he was waiting for something. "Now, I haven't reached my goal yet. But I am pleased to say I am one step closer to accomplishing it."

Silence. And for the first time, I wondered what this was about.

"Arsen, you may bring the prisoner."

The word made my hands immediately cold. Branch. They had found Branch. Panic and dread and fear washed over my mind like water.

I whirled around in my chair, my hands gripping the sides,

and the flood of feelings hit a wall.

Erika?

The woman was walking down the aisle slowly, her hands pushed tightly together by a thick rope. Her hair was still twisted into four strands and hanging down, thorns on the sides of a stem, like it had been in the world above. Her eyes were wide, slightly off, like she wasn't sure what was happening or where she was. She was cleaner, which was strange, her skin slightly lighter than it had been. But I would have recognized her anywhere.

I blinked, frozen to my chair.

The woman who told a story about drowning her child, and then smiled. The woman who led us to the dead boy with red hair in the woods. The woman who had kissed a man next to the trees with blood-stained hands. And the woman who had run after Gavin untied her, had sprinted into the woods and was never seen again.

Until now.

Arsen pulled Erika up the aisle slowly, walked proudly in front of her, like she was a prize. Erika was breathing deeply, but everything else about her was calm. She turned suddenly as she passed, and her eyes locked on mine. Blue, like ice. She held my gaze for a few seconds, and I was frozen, couldn't look away. Then she turned, her feet scraping the ground as she stepped up onto the center of the podium and then fell on her knees next to Mr. Dabir.

Arsen was beaming, and I remembered the way he had kicked her, again and again, screaming when Gavin let her get away. He was finally getting his chance. The thought sickened me, and I watched in horror.

"Ladies and gentlemen, I give you Erika." Mr. Dabir stepped forward and nodded at Arsen as he took his seat. "We may not have found the precise person we were looking for in the world above, but we found her. And she's going to tell us what we need to know." Mr. Dabir's eyes fell on the woman standing in the middle of the platform, staring at the back of the room. "Isn't that right?"

Erika didn't move. But one quiet, firm sentence came from her lips. "I will never tell you anything."

A few seconds passed before I realized I hadn't taken a breath. Something was different about her, but I couldn't say what. She seemed...calmer. Slightly less crazy. And it confused me.

"Erika, you know the consequences if you choose to withhold information from us." Mr. Dabir's eyes narrowed. "If anything, you should be sharing everything! These living quarters are a million times better than that dump of a river we found you by."

She had been by the river. The river just a short distance from the Dome.

"You know nothing of beauty." Erika looked up, and her eyes locked on his.

Beauty? Did that word just come from her lips? This wasn't the Erika I knew—the crazy, strange, hollow woman who did things that terrified me. Something had changed. My eyes dropped to the people, the leaders. No one looked surprised or even phased at all.

Mr. Dabir's laugh cackled across the air and bounced on the walls. Then his mouth pulled into a line again, annoyance flashing across his eyes.

"Erika. Where is he?"

Erika took a breath, slowly, and looked out at the chairs.

Looked at me.

My heart was pounding, and I didn't know why.

"Where is Branch?" Mr. Dabir's words pounded the air, and I clenched my chair tightly.

Why would Erika know where Branch was? This was crazy. Mr. Dabir was crazy.

"I saw your backpack, Arsen showed it to me. A container of water. Food. A flower. *The backpack in general.* And this!" Mr. Dabir reached behind him suddenly and revealed a light purple blanket, tattered and worn, with faded yellow dots. Like lavender. I recognized it immediately.

"This blanket belonged to Alese!" Mr. Dabir's voice

thundered. "I should know, I issued them to each person before the journey to the world above. And if you have her blanket, that means you know about them. Know where they are, perhaps?"

Mr. Dabir was pacing now, his face a light shade of red. "Where are they? Where is Branch?"

I had never seen him become this frantic in front of everyone before, had never heard his voice rise up in pitch every time he spoke.

Erika said nothing. Seconds passed. And then, slowly, a small smile touched her thin lips.

Mr. Dabir stopped. He looked at her, seemed taken aback by her reaction. "Stop it." The words sputtered from his lips. "Stop smiling."

Erika didn't. And I saw Emily shift slightly, watch with wide eyes. The rest of the room was so quiet I could hear myself breathing.

"He was kind to me." The words were so soft at first, I hadn't realized Erika had said them.

"What?" Mr. Dabir's face was white.

"He helped me." Her voice grew stronger, as calm as water on a day without wind. "They all did."

Mr. Dabir didn't move. He looked at Erika, at Emily's reaction, at us, and then back at Erika. For the first time in his life, he didn't know what to do.

"Will you not tell me where he is?" They were the first words that came out of his mouth quietly, without demand. He looked tired. And once again, it felt like everything had changed.

Erika shook her head firmly, without hesitation. "Friends don't put friends in danger."

Friends. She said the word in the dark, gray Dome like it was the most normal thing in the world.

Branch had been kind to her? She considered him a friend? I breathed in a deep, shaky breath. Of course he had. That was Branch. That had *always* been Branch.

I blinked back tears that suddenly sprang to my eyes.

Even crazy Erika could recognize kindness.

"Fine." Mr. Dabir took one step back. "Nash, will you do the honor?"

Erika's eyes shot up, and she put her hands on her chest.

Do what honor?

Nash stayed seated for a second longer. And then he stood, walked three slow steps until he was next to Erika, on her left, slightly in front.

He paused for a second, and I sat taller in my chair, my eyes just above the bun on the person in front of me.

Nash pulled a knife from his pocket.

What?

Mr. Dabir's mouth twitched and he stepped back once more, then folded his hands in front of him. Erika shut her eyes and started rocking back and forth.

"Friends don't put friends in danger. Friends don't put friends in danger." She repeated the words in a whisper, over and over again as Nash lifted his knife in the air.

And then it hit me like water, like stones.

No. Nash would never kill. He, of all people, would never kill anyone or do anything to hurt them. He wouldn't.

Nash held the knife in his hand firmly, his arm not even moving. He didn't blink. Didn't tremble. Didn't even take a breath.

"Nash." The word pierced the air, and I realized it had come from my lips. "Nash!" I was thinking frantically of other words to say, but nothing was coming together, nothing else formed in my mind.

Mr. Dabir's eyes shot up, his expression locked on mine.

And he smiled.

I couldn't hear myself screaming, couldn't feel my throat as arms grabbed mine, started pulling me from the room.

Everything was water, colors blended into one, the air not air and the floor not floor. I tried to push the arms away, tried desperately to make my legs work, to run past the gray eyes and gray walls to the girl rocking back and forth and the boy with dirty-blond hair.

And then for one long second, the world snapped into focus. Nash turned, the knife gripped firmly in his hand, his chest moving in and out. His mouth in a line.

His eyes met mine, once, before I was pulled through the door.

21

THEN

Exactly three years ago today, I saw a man die.

I was thirteen, the top of my class, and the most promising new teenager for miles around. Never mind the fact that I was going through some of the most embarrassingly sudden voice changes—I sounded like the ducks that visited my pond when the weather was mild and the sun melted at the edges. But, my childhood humiliation is another story for another day.

The day I saw a man die, my mother had asked me to get groceries with her, and I went without hesitation as I always did. We were walking through the town square, a little open area with stone benches and grass in neat rectangles, when we saw a bunch of people standing in a circle. I kept going, of course—never waste a step. But my mother stopped.

"Jonathan Dabir," she said simply. So I stopped too.

I remember I couldn't see for a good two minutes. There were tall people standing in front of me, and I hadn't hit my growth spurt yet. But I could hear.

"All in favor of the latter? Giving this man the punishment he deserves?" A deep, confident voice split the air, and the crowd erupted suddenly. A woman next to me shook her fist, her gray hair so long it was almost touching my arm. I sidestepped away.

"Quiet." The voice in the center commanded attention. I

wondered who was speaking, and I thought he must be a very respected leader to have a crowd eating up his every word. I remember thinking I wanted to be like him someday.

"All in favor, lift a hand please."

The people hushed, and slowly, everyone next to me raised a hand. My mother shifted, and then she put her hand in the air like everyone else. I wondered what they were voting for, and I strained to see. I should lift a hand too, right? But before I could put it up with everyone else, the voice in the middle spoke again.

"Michael, will you do the honor?"

Who was Michael? And what honor? I stood on my toes, silently cursing the disadvantage of being a child. The man in front of me had wide, impossible shoulders, so I used our *no touch* rule to my benefit. There was a space in between him and the next person. And it was enough. I wanted to pat myself on the back, to celebrate my victory, but instead my eyes fell on the man kneeling in the middle of the square.

He was younger than I thought, maybe in his twenties. He had jet-black hair, like the streets. And he was staring up into the crowd, his chest moving in and out so quickly I could see it from here.

A tall, skinny man suddenly stepped into the circle, his eyes eager balls of gray. Michael. It must be. I had to blink twice before I realized he was holding a knife.

A man behind Michael stepped back and nodded once, a pleased look on his face. He must have been the one talking, taking the vote. And my mother didn't move, didn't say a word, as the man named Michael sliced the neck of the man on the ground.

It was only when people started moving away, satisfied expressions on their faces, that I noticed the flower lying on the gravel in front of the dead man. It was yellow, crumpled slightly, like he had been holding it in his hand while they killed him.

I later learned that the man died because he had given a flower to a girl—placed it in her hair as he passed her in the grocery store. Someone had seen, had stripped her of the flower, which had somehow ended up in the man's hands again. And then he died.

I don't know why I remember that day, but I do. I always have. Because for some reason, I felt bad for the people in that square—eager eyes and faces hungry for justice. A man was killed right in front of them. The least they could have done is turn their eyes away. Yes, he deserved to die. But not like that. Not like an animal on display.

I reach over and flip the photograph over in my hands once, the one Hope gave me last night. I know I need to give it back, but I'm not going to just yet.

I remember the rain and the drops of milk in the sky as I walk down the hallway to the large gray door. My heart starts beating faster when I see it in the distance, and I wonder if anyone will be able to tell that it was used last night. Opened to the world. I push the beating back. Of course not—it's just a gray door.

I blink as I step through and the sunlight blinds me. I'll never get used to this—living in darkness ninety percent of the time and only coming out into the sunlight ten percent. Well, twelve percent for Hope and me. But no one needs to know that. Even I won't think about it. Today, I hit restart. No more hot-and-cold feelings, no more mind being pulled back and forth, or stupid decisions. No more crazy. Today I am Jonathan Dabir, future leader of the Dome. Nothing more, nothing less.

"Thank you, silence please." Yep, definitely a script. Glasses Lady stands in front of the building with her hands folded across her stomach. The eleven people left—including me—all step into the space surrounding her. I notice several others are squinting into the sun that hangs high behind Glasses Lady's head.

"Follow me."

And we do. Glasses Lady leads us through the Oval and to the hill with the caves, right in front of the red wall. We've been walking for four minutes and twenty-three seconds. The

Oval is bigger than it looks.

I shield my eyes and steal a glance around me. The replica Dome looks small now, a brown building dropped in the middle of green. Several trees dot the grass to my right, and to my left I see the thick circle of bushes and trees where Hope brought me last night to get away from the footsteps. It all seems ridiculous now, in the light of day. In fact, the sky is so bright and the grass is so dry, it's like it never even rained.

I breathe in deeply, and the fresh air feels good. Today is going to be a good day. A normal day. That is not too much to ask.

"I need my photograph back." The words come from behind me, to my left, and then Hope steps into view. Of course.

I keep my eyes straight ahead, on Glasses Lady's and Pimples's and Hairless's backs, and shrug. "What makes you think I have it?"

"I gave it to you." Hope hisses the words, and her breath in my ear makes me strangely warm. I shake it off—it's nothing but the sun.

"You have it, don't you?" Her voice gets suddenly nervous, but I still don't turn my head.

I say nothing, and I can't help when the corner of my mouth turns up slightly.

Hope lets out a breath. "You think this is funny!"

I keep walking, and I push back my hair as the heat from the sun reaches my neck, my forehead. Glasses Lady stops.

"Jonathan, if you don't give me that photo back right this minute—"

"We have arrived." Glasses Lady turns to face all of us, Pimples and Hairless by her side.

"It's *Jonathan Dabir*," I whisper back, simply. And I stand there, content, because I know she can't say anything else. I praise myself for getting under her skin when she is so hard to break. After all, she deserves it. She has so often gotten under mine. If it's my possession of an illegal photograph that does it, well, so be it.

142

Silence hovers in the air, and I can hear Hope's breathing beside me. Glasses Lady looks out at all of us, dwarfed by the caves directly behind her, and then the wall behind them. I remember that first day, the first challenge, sitting in a cave for three days. *Learning to survive, to thrive, in darkness.* In the replica Dome, that has basically become my normal now.

"Challenge number six." Glasses Lady speaks suddenly, and I see a bead of sweat on her upper lip. "The challenge of speed."

Speed. This will be easy. Silence and speed go hand in hand. Without one, the other does not exist.

"The first person to make it around the perimeter of this brick wall in its entirety wins. You are standing on the finish line."

A few people look down. It's a figure of speech, geniuses. She just means the finish line is here, right where we started.

"The leader of the Dome will need to be fast, as it is vital that they make it in the midst of the chaos that will be happening all around." Glasses Lady doesn't move. "Without you, there is no future."

For the first time I realize Glasses Lady said *leader* and not *leaders*. Her eyes meet mine and stop. And as if reading my mind, she nods.

"The winner of this challenge will be the leader of the Dome. You are all leaders, but this person will have the final say. He or she will be in charge of the Dome, its leaders, and its survivors."

I hear a few people let out a breath. I don't move, don't blink. This is what I've been preparing for. It's finally my day.

Glasses Lady looks briefly at Pimples and Hairless, and they both nod. Her eyes fall on us again.

"One line, please." She gestures calmly to the patch of grass in front of her.

We all step into a line, perpendicular to the wall, side by side. I can see the wall on my left, stretching farther and farther into the distance until it curves off into a circle that eventually leads back here. I see the slope of the hill, then a

143

large stretch of flat grass, then trees. I feel the sun, hot on my back, and I think for a moment about how it wouldn't be terrible if there was a small wind or a light rain. But it doesn't matter. I'm going to do this. I was born to win.

"This challenge is of the utmost importance." I hear Glasses Lady speak behind me, but I don't see her. I keep my eyes ahead, on the smooth red wall. "Remember: Don't stop for anything. The finish line is your priority."

I tense my arms, prepare to run. Oh, I won't stop. I won't stop until I'm the leader of leaders. The *top dog*, as Pimples said. This is my day.

I feel the other leaders beside me, jumping up and down or rolling up their sleeves. I hear the tap of a finger, and a stopwatch lets out a small *beep*.

I breathe in.

"Begin."

All I see is red when I start running. Red wall, reaching beyond me constantly. I imagine the bricks are running, are racing me, and I need to chase them. I don't see anyone else, but I hear them—hot breaths and feet pounding the grass behind me.

Thirty seconds in, I calm my breathing and reach a steady rhythm. This is going well. Most of the sounds behind me have even fallen back, distanced themselves. Haven't these people ever run before?

I reach the bottom of the hill and run straight out onto the flat field. I stay close to the wall at all times—less than a foot's distance away. If I'm going to win, I need to do it right.

I'm two minutes in, weaving through some scattered trees, when I notice footsteps coming up behind me. Then a body appears to my left, in the corner of my eye—gray clothes, white skin, blond hair. I close my eyes for a split second.

Unbelievable.

"Give me back the photograph"—Hope's voice comes out quick, in spurts—"or I'll beat you."

Does she think this is a joke?

"Not possible." I push the words from my lips and

quicken my pace. Hope matches it.

"I ran twice a day before I came here, *Jonathan Dabir*." She says my name sarcastically. "I can win with my eyes closed."

I shake my head and keep moving. This girl—she really is making me crazy. But I'm not crazy today. Today is *my* day. Not Hope's. Not anyone else's.

"Hope, if you think this is a game to me..." I let my words trail off, hoping she'll get the point.

"If that's the way you want it." Hope says the words matter-of-factly, and I see her shrug next to me. "But let the record state this: I tried to give you what you want. I offered to let you win."

She pushes off, and I suddenly remember last night, in the trees. I was breathing heavily, and Hope was barely panting. Barely tired at all.

Seriously?

I up my speed, try to match hers. And I'm almost there, almost next to her, when I hear a sound. At first I think it must be someone behind me, so tired they cried out in exhaustion. But we are only a fourth of the way around the wall—even an extremely out-of-shape person wouldn't give up that soon.

I run a few more steps before Hope hears it too.

Eyes ahead. Every step counts.

I keep pushing, keep running as Hope whirls her head around in front of me. And just as I close the distance between us, I hear another scream. This time, it's from her.

A body comes from above—from over the wall—and lands on top of Hope, pushing her arms and legs to the ground. I stop out of confusion, and in that split second, the body looks up.

His eyes are a deep, deep black.

Suddenly I don't see red anymore.

145

22

NOW

I have felt many things since I stepped up the stairs and into the world for the very first time.

Nervousness at what was waiting beyond the gray door. Disbelief at what lay outside it, at what spread past my eyes and beyond the deep canyon. Confusion when Alese smiled. Worry when Theodore was lying on the ground, blood splattered across the damp grass. Hope when Alfred stood in the middle of the gray eyes, when we led everyone from the gray world into the world of color. Fear when the first person was taken. Contentment when I soared above the trees, attached to a wire. Devastation when I was announced the traitor and I saw the look in Theodore's and Alese's and Branch's eyes.

I have felt things most people haven't felt in almost a century, breaking some feelings and piecing them back together, holding others close, feeling others squeeze my chest until I couldn't breathe or speak.

But in all the things I've felt, I don't remember ever feeling so numb my heart seemed to stop beating altogether.

The seconds ticked by, but they weren't seconds. They moved so slowly it was like the whole world was underwater. I couldn't feel myself breathing, and I wondered how my lungs were still pulling in air if I wasn't. The air wasn't air, the gray not gray. The room was a blurry haze of watery edges and lukewarm floors.

He killed her.

The thought rose to the surface, and I suddenly felt cold. The air was stripped from my lungs, and I gasped. I couldn't breathe. I was underwater, and I was drowning.

I pulled my knees in tightly, pushed the thought from my mind. He didn't know what he was doing. Mr. Dabir brainwashed him. He couldn't have known what he was doing.

It was Nash.

The boy who took on the world with bright eyes and smiled by the fire in the trees. The boy who held my hand through a field of wildflowers and spun me in the house in the woods. The boy who carried Theodore all the way to the Dome, even when he had to sling him over his back.

That boy wasn't a killer. That boy was a dreamer, an adventurer. A boy who wasn't afraid to love.

I shut my eyes, but his clenched cheeks and stone face stared back at me.

And for the first time, I didn't have a plan. I didn't know how to get him back.

The door opened, and Emily walked in. She looked at me, huddled in a corner of the room next to the wall. She set a plate down next to the cart slowly, and then she started to walk out. And suddenly another thought broke through the rest. The photograph. Emily pushing it into my hands and walking out the door.

"Why did you give it to me?" My words came out desperate, hoarse. She stopped. Looked back.

"What? The photograph?" Her voice dropped to a whisper, like she didn't want anyone to hear. "I don't know, I..." She paused, looked at the door, then back at me. "I was trying to help you. Did he promise Branch's safety?"

"Are you serious?" The numbness was rising from my chest, turning to anger. "Mr. Dabir was furious. He demanded it from me, asked where I had gotten it." I sucked in a deep, sobbing breath. This was too much. It was all too much. "Were you trying to get me in trouble?"

Emily looked confused, and her eyes flicked to the blue-gray stone, still lying on the ground. "What?"

"The photograph wasn't the prize, Emily." I looked up, frustrated. "I'm not sure what it was, but it was something Mr. Dabir didn't want anyone to see."

Her face turned pale. "Really? I...really, I thought I was helping. I didn't mean to get you in trouble." She seemed nervous, but her eyes were clear. "You have to believe me."

I watched her, and then I lowered my head again. She seemed like she was telling the truth. Maybe it really was an accident. But then again, it could all just have been another of Mr. Dabir's stupid games.

I heard Emily let out a breath, take a few steps to the door. Then she stopped. "Don't try anything tonight, okay?"

I looked up. Her eyes locked on mine.

"Just for tonight. Be here."

I didn't answer for a second, confused. "I'm locked in. Remember?"

Emily nodded, as if she hadn't thought of that. She turned to the door, opened it. She looked back at me once before she pulled it shut and clicked the lock.

Watery seconds passed, and I didn't move. I was too tired to sleep, too hungry to eat. If this was feeling, I didn't want anything to do with it.

I drifted off once, dreaming of a long gray wall that never ended, and I was chasing it. Running alongside it. I knew I needed to get to the end, to beat it to its own destination. But it never stopped. And the funny thing is, even though I knew it was impossible—catching up to a wall that never ends—I didn't stop either.

I jolted awake when I heard a click and something sliding across the floor. It took me a few moments to realize it was the door.

The room was pitch-black, and I couldn't see anything. I placed my hands on the ground, bracing myself to get up. Who was coming in my room in the middle of the night? My heart started beating, and the feelings flooded back, one of them pushing harder than the rest: fear.

"Hello?" I heard my voice in the air, and it wavered slightly. Nothing. Maybe I had imagined it. Maybe the door hadn't opened after all.

Then the room lit up in oranges and yellows and reds.

I gasped, shielding my face on instinct. The colors filled the air, and I saw shadows and corners and edges bouncing up and down. It was like a room, broken apart and almost pieced together, but not quite.

The colors seemed to calm, to get a little smaller, and I looked past my fingers. A face hovered next to the torch, gray from the shadow.

I blinked.

"Nash?"

He didn't say anything for a second. I could see the line of his lips, the top of his chest, breathing in and out.

And something crossed my mind, something terrible and chilling and true: he had just killed someone.

I stood slowly, keeping my hands against the wall for a sense of balance. If he had gone that far, I didn't know what he would do now.

"Help me."

The words came and left as quickly as they touched my ears, and for a second I wondered where they had come from.

"What...what did you say?" I asked the question slowly, and I had to remember to take a breath.

I saw the oranges and yellows move through the air as they were lowered to a corner. The whole room was lit up in shadow now, and I could see his clothes, the way he stood there with his hands clenched at his sides. The hair on his head, slightly damp.

Then, in the grays and blues and purples of the shadow, his face crumpled.

"I almost killed someone." The words fell from his lips and shattered.

I stopped moving. Almost?

"Help me, Laney. Help me come back." His voice came out as small as a whisper, but his words were desperate.

"Erika's alive?" Even as I said the words, my head pounded. But I saw him. I saw him raise his knife, and—

"Yes." Nash looked exhausted, torn apart. But that word alone made me feel like I had felt when I first saw sunlight, first breathed in fresh air.

"But how? I saw you with a knife. And she was—"

"I almost killed her." Nash's voice stopped me. "I stepped up to her, pushed every feeling I ever had to a corner. I was one of them. I wanted to be one of them. No pain, no hard decisions. They just *do*. Without feeling anything." His words were coming fast, like he was trying to explain it to himself. "But then I heard you shouting my name. And I knew I couldn't..." He trailed off. "I could never kill someone, Laney. She's not dead."

Relief flooded me like water. He hadn't killed her. Nash was still there, like rain and flowers and trees.

"But I was up there. Holding a knife. And she looked so confused, so scared. She held my gaze until I couldn't anymore." He took a deep breath, his eyes lost, like he couldn't get the moment out of his head. "So I faked being sick. I left the stage, and Mr. Dabir changed his mind suddenly and took her to a cell, decided she might be of use to us. I almost killed her, Laney. I almost killed someone."

He was taking deep, panicked breaths now. He pushed back against the wall and sank down, his head in his hands. "Help me. Bring me back. Please. I can't— I don't know what to do."

I was frozen against the opposite wall, wondering for a split second if I was still dreaming. But I felt the coolness of the wall on my palms, the slight warmth from the flames in the corner. And I saw Nash, crumbling before my eyes.

"Erika's alive." I let the words hover for a moment, to sink in for me as much as they would for him. "She's alive because of you."

Nash shifted, lifted his head slightly. "What happened to me?"

I didn't expect the question. I didn't know what to say. Mr. Dabir had happened. The Dome had happened. *I* had happened. And suddenly my heart broke for the boy in front of me who once held the world in his fingertips, but left it in a pile of stones.

"Nothing happened." I took my hands off the wall, took a step toward him. "You're still you. You, of all people, would never become one of them."

He lifted his head all the way this time. My words seemed to surprise him, like he didn't expect them. A hand squeezed my chest. I had been such a terrible friend.

"Can you teach me how to smile?" Nash was looking at me, and his eyes were pleading. "I mean, again? I just need to smile again."

I stood in the center of the cold, gray room. Silence surrounded us, and the flame twisted and turned in the corner. He looked so lost. So broken.

"Of course."

I didn't speak for a few moments. I searched my mind for things to say, for anything that might make Nash smile. And then Alese's voice filled my thoughts, from that night we sat for hours reading books by the fire.

"Think about something. Something that makes you happy. Then just open your mouth, let it fill your cheeks." My voice was soft as I thought about the moment, thought about her words. "You'll feel it filling your whole face."

Nothing moved. I knew Nash needed more than that. He needed something happy to think about. And then I remembered the memory that had made me smile for the very first time.

"I found a baby bird in the field of flowers outside my house once."

The words touched the air, and Nash's eyes met mine.

"It was next to a large yellow-orange flower and an overturned pocket of twigs. A nest. I picked the tiny bird up

151

in my hands and then ran up the stairs, into the house. I was so surprised, to find a bird. But my mother was nervous. We weren't allowed to have any animals. But when she saw the baby bird in my fingers, her face softened." I took a breath. Felt the relief of her gaze like I was there again, on the soft carpet, next to the peeling wallpaper.

"We nursed the bird back to health, together, for a month. And the day we set it on the green grass and it wobbled, paused, and then leapt into the sky, disappeared into the clouds, was a day I will never forget. My mother had her hands over her eyes, shielding them from the sun. But I had looked into the sun and watched the bird until I couldn't see it anymore."

I paused, could hear my breath. Could feel my pounding heart. That memory—and my mother. I twisted my hands in front of me, suddenly feeling vulnerable. I dropped my eyes to Nash, and he was looking up at me.

There was the faintest trace of a smile on his lips.

"Thank you." Those were the only words he said. But it was enough.

I didn't think anymore. I pushed back everything we had been and every feeling I had broken with him, every feeling I had held close to my heart. I stepped across the room, from one world to the next, and sat by him, my back against the wall.

"You're welcome."

We sat there in silence for a few moments. We were inches away from each other, still apart, but it felt warmer just to have another person in the room.

"It's a miracle you ever made it to this Dome in the first place." Nash spoke suddenly, quietly.

I blinked. "What?"

"Nursing a bird back to health should've gotten you ten years in jail, at least."

I turned to him. His smile was still small, but there was something in his eyes—a sparkle I hadn't seen in a long time.

I pushed him lightly, completely surprised. "Seriously?"

And then Nash let something fall from his lips—soft, barely a sound in the silent air. But it was laughter. I knew his laugh better than anyone's.

I blinked, my eyes still on his. Brown and soft. "I knew Nash was still in there somewhere."

He looked back at me. And there was something in the warmth of his eyes, in the comfort of his face, that made me reach down and take his fingers in mine.

Surprise touched his eyes, and he looked down. "I'm the reason you're here, Laney." Something filled his voice—pain. "I'll never be able to forgive myself for that."

I looked away, the bluntness of his statement making tears spring to my eyes.

"But I can fix it. I can do what I should've done a long time ago. And I will." His voice was determined now, and he stared straight ahead, into the gray. "I'm so sorry."

I breathed in, this time my throat a little tighter. "Everything is going to be okay."

That's all that came from my lips. That's all I had. Still, he squeezed my fingers in his, grateful for my response.

And the room was water again. It flooded me, a dozen feelings pressing down on my chest. But I pulled just one out, one I hadn't allowed myself to feel in a very long time.

I closed the space between us, the warmth of his arm on mine. I let my head sink to his shoulder. We sat there, in a cell, in the darkness, so deep underground that no one above could hear us if we screamed.

And, for the first time in a very long time, I felt safe.

23

THEN

There are a lot of things I've felt in my short life.

Confidence in my steps, my decisions, my mind. Determination to become a leader of the Dome, then to become *the* leader of the Dome. Pride when I stepped away from my mother to do more, to be more. Frustration, confusion, and resolve around this girl Hope. Amusement at the fact that no one in this place is more qualified than me.

But in all my years of living, I've never felt anything quite like this.

Fear. Sudden, striking, blinding fear.

I blink as a siren pierces the air, wailing through the large field and disorienting me even more. I whirl around, trying to make sense of my surroundings. It's all a blur, bodies jumping on bodies and people screaming and the sky still blue, so blue. How is the sky so blue?

I think of every possible explanation. The military accidentally came to the wrong training place, has jumped on us by mistake. Yes, that must be it.

But his eyes were black. Blacker than a sky without a single star.

All at once, the world rushes back in sights and sounds and breaths. And only two things flash at the center of my mind, screaming as loud as the siren is. It's happening. Everything they told us—the chaos, the destruction, the men with black eyes—it's happening *right now*. And the second thing that crosses my mind is this:

Hope.

I breath in quick, ragged breaths and close the distance between me and the man—the snarling, laughing man—who has Hope's arms and legs pinned tightly to the ground. And I know I should think about what I should do, should form a plan or map out a strategy.

But I don't.

I crash into the man's side, head-on, and he grunts and falls onto the grass. Miraculously, he doesn't spring immediately back into action. I don't think again. I grab Hope's hand and pull her up—forcing back the electric feeling of her touch—then start running.

"What do we do?" Hope screams the words over the sounds. So many sounds.

Since I didn't think anything through, I don't have an answer for her. *Away*. I just know we have to get away. Where do you go when the world is being destroyed right in front of you? The Dome. I curse silently. They never actually told us where the real Dome is. Stupid, so stupid. Do they even want us to survive?

"The replica." The words push from my lips when the next thought rushes through my mind. It's the next best thing. Exactly like the Dome in all ways but one: it isn't. But right now, it's all we have.

"We have to get inside!" I yell the words, still running, Hope's hand still in mine.

"Inside?" Hope is breathing hard, her words coming out quickly. And I'm shocked—she's scared.

"They're coming over the walls, which means they're not in the building yet. There's a lock on the door, I saw it last night."

Last night. It seems worlds ago now.

Hope nods next to me, and we run. Grass and trees and people rush past me as we run to the brown building in the middle of the walls. How perfect was Glasses Lady's timing, to have us all outside for the second time ever when the world just decides it's going to end? I shake my head at our horrible luck.

"Jonathan!" Hope stops suddenly, abruptly, pulling me next to her.

"What?" I look at her quickly, wondering if another black-eyed man I didn't see grabbed her leg or something. She looks fine, and I pull her hand again. "Why are you stopping? We don't have time!"

"We can't leave them." Hope's words are soft, and they rise just above the sound of the siren. I look back.

I see people—other leaders and wild-eyed men—wrestling in the grass or running or trying to get over the walls. It's chaos, pure chaos. No one is thinking. There are probably scores of other men with black eyes over the red wall if that's where they *came* from. And staying in the field, fighting these guys, isn't safe. From what I can see, there are at least a dozen more of them than there are of us. I turn back to Hope.

"We don't have time. There's no way we can save all of them, and if we try, we won't be able to save ourselves."

I pull her hand again, but she doesn't move.

"The future needs all of us." She shouts the words, her eyes on mine. "*All* of us. Any leader would recognize that."

I know she doesn't mean to offend me, but the words hit hard. I look at her, frustrated. This is impossible, a death sentence. Doesn't she realize that? I want to pull away, want to save my own life even if it means all of them will die. But I can't get the thought out of my head that if I go inside, Hope won't. She'll die with the rest of them. And I have no idea why, at the end of the world, that thought is even in my head.

"Tell them to get inside." I can't believe I'm saying this.

Hope's eyes widen, like she's shocked I'm actually going to do what she suggested. Like she can't believe I'm going to *help*. I can't believe it either. She nods quickly, her face flushed.

"In exactly three minutes, we'll meet at the door. Promise me, Hope! Even if you don't save everyone, you'll run, and

156

you won't stop running until you're there."

I realize her hand is still in mine, but I don't let go. For some reason, the shouting and the chaos and all the colors blending into one makes touch not seem like the worst thing in the world anymore.

"Okay." Hope looks around her, breathless, and then her eyes meet mine again. "Okay. I promise."

I nod, hesitate. I look at her for two seconds longer before I drop her hand and run.

Two minutes, fifty-nine seconds.

I look around frantically and I see two scruffy, dirty men on top of the wall to my left, preparing to climb down. A scream suddenly stabs the air in front of me, in the clump of trees and bushes Hope and I were in last night. It seems like something always leads me back there.

I sprint to the greenery and push myself into the branches and leaves, my heart beating like I imagine the black bird's must have when the coyote pounced.

I look around, sucking in deep breaths. *Silence*, I scold myself. All my training has led to this moment—I can't have it all be for nothing.

A flash of brown rises and falls behind a bush to my left. I hurry over, careful not to step on a tree branch. My mind is finally clearing, finally feeding coherent thoughts to me. *Took you long enough.*

The flash of brown screams, and I round the bush to see another man pinning down the legs of a girl, just like one did to Hope. I close my eyes, clench my fists. Brace myself. And then I slam into him just like I did before. When the man's head slaps against the side of a tree trunk, he moans and releases his grip. I lean down and grab the shirt of the girl before I even know who it is.

"Jonathan?"

I look down as I pull her from the trees. It's Geena. The one other person here whose name I know. Her clothes are streaked with dirt, and she's trembling. There are sticky tearstains on her face.

157

"Geena, you need to run. Go to the replica Dome and get inside."

She blinks, and I swear her face lights up slightly when I say her name.

"Go! Now!" I push her toward the brown building, and she sucks in a sobbing breath and runs.

It's debatable whether small, crumble-apart-at-any-moment Geena will actually make it, but I try not to think about it.

One minute, thirty-five seconds.

That took too long. I don't have time to save people one by one. I'll just have to hope that a little encouragement will make them save themselves.

I take off, sprinting across the green grass. The moment I'm within earshot of a girl cowering against the wall and rocking back and forth, I call out.

"Run! Get to the replica Dome! It's safe there!"

She looks up, sniffing, her face in shock at the disastrous turn challenge six took. But she stands, so I keep running.

I pass another person, then another. One is seconds from being pounced on by a man with black eyes, but when I scream the words, he takes off toward the replica Dome. I recognize another as the blond-haired boy with the scar on his face. He shoves a man off himself and looks at me when I pass by and shout over the sound of the siren. He nods and pulls a man off another boy nearby, and they both sprint toward the brown building. I feel the tiniest bit of pride when I see him do that. I knew he was promising from the start.

Forty-six seconds.

I see Hope out of the corner of my eye, a hundred feet to my left, four other leaders following close at her heels. I whirl around, scanning the grass and the trees and the wall. I don't see any more gray outfits. I see ripped jeans and stained shirts and long, gritty hair. None of ours. And they seem confused by the tiny, imperative fact that suddenly all the normal people have disappeared.

Thirty seconds.

I see three crazy-eyed men watching me, and then they look past me, at the brown building. At the people running to the brown building. I take a deep, breathless gulp of air, and run.

I've never felt the wind twisting my insides, the air filling my lungs and legs and chest quite like this before. I've never felt my legs pushing so fast, so hard they start to become numb. I've never had my eyes more set on a destination, never felt more desperate or determined to get somewhere.

Nine seconds.

I hear feet behind me, the sound of laughter rising from the clump of trees.

Four...three...two.

"Shut the door!" Hope's voice, and she says the words just as she sees me.

"You made it." I don't mean to sound surprised, breathless, but I do. Exactly three minutes. If the world wasn't crumbling to nothing behind me, I would be impressed.

Her wide eyes meet mine, and she nods. I put my hands on the thick knob and pull, my heart pounding again as six men charge straight for us.

"They're coming!" someone screams, and I feel Hope's hands suddenly on top of mine. I close my eyes from the searing reaction of her touch. *Not now. This door needs to be closed.* I push the feelings away and we pull, together. The large door slams shut, the wild eyes and laughter and blue sky shut out with it.

For a second, there's only gray walls and darkness and silence.

Hope stares at the door, and I brace for bodies crashing into it, or screams when they realize they weren't fast enough.

Nothing.

Ten seconds pass before I turn and look behind me, into the replica Dome. I see bodies—white eyes and tight skin— staring back at me, breathing heavily but otherwise silent. Only Geena lets out a small sob, but she quickly puts a hand over her mouth.

"...Nine, ten, eleven." Hope stops, eyes bright. "Unbelievable. Everyone made it."

I blink. I sweep my eyes across the room, see nine dirt-stained sets of gray clothes, nine other heads, besides Hope and me. She's right. And I wonder how in the world this actually worked.

"So...what do we do now?" The boy with blond hair and the scar speaks.

I remember what he did before, crashing into the black-eyed man to save another leader with dark black hair and thin arms. I've never respected someone my age, never really related to them. But after that, I'm actually kind of proud he's one of the leaders on this team.

Hope turns to me, her eyes round, like she's still trying to understand what just happened. I stand there for a moment, thinking about the black eyes and the chaos and the world. And I know there's only one answer to that question.

"I know that came out of nowhere, to all of us." My words touch the air, the gray room, and I swallow. "But we all made it, and we're safe here. And now, there's only one thing we can do." I look at Hope, and then back at the others, my heart beating faster, stronger. "We survive."

The sudden sound of someone clapping makes me snap my eyes up and clench my fists. I look around, into the darkness, and the others whirl around too. Maybe I was wrong. Maybe the men with black eyes made it in here after all.

The clapping continues as three bodies move from the shadows and into the dim light of the torches on the walls. I try to swallow, but my throat feels like the bark on the Oval's trees.

Glasses Lady. And Pimples. And Hairless.

What's going on?

Glasses Lady pats her orange hair once before she clasps her hands in front of her. Her lips are stretched to the edges of her cheeks, and her eyes are bright. She's not frightened, not questioning why the world just decided to turn itself inside out right in front of us. Standing there, in the middle of the trembling group, she almost looks…proud?

"Well done. *Well* done." Two words. Two words that should not be said in this situation, ever.

"I could not have predicted that would go so extremely well. We are impressed, to say the least."

"What are you talking about?" Hope speaks, confused. Her words are still rushed, still shaken. "Didn't you see what just happened?"

"Yes, I did. It was quite extraordinary." A sound bubbles up from Glasses Lady's lips. She turns suddenly to the door. "Boys? Please."

I turn slowly, my eyes on the thick gray stone. Someone from the outside opens it, and Geena shrieks. "What are you doing? They'll kill us!"

But I don't stop them. Something fills my chest, my mind. A nagging feeling that I can't ignore.

I watch as two black-eyed men pull open the door and step inside, followed by another, and then another. A few people in the room gasp, press themselves to the wall. But they keep coming. And once they're all inside, breathing calm breaths and nodding to each other and looking out at all of us with the same expressions Glasses Lady has, my eyes snap to her again.

I can't believe she went to such lengths for a simple challenge.

"Actors." Glasses Lady calls out the word like it's the most normal thing in the world. "They're not really men with black eyes. They won't hurt you. They were just ordered to chase you, to pin you down, if need be. Nothing more."

Pimples and Hairless share a look of pride, like their plan was perfectly executed and they should receive an award or something. Suddenly I can't stay silent anymore.

"This was all fake." I say the words confidently, matter-of-factly. I can't help that my voice sounds slightly angry. "The world isn't really ending. It was part of the challenge."

161

The fear, the screaming, the panic—all for nothing. The world isn't ending. It's still silent, untouched, with that unnaturally blue sky.

Hope shifts next to me and her eyes land on Glasses Lady, who parts her lips once more.

"I told you this challenge is of the utmost importance. And so it was." She looks around at us confidently. "Well done to you all for figuring out the finish line was actually the Dome. It will *always* be the Dome." She spreads her arms out widely, and I can't tell whether she's prouder of us or this place.

"Jonathan Dabir."

Her eyes land on me, and I look back at her.

"In the midst of chaos, absolute chaos, you stood strong." Her words ring in the air, and a few of the black-eyed men—colored contacts now, I can see it clearly—nod. One of the men, the one I must have pushed into the tree, rubs his head and salutes me.

Glasses Lady raises her hands in the air, Pimples and Hairless looking satisfied next to her, like they haven't just taken us all by surprise, haven't just hired actors to chase us and tackle us and terrify us. These people are crazier than I thought, and those are the words that are running through my mind when I hear hers.

"On behalf of my colleagues and myself, we hereby name you, Jonathan Dabir, leader of the Dome. *The* leader. You fought today, you saved the others. And you will save humanity in the future."

Her words strip me of my breath a little, but I stand tall. The words I have wanted to hear since I came to this place—to be named winner, leader—have just been said.

I did it. I won.

I look across the room as the clapping begins again, echoes against the walls and sounds much louder than it is because we're in such a small room.

I see Hope out of the corner of my eye, clapping along with the rest. And I can't help but think that the only reason I went back, the only reason I saved the others, was because of her.

If it had been up to me, I would be standing in this replica Dome alone right now. Just me. The others fake dead outside the door.

24

NOW

When I woke the next morning, legs stretched out in front of me and head against the cold wall, Nash was gone.

I blinked, and the night slowly came back to me. He came to my room. I made him smile.

He didn't kill anyone.

I didn't know it was possible to feel such relief, like a stone being lifted from my chest. I stood slowly, hands pressed against the wall, and I almost smiled. I knew the temperature hadn't changed down here—it never did. But for some reason, I felt warm.

I noticed the rectangle of black on the small table by the cart as soon as I stood. It was next to the untouched plate of food, and the color was harsh against the gray. My heartbeat quickened as I stepped over to it and realized immediately what it was.

A paper book.

But not Adrian's paper book, or the one Nash had given me in the world above that was destroyed when Emily pushed me in the water. That one had been red, like the sky just after sunset. This one was as black as a sky without stars.

I picked it up in my fingertips and swallowed back the thought of Adrian's paper book and everything it had done to me. I thought that one was the last to exist—so how was this here?

I ran a finger over the shiny cover and felt the ends of the pages, my heart suddenly in my throat. Paper was such a rarity, such a treasure. It was banned from the Dome the moment we stepped into the darkness, so the fact that any of it even still existed…

I flipped the cover to the first white, crisp page, and was surprised to see a note. The handwriting was rough, like the person had been practicing and hadn't quite gotten the hang of it yet. It was one of the most beautiful things I had seen in weeks.

Laney-

I found this in one of the back rooms of the Dome when Mr. Dabir sends us on our daily rounds to make sure no one is out of hand. I know I gave you one before, in the world above, and I'm hoping this can be a do-over for how that one turned out, because I saw how much you liked the first one. And I thought maybe this can keep you company while I'm gone.

I won't be long, and I told Emily to keep an eye on you until then. She's okay, Laney—she's on our side.

Last night was everything I needed. Thank you. I can't say I'm sorry enough, but I can say I'll make it up to you. I promise.

I'll see you soon.

-Nash

So Emily could be trusted after all. I thought back to what she had said, about staying in the room last night. Maybe she had known Nash was coming.

I touched my finger to the last sentence. *I'll see you soon.* Where was he going? I swallowed, the thought of being alone again making my head light.

I pressed the paper book to my chest, grateful for what Nash did. He was right—this was enough to keep me going. It was something to hold on to in the empty room.

I heard the footsteps down the hall before they reached the door, and I slid the paper book—small, about the size of two hands side by side—down my shirt, into the small of my back.

The door opened loudly, and I could hear a struggle just outside it.

"If you try to destroy this cell too, it will be your last." Mr. Dabir's voice was loud, and I cringed. A hand pressed the door open wider and pushed a body in my room.

At first I stood there, caught completely off guard. The person's knees dropped and her palms slapped on the floor. The door slammed, and she looked up, the flickering light from the hallway just enough to see her face.

It was Erika.

Her hair was no longer in knots, just a stringy heap that fell in front of her face. Her clothes—they must have found a spare gray set to put her in—were torn on the knees and elbows, and also by her neck. And she looked dirty. Brown streaks covered her face and arms and bare feet. Or were they bruises? I sucked in a breath.

In just twenty-four hours, she looked like she had been fighting for life outside for months.

"What did they do to you?" My voice came out in barely a whisper. I couldn't move—just stared at her from my place by the small table.

Erika lowered herself slowly to the floor, limb by limb. She put her arms around herself and brought her legs in until she was curled up in a ball.

"Erika?" My breath felt like a knot in my chest. This woman had always been strange to me, had always been something of a mystery. But this. This shouldn't happen to anyone.

She didn't move, her face buried in the heap of her hair. A few long minutes passed, and then I heard something rise from the curled-up ball of arms and legs in front of me.

She was crying.

I stood there, frozen. I didn't know what to do, what to say.

"Erika…" I said her name softly, but she didn't move. Her sobs were quiet, but in the otherwise silent room, they filled the air.

The woman bobbed back and forth on the cold floor for what seemed like hours. Then, somewhere in between sobs, I heard her voice.

"He loves you."

I blinked, wondering if I was imagining things. She must be delirious, down here in the thin air and darkness.

"That's why. He loves you."

I put my hand against the wall, searched for words. "Erika. Are you okay?"

"He loves you." Erika looked up now, and her eyes locked on mine. "That's why. He loves you. They all do."

Her sobs grew louder, and one of them split the air like water. I took a breath, confused and slightly nervous.

"What are you talking—"

"You know what." Her words came out suddenly, desperate. "Them."

She said the word so pointedly, so matter-of-factly. And I wondered if it was really true. If she really had been with Alese, Theodore, Gavin, Dalia, and Branch. Suddenly the thought of any information, any updates or details about my friends, made my heart clench in my chest.

"Have you really seen them? Were you really…with them?" I tried not to sound so excited, so desperate. But it was them. It was Branch. And it had been so long.

Erika looked at me, and in between shaking sobs, she gave me one long, slow nod. My throat went dry.

"Are they okay? All of them—are they okay?"

I held my breath, waited for her answer. If any of them were hurt, if anything had happened at all, I didn't know what I would do.

Erika's eyes looked sad suddenly, but at the same time, she nodded. Relief filled my chest.

I imagined Theodore in the world above, green eyes bright as he raced across the grass or climbed a tree, Alese by his side. I imagined Gavin and Dalia holding hands and taking a walk through a field of flowers. I imagined Branch watching them all, laughing. Thinking up some other crazy invention so he could fly through the trees again.

I swallowed down the pain that rose in my chest. To be up there again, with all of them...I needed it like I needed air.

I reached back and touched the paper book through my shirt once. It was comforting, and it pushed down some of the pain.

"And they...they helped you?"

Erika hadn't looked away since her eyes first met mine. It felt strange, feeling so relieved when she was in a ball on the floor. She nodded again, once.

"In the trees, by the river. I stayed with them. They were kind to me."

I nodded at the same time I heaved in a shaky breath. They were all okay. It was all I needed to hear. I started to turn, to walk to the wall so I could sink to the floor, but Erika's words split through the air.

"Friends don't put friends in danger. Friends don't put friends in danger. Friends don't put friends in danger." She said the words over and over again, just like she had done when Nash was about to kill her.

I turned back to her, saw her rocking back and forth on the ground as she chanted the words. The sight gave me chills.

"Erika?" My voice wavered slightly, and I tried to breathe.

Her voice rose, the words coming louder, faster. I pressed my hands against my ears, backed up against the wall. *Think about the paper book. Think about making Nash smile.*

Suddenly the door crashed open, and I jumped. My hands were still pressed to my ears, Erika still shrieking in a ball on the floor, when Mr. Dabir walked in.

"That is a wonderful thought, Erika. Friends don't put friends in danger." Mr. Dabir said the words loudly, over her shrieks. "But unfortunately"—he bent down and looked at her, smiled—"you just did."

The screaming, the shrieking, and the sobbing stopped suddenly. It was like it hit a wall, and the room fell into an eerie silence.

Erika looked up, dirty tears streaked down her face. "What?"

"*In the trees, by the river.*" Mr. Dabir said the same words she had said before, mocked them. And something cold rushed into my chest. No.

"Amazing how transparent these doors are. Like paper."

I thought of the paper book Nash gave me, and fear stabbed my chest. But Mr. Dabir seemed pleased with himself, pleased with making a joke about Adrian's notebook that he had so carefully pinned on me. I let out a breath.

"No." Erika's voice rose up in a wail, in one long sound.

Mr. Dabir had heard her, every word. This was another trick, a game. A way to make Erika speak, tell them everything, without realizing it. I was frozen against the wall, their bodies a blur in front of me.

"No!" Erika screamed the word, horrified. Devastated by her own betrayal.

But it was so vague. There were hundreds of trees by the river, so they could be anywhere—couldn't they?

Erika's wails turned to screams, her fists pounding on the floor, over and over again, until they left spots of red on the stone.

Mr. Dabir stood there, unaffected by it all, his lips twisted into a smile. "Shhh. Everything is going to be okay."

He stepped closer to her, stood over her flailing body. Slowly, he reached into his pocket. And in the pounding of the floor, the echoes of her screams, I realized where I had heard him say those words before. In the room filled with people on carts, when the girl had started singing.

"No." I pushed the word from my lips, a single breath.

"Close your eyes." Mr. Dabir bent gently over a screaming Erika.

"Mr. Dabir! No!" I stepped forward, and he turned. In one motion, he pushed me back against the wall and my body slammed into the stone.

I heaved in air, looked up from my place on the ground. Suddenly Erika's screams stopped, and in a blur, she planted her hands on the floor and whirled around, her eyes locked on mine.

"He loves you." Her face was wide, desperate, haunted.

And then it was on the floor.

I didn't move when two men walked in and grabbed Erika by the feet, dragged her motionless body from the room. Everything seemed fake. A game, a trick.

I tried to tell myself it wasn't real, tried to still my shaky breath and trembling body.

But all I could think about was that her last words were not *I love him* or *he loves me*.

Out of everything she could have chosen, everything she could have said, it was *he loves you*.

25

THEN

Glasses Lady gave us a five-minute break before whatever other mildly disturbed and slightly psychotic thing she had planned.

"Meet me in the center room in five minutes. The world could be destroyed at any moment—there is no time to waste!" she said, then bounced off with the fake-black-eyed men at her side.

Funny, I could have sworn the world *had* just ended.

A few of the people in the room are still breathing hard, and I can see Geena in the corner. She hasn't even looked up, her face still in her hands.

I hadn't realized my heart was still beating faster than normal, and I close my eyes for a second.

"Hey."

My eyes snap open. Hope is standing there, her green eyes on mine.

"You okay?"

"Of course I'm okay." The words rush out. "It was fake—it was all nothing. Why would I not be okay?"

A small smile forms on Hope's lips. "We all thought the world was ending. It's okay. And you—" She pauses, and her eyes drop suddenly. I wonder why. She looks back up again. "Thank you."

I suddenly remember what ran through my mind when I

thought I had reached the end of the world. Hope. I couldn't go to the replica Dome without Hope. I had tackled a man with black eyes for *Hope*.

Am I crazy?

My throat is dry. "The future needs all of us, right?"

She recognizes her words. My hand goes to my pocket and I fumble in it, looking around quickly to make sure no one is watching.

"Here. It's yours." I hand her the photograph, making sure it's hidden in my hand and no one can see.

She hesitates but takes it. Slides it into her own pocket.

"We should head to the center room." I know it's my voice, but it doesn't sound like my voice. "It's been two minutes and thirteen seconds."

Hope looks amused for a second, but she seems to push it back for once. She nods. "You're the boss now, right?"

The boss. The word feels off, somehow. But she's right. I'm leader of leaders. Top dog.

We walk in silence down the hallway to the center of the replica Dome. At one point the boy with the scar on his face passes.

"Well done, man." He almost pats my back as he walks by.

"Yeah...thanks." The words fumble from my lips.

Hope. It was Hope's idea to save you all, not me. But for some reason, I can't say it. I don't want to say it. I'm the leader. Right?

"Thank you, everyone, your timing is impeccable as always." Glasses Lady is just dishing out the compliments today. She folds her hands as we all file into the large center room with torches pulsing slowly on the walls like a bunch of yellow, throbbing hearts. To be honest, it kind of gives me the creeps.

There are no chairs in the center today, and the room looks bigger than it does normally, which is almost impossible considering how big it is already. Our footsteps echo on the long gray walls.

"You will stand on this side of the room. Yes, there

please." Glasses Lady nods once as we stop in a clump in front of her, next to the wall. She leans over and says something inaudible in Pimples's ear, and he clears his throat and shakes his head. His eyes dart past the group and land on me.

"Challenge number seven." Glasses Lady speaks suddenly, and my eyes move from Pimples to her. "The challenge of strength."

A few people shift around me, uncomfortable, I'm sure, at the thought of another challenge. Challenge six went from a friendly race to a fight for survival in just a few minutes. What would the surprise be this time?

"No surprises." Glasses Lady says, as if reading my mind. Well, that was a surprise. "The impromptu event was important to the results of challenge number six. How you *react* is important to the results of challenge number seven."

I look around at the empty room, wondering how darkness and stone walls and silence could turn into a competition. Oh wait, we did have to spend three nights in a cave.

"Now that you are all leaders of the Dome, you will need to learn how to fight. Fight for your own survival when you're running to the Dome, fight for the Dome when you've made it inside."

I hear Geena whimper. Hope leans over to me. "What are we going to have to fight off once we get insi—"

"The last challenge was successful." Glasses Lady shoots Hope a look, and she falls silent. "But if it hadn't been for our fast-thinking leader"—she gazes proudly in my direction—"many of you would have broken down and cried by the wall until you were killed by the men with black eyes."

I can't help when my mouth curves slightly. Harsh. And one of my favorite things Glasses Lady has ever said.

"The object of challenge seven is simple." Glasses Lady nods at Pimples, who takes off his watch and starts to walk to the other side of the room. "You have two minutes to get the watch from that side of the room to this one. The watch cannot break, and you must touch the wall behind you for the win to count."

So what, this is a fight for who gets to the watch first? Easy. So easy. I glance to my side. Except maybe Hope. But I gave her back the photograph, so she has nothing to hold against me now.

I press my hand against the wall behind me, and the other ten glance my way and do the same. So I'm already leader in their eyes. And for a split second before I can push it away, I wonder if it bothers Hope.

Why does it matter? I force myself to think. *She has her photograph, and she has her leadership spot so she can 'keep love alive,' whatever that means, which is all she ever wanted.*

I grit my teeth and focus on the challenge. The watch. That is what matters. Winning is what matters. I bend my knees slightly, put all my energy into my calves, my feet. I wait for the beep.

"Oh, silly me, I forgot to mention one miniscule thing."

I look up, my muscles tense. Glasses Lady is watching us all, amused. She turns to the door and claps her hands once.

"Boys?"

I follow her gaze. We all do. And when the door opens and the actors—the men with fake black eyes—enter the room one after the other and step to the center, next to Glasses Lady, I feel a sharp tug on my lungs.

Great.

Geena lets out a gasp and presses her back against the wall. Scar Boy looks annoyed that they're back. I couldn't agree more.

Glasses Lady takes three steps back, against the side wall, where Pimples is rubbing his wrist like he's second-guessing using his own watch for this. I don't blame him.

"Begin."

It takes me a second to realize Glasses Lady spoke. Begin? She's going to let those crazy actors in the room and then just say *begin*?

I take my hand off the wall, but no one else moves. The

mass of huge men with bulging muscles and fake black eyes stares back at us. I do a quick count in my head. Fifteen. There are fifteen of them, and eleven of us. Well, ten. Geena is useless.

"Twenty seconds has passed," Glasses Lady calls from the wall. She sounds irritated.

I look to my right, and Scar Boy looks back at me. On my left, Hope is the only person who meets my eyes. Well, we have three. That will take half the big boys off my back, at least.

I count to three in my mind. And then I look forward, a little to the right, where I see a hole.

"Go."

Hope steps left, staying close to the wall, and Scar Boy runs straight to the middle of the mass. I look away just before one of the actors jumps on him.

I jog to the right, then slightly to the left, then to the right again. At least seven of them are watching me, trying to predict my every move. I sneak a look back, and other than a few people creeping a few inches from the wall, no one has moved.

Come on, people. You're supposed to be leaders!

All the pride I felt when everyone was fighting and running to the Dome, gone in an instant. What happened to them?

I see movement to my right suddenly, and Hope slips through two of the men and starts to sprint to the watch. Well, I guess now is as good of a time as any.

I fake left and sprint right, pushing through a spot that opened in the last second. I blink, clear my vision, and see the watch sitting limply next to the wall. I'm fifty feet away, wide-open space, and I run.

Out of the corner of my eye, I see that one of the men has grabbed Hope's feet and she's struggling to get free. I suddenly think about the fact that these actors sure don't seem to mind touch, the way they pounce on everything and everyone like we're nothing. But this touch is different. It's cold, like ice. Like pain. The other touch, the way Hope touched me, is white-hot. Blinding. They couldn't be more different.

I swallow, the feeling of Hope's fingers on my cheek suddenly filling the air around me. Is something buzzing? I blink, try to clear my eyes, my thoughts. *Get it together. Get it—*

Pain shoots through my shoulder as someone grabs it, and the warm air turns cold as my face is slammed to the floor.

Three seconds later, while I struggle to breathe and see straight again, I hear Glasses Lady from the other side of the room.

"Time."

The pressure eases off me, and I push myself up. I glare at the man who dusts himself off and tips his chin toward me before joining the rest of the muscles.

I pass Hope, who is retying her bun into a tight knot, on my way back to the others.

"Stop it," I say, and she looks at me.

"Stop what?"

Stop getting in my head.

I just take a breath and walk back to the wall. I push all thoughts of her from my head like I pushed that crazy man off me seconds ago. This is ridiculous. The world isn't even fake-ending.

"That was one of the worst failures I have ever seen." Glasses Lady is still standing next to the other wall, but her voice carries well. "If all of you do not try this time, you will be eliminated as leaders, and you will leave this Dome immediately."

I reach the others and turn around, face her, rubbing my shoulder and pushing back the sharp pain pulsing through it. Good. Now more of the men will be occupied. I look around as the wide eyes and trembling fingers turn to deep breaths and clenched fists. If there was any proper form of motivation, that was it.

Glasses Lady's eyes are ice—I can see them all the way from here. They move to the men in the middle of the room, then snap back to us.

"Two minutes. Begin."

This time, four people get tackled before I do. I only make it fifteen feet before a large man with thick black hair and a ripped shirt charges me and slams me back into the wall. I breathe gasping, quick breaths, and for a second my mother flashes in my eyes.

"Time." Glasses Lady sounds like a parrot now, repeating the same word so much it's starting to get annoying.

I pick myself up, not having to walk back at all this time—lucky me, I'm already at the wall! I try to hide my groan as I move one of my legs back to a normal position. Geena is the only other person here; I bet she ran two feet forward and two feet back until time was called. The rest, rubbing arms or necks or faces, join me in a few long seconds.

Glasses Lady is tapping her foot on the ground, and she does not look pleased. Pimples's eyes are on his watch, untouched so far. I bet he's secretly enjoying that.

"If one of you fails, you all fail." Glasses Lady's voice pounds the air, echoes against the walls. "Remember that."

I'm pretty sure that's not tr—

"Begin."

I let out a breath and take my hand from the wall, in no hurry this time. The circle of death watches hungrily from the center of the room, ready to pounce, not even tired.

I'll let a few of the others run into that first.

Scar Boy lunges right and two people tackle him. The two leaders who look like brother and sister—they have to be siblings, I swear—run straight, try to barrel through the circle and end up a tangle of limbs on the ground. The boy with jet-black hair who stole my idea in the box-with-costumes challenge gets pounced on by two particularly large-looking men, and I can't help but be pleased with that one.

Then I hear something split the air at the end of the room.

"I got it!"

My eyes snap to a boy I've never really noticed before—brown hair, brown eyes, plain-looking—just as he thrusts his fist in the air and at least six fake-black-eyes jump on him.

Glasses Lady calls time seven seconds later, but her words are a blur. My mind is on the words she said exactly two minutes before this—*If one of you fails, you all fail.*

And suddenly I have an idea.

When the ten other leaders—minus Geena, who still hasn't moved more than two feet from the wall's side—walk slowly back to the end of the room again, I position myself next to the boy with brown hair. He's groaning softly, and his arm looks slightly out of place. But other than that, he's fine.

"Do you think you can do that again?" I whisper the words, and no one else around me seems to notice. They're too busy checking for their own broken bones.

The boy looks at me—blue-gray eyes, freckles splattered across his nose and cheeks—and his mouth parts slightly. "What?"

Glasses Lady is going to say *begin* any minute now. I don't have time for this.

"Can you get the watch again?" I say the words quickly now, but make sure I emphasize every syllable. This boy looks young, at least a few years younger than me.

He hesitates, looks at the others, then back at me. "I don't know. Even if I get it, they'll tackle me before I make it back."

"Exactly." I blurt the word, and he looks slightly offended. *Someone* has to make sacrifices for the good of the people, right?

I notice the fake-black-eyed men watching me, and I lean closer to Brown-Haired Boy, whisper the words to him so they have no chance of hearing or even lip-reading—hey, I don't know what these actors are capable of.

"Begin." Glasses Lady says the word like she's tired and she knows we're going to fail.

I pull back. "Right when you get the watch. Okay?"

The boy's eyes are wide, but I can see it clicking behind all that innocent youth. He nods.

A few people sprint toward the back wall, and I see

Hope's long blond hair streaming behind her—so much for the bun—as a man grabs her arm and she tumbles to the floor. I almost admire her persistence. I pull my eyes away, watching as the brown-haired boy slowly steps to the side wall, then stops, his eyes on the room. Waiting.

I take a few steps forward, angling myself closer to the actors but not *too* close. Then I look back at the boy. He's still standing there, his eyes doing laps around the room, slowly, and I wonder what he's looking for. If he waits any longer, it's going to be time.

Right when I think he's decided not to run, or do anything for that matter, the boy takes off. I mean *takes off.* He sprints to the back of the room, his body just inches from the side wall. And because he stood there for so long, unmoving, all the attention of the black-eyed men is elsewhere.

Impressive.

He angles off at the last second, cutting to the back wall, and the others start to notice. I see one large man pick himself off Scar Boy, and then another look up from the other side of the room, until at least six are lunging toward Brown-Haired Boy.

My throat tightens, and I take a few more steps forward, not worried about being tackled because in just a few seconds, all eyes are turned to him.

Brown-Haired Boy charges to the center of the back wall and his fist grabs for the watch. I see his face, red and sweaty, as he lets out a cry and whirls around, his eyes locking on mine.

I nod frantically, the moment causing adrenaline to course through my veins, quicken my breath.

And just before the first black-eyed man reaches him, jumps on him like *we're* the intruders, he throws it.

The world seems to pause for a second. A large man with thick black paint across his cheeks, frozen in the air. Scar Boy's arm poised in a punch. Geena midcry against the wall. Hope's eyes on the small piece of metal careening through the air.

I cup my hands, lift them up, and catch the watch in my fingers.

I turn around, heart pumping, lungs working overtime, and start to sprint to the wall. But when I do, I notice a slightly overweight monster of a man just a few feet on my left, leaping toward me.

Where did *he* come from?

And I realize, almost too late, that I'm not going to make it. I close my eyes, tighten my fingers on the watch, brace for the teeth-shattering impact, when Hope's voice pierces the air.

"Jonathan!"

My eyes snap open, and I look up. She's standing a dozen feet in front of me, one hand on the wall, the other stretched in the air.

Throw it. She wants you to throw it!

And I do. I heave the watch into the air just as Monster Man jumps on my back. As I fall to the floor, cold surging through my skin from his touch and my bones being twisted the wrong way in at least six places, I hear something that almost makes the tears in my eyes worth it.

Glasses Lady is clapping her hands.

26

NOW

Everyone has a past, a story.

It's kind of like the paper book stuffed between my shirt and my back—we all start out blank, pages of empty white stacked in a pile and stapled together.

But then, suddenly, the first page turns black with ink.

Some days are written slowly, loops and twists and curves that widen into words and lines and spaces. Other days are scribbled quickly, outside the lines, until all the white is sharp corners and crossed letters. We rip some pages out, hang some on the wall, read others over and over again with a wish that we could go back and relive that part of our story endlessly. Or at least once. We cross some pages out, crumple some up in our hands, soak others with tears until they are soggy balls of nothing. But at the end of the day, it's us. Every piece of that story—the corners and loops and crossed-out lines and rewritten paragraphs—is what made us who we are.

Before I was eighteen, I was a girl who had barely spoken a single word. Now, I was trying to help humanity learn how to love again.

Mr. Dabir was, and probably always had been, a monster.

I couldn't imagine his story, what filled up those white pages day by day. But I could imagine that every word was black, every edge was sharp. I could imagine that he never had a friend, never even knew what the word meant. I could imagine that he never knew love, or even came close to it. And I could imagine that he had always been this cruel, this selfish, this evil.

There was no other explanation for the man he was—the man who hid in the Dome and murdered people just because.

What had happened in his life to make him like this?

The door opened, and I hoped it was Nash. I needed it to be Nash.

Blakely stuck her head in. I swallowed. The girl who pretended to be crazy. The girl who pretended to be in love with Branch.

"Mr. Dabir wants everyone in the center room." Her eyes landed on me, and I didn't move. Blakely tapped her foot in frustration. "Now, Laney."

I stood, stepping around the splotchy red circle of blood, now soaked into the cement, as I walked out the door. Blakely didn't even act like she noticed.

When we stepped into the large room, torches twisting on the cold walls, I noticed the chairs in the room were pushed in stacks against both sides. Mr. Dabir was standing next to the chairs, Brooke, Arsen, and now Blakely by his side.

I scanned the room quickly. Nash wasn't here. But for some reason, no one seemed bothered by that fact.

Mr. Dabir clapped his hands, and I looked at him from my spot in the sea of gray eyes.

"Impeccable timing, everyone." His eyes swept the group of standing people. "I thought we might have a little excitement today. And—I confess—I need to get my mind off something *terrible* that just happened."

He turned, slowly, and his eyes locked on mine. Then he looked out at the sea of people again. "All of you know Laney—the kidnapper, the traitor."

A few people in the audience shifted uncomfortably. Not again. And right when they were starting to forget.

"Well, I'm devastated to say she just killed our hostage and one of the means to our goal."

What? I didn't kill Erika!

Dozens of eyes turned to me, gray and cold. My throat tightened, and I clenched my fists. Not here. Not now. Not in front of the people who needed to see love.

"Regardless, we have a group in the world above searching for Branch and the others. My hopes are high that we will find them soon."

The search party. Maybe Nash was with them. I reached behind me slowly, making sure not to draw attention to myself, and lightly touched the paper book's cover over my shirt. It was amazing how having just one secret—something to hold on to in the darkness—made me feel so much lighter.

Mr. Dabir held up a hand and pointed it at the middle of the group of people. "Everyone on my left, go to that wall. Everyone on my right, go to this one." He pointed to either wall and, after a hesitation, everyone went to their designated side.

I stepped over to the wall on the left, next to a small, thin Delma. She didn't look at me. I wondered if she thought I was a traitor-kidnapper-murderer too.

"Does anyone have a watch they would like to lend to this pleasant occasion?" Mr. Dabir's eyebrows raised as he looked from one side of the room to the other.

A blond-haired woman fumbled with something on her wrist and walked it over to Mr. Dabir's outstretched hands. A boy from my side of the room—red hair, like Theodore's—shook off his watch and did the same. His eyes were dull, empty. Nothing like Theodore's.

Mr. Dabir handed the watches to Blakely and Brooke, who placed one behind my group, against the wall, and the second on the other side of the room.

Mr. Dabir looked pleased, and his eyes were brighter than usual. "The object of the challenge is this: You have two minutes to get the watch from the other side of the room to your side. The watch cannot break, and you must touch the wall behind you for the win to count."

A man coughed behind me as I wondered what the point

of this was. We really were pawns in his game now—actual pawns, playing games for his entertainment.

"The losing team…" Mr. Dabir tapped his chin and looked at Blakely as she joined his side again. Blakely said something in a low voice, and his eyes brightened even more. "Yes. The losing team does not eat for five days."

I felt like my lungs had been stepped on. Five days? The people down here already looked like they were starving—hollow cheeks, skin stretched over white bones. A horrifying thought crossed my mind that maybe he didn't care if everyone down here but him died. It made sense, knowing everything he was. And it would make this challenge so much more than just a game.

It was now a fight for survival.

Gray faces widened, fists clenched, knees bent. All eyes were suddenly focused on one thing.

"Begin."

Mr. Dabir's voice split the air, echoed against the stone. It took me a second to realize that at least a dozen people from my side of the room had started running. And at least two dozen people from the other side of the room were running here, to this wall. Straight at me.

I sucked in a breath and took a step back, but my foot landed on something—the watch. It was right behind me. They would think I was guarding it.

I lifted my foot and the watch lay there, unbroken. I didn't know why I even cared. I started to move, started to sidestep out of the way, when ice touched my skin and plunged into my arm.

Then all I saw was stone—gray, blurry. And feet. So many feet, running and turning and skidding on the floor.

Someone had pushed me to the ground. Someone had *touched* me. A chill ran through my body, and my side ached. This was even worse than I thought. They were terrified to go without food. And terrified meant do anything they had to do to win.

Even something they were terrified of.

I pushed myself up on shaky arms and watched people defending the watch, people lunging for the watch. They were trying not to touch each other, I could tell. But if someone was standing in the way, if someone was blocking the only ticket out of five days without food, fingers clutched an arm. A fist pounded on a shoulder.

It was like the world had paused, frozen, and reversed. It was like it had gone back in time to the screaming, the crumbled buildings, the black smoke in the sky. When the men with black eyes had destroyed the world by destroying each other.

And Mr. Dabir was standing there, watching it all with a twisted smile on his face.

I couldn't breathe. I pressed myself up against the wall, closed my eyes. Counted the seconds going by until he shouted, "Time."

I heard them breathing thick, ragged breaths. I saw twisted legs and red, bloated spots on their skin. I saw blood sprinkled on the ground like rain.

"You failed." Mr. Dabir blinked. "Try again."

A few seconds after he said, "Begin," and the world was a rush of legs and arms and narrowed eyes, a set of doors on the side of the room opened.

Nash walked in.

When he saw the room, he hesitated. I could see it in his body language, in the way his hand hovered on the door for a second too long. But no one else would have noticed.

Nash walked over to Mr. Dabir and said something to him under the madness. Mr. Dabir's eyes widened, and he nodded. Then, quickly, he held up a hand.

"Stop."

The room slowed, sucked back in the sudden rush of sounds and panic, and became silent again.

"You are all dismissed. Back to your indents, immediately."

A few people let out a breath, and I saw one of the men—dark hair, dark eyes—was clutching one of the watches in his

185

fingers. He dropped it. After a pause, everyone formed a line, one after another, something that was etched in us like stone, and started walking to the door. The girl in front of me had a smear of blood on her neck.

We had just walked through the door, our footsteps echoing like one on the walls, when someone stepped in front of me.

"Not you. I have a rope for you." The voice held authority, and when I turned I was looking into Nash's eyes.

My throat turned dry. I sidestepped out of the line and lifted my hands weakly for the rope. I was too tired to think. Too tired to wonder if everything that had happened in the past twenty-four hours meant nothing.

Nash led me to the left, a longer but quieter way to my indent. We passed Mr. Dabir on the way, whispering something to Brooke, and he nodded at Nash and me. Mr. Dabir's dark eyes were sparkling; he looked incredibly pleased. I wondered what Nash had told him.

We walked down a long hallway and then came to the last turn. But Nash went left, instead of right.

"Isn't it—?"

"We don't have much time." Nash dropped the stone face, the powerful act, in less than a second. He untied my wrists and stuffed the rope in his pocket, his flushed brown eyes turning to mine. "Think you can keep up?"

Before now, my mind was a blur, a haze. But those words—his deep brown, hopeful eyes—sharpened it in an instant.

"Yes."

His eyes stayed on mine for a moment, just like when his fingers had hovered on the door for a second too long. Like when you think a page is full, written, but there is still a little more room at the bottom. A little more white space waiting to be filled.

Then his eyes tore away and he lunged into the darkness. I took a breath, and I ran.

27

THEN

I barely slept last night. I think the fact that I'm leader of the Dome now—*the* leader, head of humanity—finally hit me. Just like when Monster Man jumped on my back, except less painful.

Who cares how I was named leader? I'm above caring now. My only job is to survive, and to help others do the same. But, of course, I'm the head of the survivors. I did it. Every step I took had a purpose, and it landed me here.

If you could only see me now, Mother.

I'm done with crazy, with feelings I don't know the name of. I'm putting them out of my mind for good. Leaders do not have time for distractions.

Two minutes. I have two minutes until I'm supposed to be in the center of the Dome, for the next challenge I'm sure. Glasses Lady didn't say, but she had that look in her eyes—the one that says she knows something none of us do.

When I walk down the hall, the others stepping from their rooms and joining, I naturally fall into the lead. There's something different now, a sense of power around me that I know they feel too. I avoid Hope's eyes.

"Welcome." Glasses Lady's eyes are too bright when we walk into the room. Two dozen chairs are in the center of the room, filled with the fake-black-eyed men. I groan internally.

Not again.

We walk over to the center of the room and I stop, the others behind me. Every single chair is filled with one of the brawny, hairy men. There are no empty spots for us. I turn to Glasses Lady, and she nods gently. *Gently.*

"Not anymore. You belong on the stage now." She sweeps her hands out wide and points next to her, and we file slowly onto the wooden platform. I turn, and the black eyes are staring at me. What is this?

"Welcome, future leaders of humanity." Glasses Lady has stepped up to the podium, her voice rising with authority, like she's addressing a professional event. A few of the men in the audience nod. I look over at Hope, and she shrugs.

"We began with fifty. Fifty of the most *promising* young men and women that we handpicked from only our best cities. Now, we have eleven." Glasses Lady pauses and looks at all of us. Is that pride in her eyes?

"You survived three nights in a cave, learning how to stay sane in darkness. When faced with the choice of hundreds of animals running rampant in the Oval, you decided that *each other* is the most imperative to the survival of the people in the Dome."

I meet Hope's eyes without meaning to. That was the first day I had seen her. The first day she stepped forward and did something even I couldn't predict. *No distractions, remember?* I look away quickly, back at Glasses Lady and her speech.

"You learned that a decision to get dessert only matters if it is a unanimous vote. When faced with a choice of three people you could take to the Dome with you, you learned to choose rationally, not emotionally."

I swallow. So Hope was right about the photograph/headband-of-death challenge. It didn't matter who you picked, as long as you didn't *feel* anything.

"You survived a natural disaster in the Dome by simply getting out. When asked what a leader looks like to you, you chose, naturally, your leaders." Glasses Lady looks at Pimples and Hairless, and Hairless's face turns red. "And, ah, the challenge of speed."

188

You mean the fake end of the world.

"Even in the midst of chaos, even when you thought the world was being destroyed before your eyes, you thought rationally. You escaped to the replica Dome and survived— every one of you."

I can't help but feel a stab of pride in my chest. It *was* pretty impressive, wasn't it?

"And finally, you learned the invaluable lesson that when faced with an obstacle, you are stronger together than apart. You learned that you are a team." Glasses Lady pauses and looks out at all of us. I see Brown-Haired Boy who threw me the watch hold his head high, even though his arm is still twisted slightly from when at least five guys jumped on him after the throw.

"Each of the challenges and how you reacted is why you stand here today. We began with fifty. And now, you are our chosen eleven."

There is a pause, and I almost think her speech is over. But none of the fake-black-eyed men move. Glasses Lady wrings her hands out suddenly.

"From this day forth, you are not competitors anymore. You are leaders. Teachers." She takes a breath. "The Dome will be your home, your life, your everything. It is everything you worked for and everything that will keep you alive. Do not trust the people that you bring into it: they will be merely survivors *you* choose, people who will have barely escaped the hate, and people who will know nothing about how to live or survive. You will lead them. You were trained and chosen by us. You know what is best, and they will not. So teach them. Make them aware that you are their teachers, that you will show them how to survive, and then they will trust you."

One of the black eyes—Monster Man—shifts in his seat.

"Teach them order and contentment with their new world in the Dome. This world we live in today will never be safe. And as the years go forward and you create a peaceful, thriving humanity once again, remember this: The Dome is not only *for* you. The Dome *is* you."

Her voice stops abruptly, and I hear the echo of her last sentence bounce off the walls. The breath she takes is shaky this time as she turns to all of us, more pride in her eyes than I have ever seen before. Like she's looking at us all for the last time. And, I realize, it is one of the last times.

"The directions to the Dome—the *real* Dome—are in the packets on the table, one for each of you. Memorize these directions, and then destroy them. Share them with no one else." Glasses Lady nods at a stack of thin black folders sitting on a small gray table by the door. She takes a breath, spreads her hands out in front of her. "Congratulations to our chosen eleven. We are no longer the leaders. You are."

She holds her gaze for a moment, taking in each one of our faces. And then she takes another breath, clears her face, steps back, and begins to clap. The men in chairs join, as well as Pimples and Hairless, and soon the room is thundering with more sound than it's probably ever experienced before.

It's a graduation. A graduation for us, from simple competitors to fearless leaders. Because that's what I am, isn't it? Fearless. A leader.

I take in the clapping, watch as Glasses Lady blinks away moisture from her eyes and Scar Boy takes a bow. But I can't push away the thought that the people clapping for us—standing now, in front of the chairs—look just like men with black eyes, the people we're supposed to hate. The people who are forcing us to choose leaders and create a whole new world inside a Dome are giving us a standing ovation.

When the applause dies down, Hairless points to the old table pushed against the wall and says the word *cake*. They made us a cake? This is almost as surprising as the fake end of the world.

"We did it." Hope comes up behind me, out of nowhere as always. "And they made us a cake." She almost laughs.

"Yeah. They did, didn't they?" I still can't believe it myself.

"Hey." Hope says the word, but I can tell there's more.

No distractions. I keep walking to the table, to the cake. Hope falls into step beside me.

"I think you're going to make a good leader."

I stop without realizing it. Did she really just give me a compliment?

"I know, I'm surprised too." A trace of a smile touches her lips. "But the way you saved me…and everyone. You care about us, I can tell. And that's why you might just be the best leader they could have chosen."

Something in my mind shifts. Care. She just said I *care* about them. And her. My hands suddenly feel cold.

"The only reason I saved them is because of you." The words come out of me before I realize that might just be the worst thing I could have said. I try to save myself. "You were being your stubborn self, and I can't very well lead a new humanity on my own, can I?"

Hope's smile doesn't budge. "Could you?"

Her question hangs in the air, and I let out a breath.

"Besides, everyone knows that the definition of a good leader is smart, calculated, quick on his feet. A leader shouldn't care. It distracts his ability to think." There. That should do it.

Hope lets out a small laugh, her green eyes full of amusement. My eyes widen and I look quickly to the left, at Glasses Lady, to see if she or anyone else heard.

"Okay, okay." Hope holds up her hands in surrender. "If you don't want to be the leader of caring, I will. But we'll be working together for quite some time, so be careful…some of it might rub off on you." She winks before she turns to the cake.

I blink as I realize that Hope and I will be living together in the Dome for years, and even beyond that.

Forever.

The feeling wells up inside me again, confusion and frustration and…and that one I can't name. I close my eyes and take a deep breath. *No distractions. No distracti—*

"Jonathan Dabir."

My eyes snap open. "Yes?"

Glasses Lady is in front of me, watching me with an

expression on her face I can't read. "Come with me, please."

I follow, wondering if she saw Hope and I talking. Or maybe she heard Hope *laugh*. The thought makes my brain feel light. But then shouldn't she be taking Hope with her instead? I shake my head. I'm the leader now. I should be the one keeping order, forbidding things like that.

I can hear my heart beating as she leads me out of the room, around the corner, and into another room, smaller. When she closes the door, I see that Pimples and Hairless are in here too.

"What is this?" I look from Pimples to Hairless, and then around the empty room. It's dark in here, and cold.

Glasses Lady turns around to face me, and she tries to look confident, full of authority, like she usually does. But there's something about her expression—whiter, rounder, less sure of herself—that makes me see right through it.

They're either going to demote me as leader, or they're going to kill me. I blink. Not a funny joke.

"Congratulations on being named head leader, Jonathan Dabir." Glasses Lady twists her hands together and looks at me. "It is an honor that is only bestowed to one."

So they're not demoting me. I hesitate and look back at her. "Thank you."

She nods, her eyes flitting to Pimples and Hairless before landing on me again. Like they all know something I don't.

"The ceremony made it official. You are the leaders now. And as head leader, you are the one who must make the difficult decisions." Glasses Lady takes another audible breath. I've never heard her make so much noise before, and it's strange. I don't know what to say to that.

"I understand." The only sentence I can think of that makes sense in response. But she's acting like I'm making a decision right here, right now. "Did something happen?"

The room falls silent. Glasses Lady looks down, runs a hand through her hair, then looks up at me again. "Not yet. But something will."

Something...will? I can't help it. The dark room, the

nervousness, the three leaders. They really are going to kill me, aren't they? I take a step back as Glasses Lady realizes what I'm thinking.

"Jonathan Dabir, no. We would never hurt our leader, the person who will bring humanity back from the ashes." She shakes her head, confident, and some of the authority returns to her voice.

I stop. Somehow, I'm less reassured than I thought I would be.

"Okay...thank you." Thank you? I can't believe those words just came from my lips. I look at Pimples, at Hairless, at all of them. And I suddenly realize that the cake is probably gone by now. I haven't had cake in years. Instead, I'm standing here, wondering what on earth is going on. "If you're not killing me, what is this about? Why the dark room? The jumpiness?" There. Finally. It's out.

Glasses Lady takes a deep breath and seems to breathe back in the poise, the importance, the all-knowing and all-seeing person that she was when all of this started, and has been every day since. Her face sharpens, her chin lifts, her back straightens, and she looks like she's remembering why she's here. Who she is. And who she's not. She folds her hands in front of her, casually, and her eyes lock on mine.

"You, Jonathan Dabir, are going to kill us."

193

28

NOW

A year ago, if someone told me I would be running through the Dome following a boy with no idea where I was going, I would say they were crazy. Well, I guess I wouldn't *say* they were crazy because a year ago people did not talk. People did not run. People did not follow boys.

But here, now, it was the most normal thing in the world.

There was a time, once, when I watched Nash run ahead of me, his eyes set on a sparkling pool of water and his arms lifted in the air. I watched him, sprinting across the grassy field with laughter in his eyes, and I remembered thinking he looked so out of place, gray clothes against a backdrop of greens and blues and purples and whites. I never thought of gray as beautiful, always thought of it as the color of silence and steadiness and something that just had to be in order for us to be.

Here, in this Dome, my breath hot and feet pounding the floor, all I saw was gray. Gray walls rushing past my skin, gray ceiling that sloped forward as far as I could see, and Nash's gray clothes a blur in front of me.

And it was beautiful.

Maybe gray itself was still ugly. But when you added layers—rushing feet and wide eyes and the hope of something new, something better—maybe that's what made it different than it was before.

We ran down hallways, passed closed doors and winking lightbulbs, and I noticed we were going a way I had never seen before. It was emptier, echoed more than the other hallways did. I wondered how Nash had found it—just how much of this Dome had he seen when he and Mr. Dabir and the others made their nightly rounds?

How big was this Dome, really?

We wound around corners and passed through the hallway that led to the staircase. My heart was beating quickly, my breath too short to stop and think. I just ran. If there was anyone I could trust, it was Nash. I knew that now. He had made a mistake trusting Mr. Dabir. His heart, his intentions, had always been good. He was good, to the core. He could try to be one of them, but he would always fail. I hoped he knew that, and I hoped he clung to it.

At the top of the stairs, in front of the door to the world, he stopped. He turned to me, his face flushed and hair pushed back from running. His eyes were wide, but he didn't seem nervous. He looked around, at the walls and door, back at the walls again. His eyes moved past me, down the staircase, then to the walls again. The room was silent. He turned and looked at me, and his face fell.

"He's not here."

I stood there, at the top of the stairs. "Who?"

Nash didn't answer. He jogged to the top of the staircase, looked down, then looked at the door. He turned his wrist, and I saw a watch strapped around it, small and brown.

"I don't understand. He wouldn't be late, not for this."

I looked at him, confused. Something moved behind me, on the stairs, and I heard footsteps. Nash's eyes widened and he turned to the door. I stepped away from the doorway and pressed myself against the wall on instinct. But when the footsteps stopped next to me, Nash let out a breath.

"Emily."

I took a step away from the wall, saw the girl with red hair look at me, then at Nash. She shook her head in between short breaths: she had been running.

195

"I tried to catch you before you came up here. He's not coming. Something came up, something he had to do for the plan." Her eyes fell on me. "I'm sorry."

Nash didn't say anything for a second. He was staring past Emily, at the stairs.

"Who?" I looked at Emily, then back at Nash. My heart was beating quickly still, from the run.

Nash turned to me, the confidence and excitement in his face gone. He looked apologetic, and I didn't know why.

"He wanted to see you—he asked for this one thing—and I knew you would want to see him, so..." He paused, took a breath. "Branch. Branch was supposed to meet you here."

Something squeezed my chest. "Branch? But how—"

"When I told you I was going somewhere, I went out looking for him." Nash's eyes met mine. "I was with the search party Mr. Dabir sent out, but I snuck away when they were sleeping one night. I found him—I found all of them. We talked. And he—he was supposed to be here."

I tried to speak, but I couldn't. The room was suddenly silent. He was looking for Branch, for them all. He had *found* Branch. Talked to him and Theodore and Alese and Dalia and Gavin.

Nash sank to the ground, like the walls and ceiling were crushing him. "I was trying— I wanted— I knew it would make you happy. To see him. I'm sorry."

Branch was supposed to be *here*. I blinked, still hoping he would appear in the corner, that half smile on his face and torn sleeves pushed up around his shoulders, those golden eyes looking into mine.

"Mr. Dabir will know you're gone soon." Emily shifted in her place by the stairs. "You should get back. And sorry, Laney, we would let you leave the Dome, but—besides the fact that Mr. Dabir would completely flip if you were gone— Branch needs you here. It's all part of the plan. Until the moment is right." Her eyes fell on me once, and she actually looked like she was sorry.

"Plan? What plan?" I pushed a stray piece of hair behind

my ear. My palms were wet.

Emily turned to me, and I saw something there, in her eyes. "The plan to save us." Her lips turned up slightly. "That's all he would say—we don't know anymore. But it's soon. That much, we do know." She looked at me a second longer, then she turned and walked down the steps. This time I didn't hear her leaving.

We stood there, at the top of the Dome, the shadows even darker than usual. I didn't move, and neither did Nash.

It was like I had known it all along, but then I hadn't. The note from Branch, the drawing on the wall. There was always a plan, wasn't there? And Branch and the others were behind it. I was finally going to get out of this terrible place—we *all* were. I didn't know whether to laugh or cry. In this dark room, I didn't even know if either of them was possible.

Suddenly Nash stood. There were shadows on his face, and I couldn't see his expression.

I looked around the room one more time, just in case, and then turned to the door. If what Emily said was true, I would see him soon enough. I would just need to hold on to that.

"Ready?" I forced the word from my lips, shook the disappointment from my mind.

Silence.

I looked behind me, and Nash still stood there, his face bathed in gray.

"Nash?"

"No." He pushed his sleeves up his arms. "We're not leaving yet. Wait here."

Nash stepped to the bar next to the door, took a breath. And then he grabbed it firmly and pulled.

I stood there as the door groaned open, the sunlight cut a sharp line through the middle of the room, and dust filled the air, winking like stars. Slowly, as minutes passed, the yellow grew, swallowing up the darkness and creating a room that didn't look like the room we had been in moments ago. The corners were too soft, the walls too smooth, and the entire room a hazy yellow-white. The gray was gone.

The door groaned for the last time, and then there was silence. Silence, and a big, wide-open space that was sunlight instead of stone.

I blinked away the last bit of darkness, my throat tight. "What are you doing?" The words came out of me in a whisper, and Nash turned from the sun to me.

"We're going to take a little detour." He swallowed, his eyes suddenly hesitant, like maybe he should change his mind, maybe he shouldn't be doing this. But then he looked out the door, and his lips turned up into a smile. He reached out his hand, and it looked orange in the light. "We don't have long. Ready?"

I blinked, moved my eyes back to the sun. The warmth touched my skin, flooded through my veins like when Nash held my hand up to the ceiling of the Dome that first day. I could see the soft white clouds, could hear a bird singing in the distance. I took a deep, shaky breath.

"Yes."

When I stepped up to the door, I took his hand, threaded my fingers through his. I didn't know why I was nervous— didn't know why I felt like this was the first time I was seeing the world. I had been waiting for this moment for so long. But day after day in my cell, day after day of seeing nothing but gray walls and cold food and dark eyes and white skin, this world seemed like something foreign, somewhere I didn't belong.

First, we stepped through the door, silent and soft and cautious. Then, we were running.

The deep brown of the canyon wall and the blue of the sky filled my eyes, blurred together into a watery picture, focused into edges and lines, and then blurred again. The air was clean—*so* clean. I took a breath and it felt like water was pumping through my lungs. The ground under my feet was hard, unsteady, my shoes not used to loose stones or uneven surfaces, but it only made me want to run faster. Nash was a blur next to me, and we ran, hand in hand, two not-so-ugly blobs of gray against a smear of bright colors.

The blinding sunlight, the colors, and the air suddenly caught up to me and I sank to the middle of the canyon floor, pulling Nash down with me. And I noticed for the first time—he was laughing.

I looked at him, at the smudge on his face and the canyon walls surrounding him, and I couldn't help but smile. It wasn't grass, or trees, or water, but it was its own kind of beautiful.

"That." Nash stretched his hands on the ground behind him, his eyes on mine. "*That* was all I wanted today. One LP."

"An LP? Seriously?" I put my hands out next to his, caught my breath. We were here, out in the world, and he was bringing up love points—the thing Alese had created to teach the people how to love.

"Yes." His expression looked playful now, and I loved it—loved seeing the Nash I always knew. He looked forward again, at the opening of the canyon. "I wanted to make you smile."

I fell silent, following his gaze. My heart was beating quickly again, from our run. I took in a deep, clean breath.

"Thank you for this."

His eyes stayed on the canyon walls. "This is nothing."

Something pressed against my back, and I suddenly remembered the little black square that had kept me going through this day.

"And the paper book—I never got to thank you for that too."

Nash turned to me, his eyes browner than I had seen them in a long time. He suddenly seemed to remember something.

He stood, brushed off his hands, started walking.

"Nash—?"

"Just wait here."

And for the second time that day, I did. I watched as he walked to the edge of the canyon wall, bent, picked up something, then dropped it. He did this several times, until finally he jogged back over to me and held out his hand, closed in a fist, with something inside. Then, slowly, he opened it.

I blinked, tried not to laugh. "A rock?"

He shook his head firmly, his eyes sparkling. "Come on, Laney. You're smarter than that."

I looked at him, back at the rock—black, with sharp edges. I shook my head finally. "I give up."

Nash let out a pretend breath of frustration. "Not *just* a rock." He took it in two fingers, swept it up and down and sideways, scribbled in the air.

And I got it. Just like the rock I had used to write with my second time in the world above, before the paper book was destroyed.

"A pencil."

Nash smiled and dropped it in my hand. "A paper book is pretty useless without it."

For some reason, it hadn't even occurred to me that I had no way to write. Just having the paper book was enough.

"And no more *thank-yous*, okay?" Nash sat down again, stretched his legs out next to me. "If anything, I'm the one who gets to thank you. For giving me another chance."

We sat there for a few moments, our faces bathed in sunlight and our hands pressed against the rocky floor of the canyon.

"Do you remember the first time we met? Officially, I mean?" Nash spoke suddenly. I looked at him, wondered why he was thinking of that day.

"Of course. When you asked me to come onstage with you, to hold your hand."

"Yes, but no. That's not what happened."

I turned to him, and his eyes met mine.

"Yes, I asked you to come onstage with me. But I never told you why. I never told you I was going to take your hand. And still...you came up anyway. With no idea your world was about to change." His lips went up in a half smile.

I rolled my eyes, a half smile on my own face. "The day *everyone's* world changed. I had never seen the audience look like that before, go into such a panic. Actually make *noise*. And anyway, it's not like you gave me much of a choice."

"But that's just it, Laney." Nash turned to me, his eyes suddenly serious. "You did have a choice. And you did it anyway. Why?"

I looked back at him for a few seconds, then dropped my eyes to my lap. Why had I trusted him that day, when I had no reason to? When it was going against everything I had ever been taught?

Nash squeezed my hand, and I looked back up at him.

"That's what I like about you, Laney. You were brave, even when you had everything to lose. And that's how I know you're going to make it through this." His expression didn't move, smile didn't budge. "You're going to get out of here. I promise."

I blinked. And I believed him.

"Why did you pick me that day?" I shifted, sat up a little straighter. "Of all the people in our class?" It was something I just now thought of, something I had never thought to ask.

Nash shrugged. "You were the only one that hadn't left the classroom yet."

I stared at him, and he turned his head toward me. Then a smile broke out over his face.

"You're unbelievable." I scooped up a pile of dirt next to me and threw it at him. "You could have at least made up a better answer."

Nash chuckled and ducked, and the dirt landed on his arm, a smear of brown against his skin. He brushed it off. "You're right. Do-over. Why did I choose you, of all the fine pale-skinned, gray-eyed people in the Dome?" He stood, bowed, and held out his hand in front of him. "So I would have an excuse to hold your hand."

I laughed—I couldn't help it, the feeling bubbled up through my stomach—and took his hand. "Much better."

He pulled me up in front of him, and I blinked back stars from standing so quickly.

"You'll get through this, Laney." Nash let go of my fingers

and brushed his hands on his pants. He was looking at me again, and I liked that he could be so sincere—so real—without even trying. He smiled. "Branch has a plan. And if there's anyone you can trust, it's Branch."

Branch. I realized I hadn't thought about him since we stepped into the sunlight, stepped into the world. I looked away, nodded. He was right. We could trust Branch.

Nash was silent for a few seconds longer, his eyes forward again, on the exit to the canyon. I wondered if he was thinking about leaving—wondered if he wished he could.

"We should get back."

My stomach clenched when he said the words, but I knew he was right. Mr. Dabir was probably looking for us—and who knows what that crazy man would do if he found out Nash and I left the Dome, just walked through the door. I stood, wiped my hands on the bottom of my shirt. There were small indents on my palms, from the rocks, and I smiled.

When Nash turned to me, his eyes were bright. "Race you."

He took off, kicking up dust as he sprinted back to the Dome's door.

"Nash!" I couldn't help but laugh as I ran after him, savoring the last few seconds of the sun on my arms and the sound of the wind and the way the blue sky looked like water.

A year ago, if someone told me I would be running through a canyon following a boy who was racing to the Dome, I would say they were crazy. Well, I guess I wouldn't *say* they were crazy because a year ago people did not talk. People did not run. People did not follow boys.

But here, now, it was the most normal thing in the world.

29

THEN

A year ago, if someone told me I would be standing in a replica Dome, recently named the leader of humanity, and the very people that named me leader asked me to kill them, I would say they were crazy.

No, more than that.

I would say they were insane. Messed up in the head.

Not about the me being named leader of humanity part, of course—that wouldn't be so hard to believe. But the killing the leaders' leaders part? Fiction. Fable. A lie. The thing is, no one would be crazy enough to even dream that story up.

I stare at Glasses Lady, at a single orange hair that's sticking out from her normal hairdo. It's not right. None of this is right. The dark room when I should be celebrating graduation, the orange piece of hair that should be plastered down with hairspray like the rest of her head. Something's off about it all. And I realize, for the first time, that maybe the games aren't over yet.

"Is this a test? Because I don't know what you want me to say."

Glasses Lady isn't nervous anymore. She calmly reaches her long white fingers into her pocket, revealing three gray straws pinched in her fingers. She looks at Hairless and Pimples, lowers her voice slightly.

"The shortest straw will go first. The middle is second.

203

The tallest is last."

I stare at them. I'm right—of course, I'm right. It's some sort of sick test she has prepared for the grand finale. Well, if it will affirm their faith in me even more, I might as well play along. Though after all they've put me through, I can't believe they even need it.

I cross my arms slowly over my chest. "I'm not killing you. There. Did I pass the final test? *The test of loyalty? The test to make sure he's not actually a violent psychopath*, maybe? I'm going to have some cake."

I turn around, take a step toward the door, hoping they won't demote me for being rude. But this—this is ridiculous. A little too far, if you ask me.

"Jonathan Dabir."

Glasses Lady's voice isn't necessarily loud, or stern. But it has a coldness that makes me stop.

I turn around slowly, and I see Glasses Lady, Hairless, and Pimples standing side by side now in the darkness. Their hands are in front of them, each holding one of the three straws—Hairless, the shortest. Glasses Lady, the middle. And Pimples, the tallest.

Glasses Lady's eyes are staring into mine, and I never realized how gray they really are—not like clouds or rocks, but deeper, like the ice on the edge of a lake in the winter.

"This is not a test, Jonathan Dabir." If Glasses Lady is breathing, I can't tell. Her chest isn't moving—nothing about her is moving.

"Do not forget to read the instructions on how to get to the Dome. Memorize them. Lead the others there." She doesn't blink. "There are eleven backpacks filled with books in the small room next to the replica Dome's door. They are books that will be useful to your new life in the Dome. Have you and each of the other leaders take them with you when it is time."

She's talking slowly, calmly, but I can barely keep her words straight. Why is she telling me this, like she won't be there when the time comes? And books? I guess that makes sense, making sure *all* the books in the world don't get destroyed, but—

"Now is your final chance to prove yourself as head leader." Glasses Lady pauses for a moment. The room is silent, but my head is pounding. She nods toward Hairless, who wrings his hands together and sets the straw down slowly, on the ground. He stays there, kneeling on the cold, hard floor. "He is the first of your final three-part assignment."

Hairless is my assignment? I shake my head, realize it feels suddenly light, take a step back. It can't be—she can't be serious.

"Jonathan Dabir." Glasses Lady's eyes lock on mine. She reaches behind her, pulls something from under her shirt, by her back. I swallow, but my throat is dry. A small black gun. She places it on the top of a dusty gray desk in between us, slides it slowly across the surface. "Do you have what it takes to be head leader?"

Her question hangs in the air.

"This is real. You're serious." Those are the only words I can think to say. I look up from the gun, see her nod. Suddenly I'm very cold. "Why not just wait until the end of the world, like everyone else? Why now?"

A second of silence passes, and I think maybe I've convinced them. But she tips her chin, does the slightest shake of her head.

"Right now, we have a choice. To die by the hand of the future leader of a new and thriving humanity who *will survive*, or to die by the hands of the men with black eyes. And the choice is simple." She's talking so simply, so matter-of-factly. "It will be an honor to die by the hand of our leader."

I swallow, the chill still in my blood. Maybe I was wrong. Maybe she really is crazy.

"Why don't you just come with us? You taught us everything we know. The Dome will have room, they're making it big enough for—"

"We cannot come with you." Glasses Lady kneels now,

Marissa Howard

her gray skirt wrinkling when it presses to the floor. "We have done our job. And it is time." She nods to Pimples, who kneels next to her and dips his head toward the floor. "*Now*, Jonathan Dabir. Your fellow leaders will be wondering where you've gone."

I look at them all on the ground, my heart pounding. "I'm not— I can't—"

"*Now.*"

I take a deep, shaky breath, my palms wet. It's so quiet in here—the silence is pressing down on me like water. I can hear my heartbeat as it counts down the time.

Ten.

Nine.

I take the gun.

Eight.

They're my leaders. They're my leaders, and they asked me to kill them.

Seven.

I lift it slowly, the metal cold in my fingers. My hand is shaking, my arm is shaking. *Everything* is shaking.

Six.

I aim the gun at Hairless's head. Shut my eyes.

Five.

This isn't real. None of this is real.

Four.

I can feel the trigger, cold on my index finger. I start to squeeze.

Three.

Something clatters down the hall, and my eyes snap open. I listen, and nothing. My eyes fall on Hairless's head, face turned to the ground, and I see a few single gray hairs on the top of it. So he's not hairless after all.

"*Now*, Jonathan Dabir."

Two.

I shut my eyes again, breathe in, breathe out, and in again. I think of my pond, imagine diving into the water and sinking farther, farther, until I reach the bottom and the world is silent. This isn't real. I breathe in, slowly, and start to squeeze.

One.

This is crazy. I'm *not* crazy.

I open my eyes, let the gun fall to my side while I try to still the shaking. "I'm not going to kill you."

No one moves for a second.

Glasses Lady looks up, and there's an expression of genuine disappointment on her face. She opens her mouth, but another voice cuts through instead.

"Wait."

It's Pimples. I breathe a sigh of relief. I finally got through to one of them. I won't have to do this. I set the gun down on the table and step back.

"Maybe I...maybe I can do it." He swallows audibly, wrings his hands in front of him. "I am supposed to go last. So I will kill myself last."

Glasses Lady doesn't move for a moment. Then, slowly, she nods.

"You can't be serious—"

"Jonathan Dabir, you have no right to speak anymore."

I swallow my words, and Glasses Lady looks at Pimples again. She pauses, like her entire plan has changed, like this is not what she wanted. But she nods again, opens her mouth slowly. "Do it."

Pimples doesn't move for a second. Then he places his hands on the ground and stands, steps over to the gun slowly. He breathes a deep, shaky breath, and then he closes his eyes. A moment passes, and when he opens them, he takes the gun in his fingers.

I step back slowly, my throat tight, not completely believing that this is happening. I need to get out. I need to get out *now*.

I take a step back, then another, put my hand on the door and pull.

"No." Glasses Lady speaks again, and I turn, see that her eyes are on the gun in Pimples's hand. They shift, slowly, until they're on me. "You will watch."

Watch? I was so wrong—she is so much more than just crazy. Psychotic, maybe?

"You can't be serious."

For a woman who is about to die, she's so calm. She shakes her head slowly, doesn't move her eyes from mine. "You are a coward, Jonathan Dabir. We chose wrong."

Her words make me forget, for a moment, what's happening. Something stirs inside me, something hot. I'm the best candidate of anyone by far. I *deserved* to win, and no one is going to say otherwise.

I take my hand off the door, let it shut with a click. I turn around slowly, my eyes on Glasses Lady, and fold my arms in front of me. I say nothing, my eyes locked on hers.

She watches me for a moment, and then the briefest flicker of pride flashes across her eyes. She nods at me, once, then looks back at Pimples. He takes his eyes off me and lifts his arm, aims the gun at Hairless's head.

A few seconds pass, and then it seems like a whole minute. I stand there, trying not to cringe, waiting for the sound of the gunshot. My palms are wet, my heart is pounding in my head.

I saw a man die once. Then, a whole crowd of people had watched him fall. Now, it's just me.

The air is hot, heavy. Silent. I see Hairless shift, probably wondering what's taking so long. He looks up, at Pimples.

Bang.

My breath leaves me, the sound so loud that for a second I think something else has happened. Has the world ended again? Then I see Hairless fall, see the blood pool on the cold floor in front of him. I can't breathe.

I look at Glasses Lady, and her eyes are on Pimples. She turns suddenly and looks at me. And I see something in her eyes—something that wasn't there before.

Fear.

She opens her mouth, but then all I see is red. Red splattered in gray, a body crumple to the ground. Her head rolls once, her orange hair still perfectly in place.

"What did you— She was going to say something!" The words sputter out of me, like there's not enough oxygen in my lungs to speak.

Pimples looks at her for a moment longer, then turns to me. "This is what she wanted."

He's shaking—I can see it from here. The gun lifts slightly in his hand, then falls back to his side. He's breathing quick, short breaths. And standing there, I can't help but wonder how a man like this was chosen to lead the future leaders of humanity. He's just...not what I imagine a leader would be.

Pimples lifts the gun to his head, presses it against his temple. I suck in my breath. I want to shut my eyes, but I don't. They asked for this. They want me to be their leader, and a leader wouldn't look away.

Pimples stares at me, his face pinched and white and his breaths audible in the silent room. Five seconds pass. Ten. I wish he would pull the trigger. I wish he would get this nightmare over with, so I can finally leave the room.

Fifteen seconds. Twenty.

We're staring at each other, none of us able to move our eyes. I'm the last person he will see. And he—he is the last non-black-eyed person that I will watch die.

The silence, the stare contest, is crushing. Pimples shifts suddenly, and I see something change in his eyes. The nervousness—the unsureness and weakness and twitchiness about him—disappears suddenly. I blink. But it's still gone. Goose bumps prick my skin.

And then he smiles.

It's not the smiles I remember people talking about in the past—the ones that fill your face, that light up your eyes. No, this smile isn't like that. This smile is twisted slightly, his cheeks too wide and his eyebrows too close together. I saw this smile on the man with fake black eyes, when he pounced on Geena, and then again every time they stopped us from taking the watch.

This smile is bad.

A laugh erupts from Pimples suddenly, and I flinch. His

lips twist again into that awful smile.

"You didn't think I was actually going to kill myself, did you?" His voice is too loud against the silence, too sharp.

My throat is dry. What is happening?

Pimples slowly lowers the gun, observes it in his fingers. "It is such a relief to finally be rid of those two. And to finally stop playing the *smarty-pants, nervous leader who is afraid of everyone and everything.*" He smirks at those last words and faces the dead bodies on the floor. "Idiots."

I swallow slowly, my hands on the door behind me. This isn't the Pimples I know. It's like the whole room has been turned upside down.

"I knew you would be too weak to kill us." Pimples swings the gun around in his hand a few times and steps toward me. "That's why I recommended you as leader. It worked like a charm."

Heat flashes across my eyes, and I blink. "What do you want?"

"What do I want?" He scoffs. "Well, I certainly don't *want* to hand humanity over to you, a *child*. No. My time isn't up yet." Pimples stops again, the smile stretching across his face suddenly, wider than before. He pauses for emphasis, then bows.

"Jonathan Dabir, meet the new head leader of the Dome: me."

30

NOW

The Dome seemed a little less gray when the door shut and the sunlight and air and colors disappeared. It was strange— shouldn't the Dome have seemed even darker, colder, after spending time outside the door? It was funny how the world worked. It was like the sunlight could reach down through the ground, could light up even the deepest and grayest places, if just for a few moments.

I could still feel it, in my skin.

Nash jogged softly ahead of me, peering around corners before he motioned for me to follow. It was quiet, and for a second I wondered if something was wrong. But then I remembered Mr. Dabir had ordered everyone to their indents before Nash took me to the world above. In just a few minutes outside, I had forgotten how silent silence could be.

Nash slowed to a stop as we reached the door to my indent. He looked around the hallway once more, to be sure. Then he looked at me. I swear, it was like we were still outside, his face a mix of flushed pinks and oranges and yellows.

"Will you be okay?" I could hear his breath against the quiet air.

I put my hand on the door and turned back to him. "Yes."

His lips curved slightly. "Good." He turned, started heading down the hall.

"Nash?"

He stopped, looked back at me. "Yeah?"

"Thank you." I swallowed. "I needed that more than you know."

He watched me a second longer, the hint of a smile still on his lips. "No more *thank-yous*, remember?" He dipped his head at me once, then turned again and disappeared into the darkness.

I slipped past the door and shut it behind me, the light in my room fluttering softly against the gray. Then I saw it: a shadow in the corner, a sharp intake of breath.

"Laney?"

I stopped, my body suddenly awake, alert.

The shadow stepped closer to the light, closer to me. I blinked. And suddenly it was like the whole world un-paused, the walls and gray and air rushing back at me in one breathless push.

"Branch?"

His face was sprinkled with shadows, but it broke into a grin—one end slightly farther up than the other, perfectly crooked. Perfectly crooked, and in my indent, underground, right here. In front of me.

"How did you—?"

He closed the space between us, rushed across the room before I could finish my sentence. My head was pounding, my body suddenly light. This was a dream. It had to be a dream.

When he reached me, he wrapped his arms around me, lifted me in the air. I laughed suddenly, a sound that erupted from my lips. He set me down gently, and I felt his fingers brush against my chin. His eyes—those golden eyes, like fire, like the sun—were so bright, even in the darkness.

"Are you okay?"

His voice. Branch's voice. Something I had waited so long to hear.

I nodded—the only thing I could do was nod. The smile filled his face again, filled his eyes. I reached my hand up, touched his golden hair. I could feel the heat from his skin, could see the ripped sleeves and the softened look of his clothes from being in the sun.

"I missed you so much." Five words, and then he pulled me in, touched his lips to mine.

I could smell him, the outside air—the smell of the leaves and the trees and water—were on his skin, in his touch. It was strange, kissing him underground, when every scenario I had imagined was in between canyon walls, or under tree branches, or with soft grass brushing against my heels. But here he was, finally, in my arms.

Branch pulled away and smiled, laughter playing at his lips, even in all this gray. "Lesson number three about love, Laney. *Never* leave someone for more than an hour or two, at the most."

I laughed. "Like I had any say in this."

Branch's eyes held mine for a little longer, then he looked me up and down, touched the gray plastic device on my head. "What is this? You sure you're okay?"

I hesitated, nodded.

"Good." Branch took a breath. "Because we're getting you out of here ASAP. Where were you? I almost died waiting in this deep, dark room. All this silence and gray."

"Welcome to my life." I smiled, my heart still pounding, my palms wet. "I was upstairs, looking for you. But you—you were down here?"

"Of course." Branch smiled. "Sorry I played a little switch-a-roo on Emily and Nash. I knew I would find you alone here, and I thought you would come right back down to your room. I've been waiting for you."

"Nash took me out in the world." I smiled, the warmth of the sun filling my thoughts. "I'm sorry—if I had known you were in here, I never would have —"

"Nash?" The smile from Branch's face disappeared. "Are you okay? Did he hurt you?"

I looked at Branch, confused. "Hurt me? No. He wanted to get me out of the Dome for a few minutes. He knew it

213

would make me happy."

Branch stepped back, ran a hand through his hair. "Laney, you know you can't trust him, right? He betrayed us." His eyes didn't move from mine. "He'll do it again."

I hesitated, my throat dry. "You don't understand. He's—he's been through a lot. He's different now."

Branch shook his head slowly. "Nash is the reason you're in here, Laney. And the reason Theodore, Alese, Gavin, and Dalia are out there. The reason I'm out there." He didn't blink. "He's the reason we were separated, Laney."

I tried to shake my head, tried to speak, but I couldn't. Not with Branch right in front of me, his eyes full of concern and determination and...and something else. Something soft. And what could I say? Even if Nash's intentions had been good, you couldn't deny the facts. Branch was right.

I let out a breath.

"How are they? Alese, Theodore, Gavin, and Dalia?" Just saying their names made my throat tight.

Branch stepped forward again, wrapped me in a hug. "They're good. We've been surviving out by the river. Erika was even with us for a while, believe it or not." He chuckled. "They miss you. *I* miss you."

I sucked in a heavy breath. He didn't know. Of course he didn't know. "Branch, about Erika..."

Branch pulled back, looked at me. Shook his head slowly. "He found her, didn't he?"

I hesitated, nodded.

Something clenched inside of him. His eyes met mine. "Listen, Laney, I can't stay much longer. Me and the others, we're the only people who know about this plan. And it's going to stay that way. We can't risk telling Nash or Emily. We'll find out soon enough what side they're really on, and then we can make our decisions from there." He cupped his hands around my cheeks. "And we can't risk telling you either. Who knows what Mr. Dabir will do if he finds out you know something he wants to know? I couldn't live with myself if that happened. You just..." He took a deep breath, like this pained him. "You just need to trust me. I'm going to get you and everyone else out of this. For good. If it's the last thing I do."

I tried to swallow, tried to memorize the gold in his hair and the creases around the corners of his eyes. My throat tightened. It was too short. It was always too short. I nodded. "I trust you—of course I trust you."

He let out a breath, and his eyes stayed on mine for a moment longer. The intensity of his gaze made me forget the room, forget the gray and the stone and the shadows, for a moment. Then he spoke.

"I love you, Laney."

I stood there, the air suddenly gone.

The door opened behind me, and at first I was confused. Branch was still in front of me, his fingers laced in mine. So how was someone at the—?

"*No*, Mr. Dabir was right. How are you here right now?"

I whirled around, saw Branch's eyes snap to the door. I let out a breath when I saw the person who had spoken.

"Nash?"

"Mr. Dabir knows you're here. I didn't even know, but somehow, he—he found out—" Nash was breathing quick, short breaths, his eyes wide and hand still clutching the door.

And I realized he wasn't looking at me. He was looking at Branch.

Nash's face was white. "You need to go, now!"

Branch's eyes flickered to mine, and I felt a sudden cold as he released his hands.

"Branch, how *delightful* of you to grace us with your presence. How positively, wonderfully delightful!"

A voice, too sharp in the silence, stabbed the air. And then a face—dark gray, covered in shadows—appeared just behind Nash. Mr. Dabir held up three broken gray straws and smiled.

"Anyone up for a little game?"

31

THEN

I had wanted him to live. I had set the gun down, stepped back, and let the hands of a monster pick it up.

I was supposed to be their leader. But I fell for it as much as the two bodies on the floor.

They wanted to die, Pimples said a few seconds after he placed the barrel of the gun against my back and pushed me through the door. *But no one else knows that, do they?*

My vision is a blur as I step back into the room where ten teenagers and a few dozen men with black eyes stand in circles, shoveling cake into their mouths. The light seems bright in here—too bright. The room is all wrong, corners not sharp enough and edges too long, ceilings too high.

Hope looks up from her conversation with Geena and I see questions in her eyes. *Where did you go? Is everything okay?*

I take a breath, press my hand against the wall behind me, and accidentally bump the table with the cake. The stupid cake. The stupid cake and the stupid men with black eyes and our stupid leaders who decided to kill themselves.

Pimples pushes me forward, the gun cold against my shirt.

The world is still spinning when I hear Pimples clear his throat, hear him call attention to the room. I'm tired, too tired for this craziness that escalated to unpredictable heights. But when everyone falls silent I suddenly feel it—the terror pricks me, buries itself underneath my skin.

And suddenly the world is sharper than a bullet.

Pimples is quiet for a moment, a fake look of horror on his face. I stand up straight, my heart pounding audibly in my ears, until I notice everyone else. The fake men with black eyes, every other leader that I brought to this moment—they're not looking at him. They're looking at me.

And then Pimples says one simple word that falls from his lips and shatters on the floor.

"Murderer."

32

NOW

My vision was a blur, the air suddenly silent—so silent.

Nash was shaking his head, his eyes tightly shut. I couldn't see Branch, who was standing just behind me. Branch—here, underground, in my cell. In front of the monster.

"I promise, it's not violent or gruesome." Mr. Dabir stepped forward, forcing Nash into the room with us. He scrunched his face up dramatically. "Trust me, I have been there, done that. No, *this* game..." He paused, and that twisted smile filled his face. "*This* game will be more fun."

I looked at Branch, my eyes wide, but I couldn't read his expression. He was watching Mr. Dabir. I tried to swallow, tried to breathe. This wasn't happening. How did Mr. Dabir know he was here?

"We'll *finally* get some proper use out of this." Mr. Dabir stepped up to me, flicked the gray plastic device on my head with his finger.

"Don't touch her." Nash moved forward suddenly.

Mr. Dabir's hand hovered over my head. Then he lowered it, grabbed Nash's arm and pulled him close. I could see his fingernails digging into Nash's arm as he peered into his eyes.

"Careful, boy. *You* betrayed *me*, remember?" He laughed suddenly, a sound that gave me goose bumps. "Your second betrayal, I believe. Now you've betrayed everyone you know. I underestimated you, didn't I?"

Nash stepped back, his mouth in a line.

When Mr. Dabir put the device on Branch, he didn't even flinch. I looked at him, tried to catch his eye, but he stared straight ahead.

Mr. Dabir had murdered Branch's brother, Lander, and Branch had almost killed him for it once. I didn't know what Mr. Dabir would do, alone with him for the first time since. This was bad. This was really bad.

Mr. Dabir stepped back, admiring his work. He held the straws behind him, and I stumbled backward, pressed my hands against the wall. My heart was pounding in my head.

Slowly, without looking, Mr. Dabir set a straw in front of me, then Branch, then Nash. My eyes snapped to Nash, and he was watching me, trying to hide the fear on his face. But his mouth was too tight, his face too white.

"Well, well."

My eyes snapped back to Mr. Dabir. He had removed the hand over his eyes and was looking at the floor, a thoughtful expression on his face. I followed his gaze, and for the first time I noticed the straws were different sizes. The longest was in front of me, the medium in front of Branch, and the shortest in front of Nash, lifeless on the cold floor. Mr. Dabir looked at me, and the edge of his mouth twitched.

"It looks like I'm finally going to solve the source of love, after all these years."

33

THEN

I remember silence, but not like this.

Every time before, silence has been the simple lack of sound, like people don't care enough to talk. It's been dull, gray, natural. A part of life that has to be so we can be.

But not this.

The moment the word leaves Pimples's lips it's like every breath from every pair of lungs is sucked from this room. This silence is hard, sharp, deliberate. This silence isn't gray.

It's black.

"What are you talking about?" Someone speaks, adds a crack to the wall of silence. I look up, see that it's Scar Boy. He's not looking at me anymore. He's looking at the gun.

"He's lying!" I manage to spit the words out, but I feel the gun dig deeper into my back.

"Unbelievable. You killed them and now you're denying it?" Pimples's voice wavers, the perfect blend of fear and nervousness and anger. It makes me sick. He looks up at everyone in the room. "We wanted to congratulate Jonathan Dabir personally, for becoming head leader of humanity, so we took him down the hall. We went to shake his hand, and he just..." Pimples sucks in a breath. "He just snapped. He pulled out a gun—I don't know where he got it from—and shot each of our dear other leaders in the head. And then I— I tackled him. Got the gun from him. He was planning on killing us all, and never telling a soul."

"This is insane. They're never going to believe—"

"Aaaagghhhh!" Pimples cries out suddenly, falls to the floor. He's sobbing now, like the event was so terrible he can't possibly relive it. I can't believe what I'm hearing—can't believe the story he's making up. And the fact that he's back to playing *poor little scared senseless leader* in the snap of a finger, the evil Pimples I saw in the room hidden behind that fake bundle of nerves, makes my head swim.

He stops slowly, sniffles twice, then stands, points the gun at me. The room is stone-cold, that prickling silence filling the air again. Someone in the room shifts.

"I don't believe you."

Finally. Hope's voice. I meet her eyes and nod gratefully, look out at the others. Geena starts to whimper. Scar Boy is looking at me, but he says nothing. Redhead avoids my eyes.

"Seriously? You guys know I would never do something like that." I let out a breath. "Listen to Hope! She knows what she's talking about."

More silence. I can't believe this. There is no way they actually—

"Do you have proof?" Scar Boy speaks suddenly, slowly.

Pimples nods, a little too excitedly if you ask me. How does no one see that? He points the gun toward the door.

"Follow me."

He never takes the gun off me, never drops his stupid act as the ten leaders and all the fake-black-eyed men follow Pimples down the hallway, turn the corner, and then reach the door.

When he pushes the door open, he just stands there in the doorway, shielding his eyes. "In there." He points, gasping the words out like his throat is too tight.

Scar Boy goes in first. He's silent when he sees the bodies—doesn't take a step back, doesn't blink. He just stares. The fake-black-eyed men pile in the room after him, each of their mouths turning into a line simultaneously. They're staring at Glasses Lady most of all, like she means

221

something to them simply because she hired them for some crazy end-of-the-world act. Geena gasps and begins sobbing right before she collapses on the ground and pushes herself up against the wall.

Hope is last. I don't see her face as she steps through the doorway, takes in the pools of blood that have spread across the floor and the bodies lying next to them. Then she turns, slowly, her green eyes on mine. A few seconds pass. I can't read her expression, can't tell what she's thinking.

There's a *thump* at the end of the room—one of the fake-black-eyed men just picked up and dropped Hairless's arm, to make sure he's really dead. I swallow bile, look back at Hope, but she's not looking at me anymore. She takes a breath and walks past me, out the door.

No.

"Hope, don't believe him— I didn't—"

"Yes, you *did.*" Pimples's voice echoes on the cold walls.

I blink, shake my head, look down the hallway. Hope is gone.

A coldness creeps over my skin and in my blood, squeezes everything in my chest, over and over again. I feel frozen to the floor, frozen against the end of the gun.

"The Dome calls for eleven leaders." Pimples meets eyes with the others who look up from the bodies on the floor. "It will call for a unanimous vote, of course, but..." He pauses, takes a deep, shaky breath. "I volunteer to take Jonathan Dabir's place, if you will have me."

All eyes shift from Pimples to me. Something has changed in the air—I can feel it. I can see it in their eyes, in the way they press their lips tightly together. The other leaders are either terrified, or angry.

"He's right." Scar Boy steps forward. "This man trained us, made us who we are today. If anyone deserves to take Jonathan Dabir's place, it's him."

"He's lying!" I shake my head, frantic now. Why is it so cold in here? "You're making a murdering psychopath your leader!"

No one speaks. Pimples shakes his head, like I'm the one who is crazy. He looks tired.

"All in favor of making me your new leader?" He says the words like this is the last thing on earth he wants to happen.

But it does.

Scar Boy raises his hand first. And suddenly the world is a blur again, a roomful of colors and people and arms raised to the ceiling, cold eyes on mine.

All of them. All nine of the other leaders who I brought to where they are today and saved from the fake end of the world.

"But, sir, it's not unanimous," Geena's voice squeaks out, small, her back still pressed against the corner. "Hope isn't here."

"I'll ask her later. I'm sure she'll agree." Pimples sounds annoyed for a second, but he catches himself. He nods suddenly to two of the fake-black-eyed men and stuffs the gun behind his shirt. "Please escort Mr. Dabir off the premises. He is henceforth banned from this building, permanently."

I don't move for a second. I breathe in a deep breath, still my shaking hands, swallow down the bile and the cold. I look back at the others, make sure I meet eyes with every one of them. And I push it all back—push back every feeling of pride or determination or loyalty I felt to them. I push back those unknown feelings I felt with Hope, every time I hesitated or questioned something or took a step that didn't have purpose. I crush them all in my mind, one by one.

That wasn't real. It was never real.

As the fake-black-eyed men follow me through the door, one word pulses in my mind, and it's strange that it's the last thing I'm thinking before I leave this replica Dome forever.

He called me Mr. Dabir.

34

NOW

I remembered silence, but not like this.

Every time before, it was just there, like something that had always been and would always be.

But not now. Now—the look on Mr. Dabir's twisted face, the shadows falling unnaturally on Nash and Branch and the gray straws on the floor—now, the silence was dangerous. It was a sick, twisted game. Silence was a threat.

And we needed to get out.

Mr. Dabir looked up slowly, his eyes dark against the pulsing yellow light that flickered on the ceiling.

"Nash. You win."

The wall felt cold against my hands—too cold.

"Don't you dare kill him!"

Silence. Mr. Dabir didn't move for a moment, and then he turned. I could see the reflection of the light in his eyes, and it looked like fire.

"Kill him?" His mouth twitched, then grew until it filled his face. Laughter escaped his mouth until he was heaving, his shoulders shaking back and forth. Then he slowed, stopped, the amused expression still on his face. "Well that would defeat my whole plan, wouldn't it? I'm not going to kill him, Laney. Not here, not now."

He acted like I was crazy. He was crazy.

I swallowed, clenched my fists. "Then what do you want

with us?"

Mr. Dabir walked over to Nash, bent slowly, and picked up the straw that was lying on the ground in front of him. He twisted it thoughtfully in his fingers.

"I want you to kiss him."

I unclenched my fingers. "What?"

"I was surprised too, of course, that Nash had the shortest straw. From what I've heard, Branch is the favorite now." Mr. Dabir looked at me, winked. "But *now* it's a game, isn't it? And if it doesn't work with Nash, Branch is next. Either way, I'll get what I want. But it's *so much fun* to see who Laney's true love really is! When you kiss them, these gray devices will tell me everything I need to know. I'm on pins and needles, myself."

My throat was suddenly dry. I looked at Branch, but his eyes never left Mr. Dabir.

"What, no response?" Mr. Dabir's face hardened suddenly, like stone. "Kiss him, Laney. Or I will kill every person in this Dome, one by one."

I didn't move. Nash's eyes were on mine, wide. He shook his head. "I'm so sorry, Laney."

"That's enough talking," Mr. Dabir snapped. He looked at me. "One by one, Laney. One. By. One."

I blinked, and my heart clenched in my chest. The air felt thinner, colder. I couldn't breathe.

"Laney, it's fine." Branch spoke suddenly, and I looked at him. His eyes were still on the man in the middle of the room. "We don't need anyone else to die."

My hands were shaking. I met Nash's eyes, and he nodded. Branch was right. It didn't mean anything. And if it meant the people in the Dome were safe for one more day, I had to do it. One kiss. And then I was done.

"Okay." I squeezed the word from my lips, but it was quiet, a whisper.

I walked the few steps to Nash, and his eyes never left mine.

"Wait!" Mr. Dabir spoke suddenly. "No quick,

emotionless peck on the lips. You have to mean it. Or I will kill someone, right now."

I bit my lip, did everything I could to stop myself from turning around.

"It'll be okay." Nash's eyes were firm now, and I could see that he wanted the same thing I did—to punch Mr. Dabir in the stomach. I let out a breath, stilled my shaking fingers. One look in his eyes and I was calm.

I nodded, showed him that it was okay. He leaned in slowly, put his hand behind my back like he always had.

We had to do this. For all of them.

Our lips met.

I didn't know why I thought of the world outside the door—brown canyon walls and green trees and black rocks and blue water. I didn't know why I thought of flowers—red and yellow and white and purple, every color imaginable—stretching across a field and bobbing up and down with the wind. I didn't know why I thought of hands stretching to the ceiling and a blanket placed over my back and books being read by a fire and soaking wet clothes and paper books with white pages and fingers clutched tightly to mine and running and sunlight and laughter, but I did.

When Nash pulled away, I couldn't move, tried to catch my breath. I blinked, and the room fell into place again, like shadows melting together.

Silence. Too much silence. I whirled around, to Mr. Dabir.

He was staring at us, an expression I couldn't read on his face. Suddenly he came to life.

"Branch. You're up."

My face was hot. This game had to stop. "No. I'm done with this."

Mr. Dabir raised an eyebrow. "Is that so?" He tilted his head toward the door. "Blakely. Go find—what was that woman's name Laney's so fond of? Delilah? Dirma? Delma?"

My face turned white.

"Ah, yes. That's it." Mr. Dabir smiled. "Find the old woman—Delma. Bring her here. She is my first victim."

"Wait." Branch spoke, firm. "We've been separated for weeks. You don't have to convince me to kiss her, game or not."

"Pause the Delma thought." Mr. Dabir called to whoever was behind the door. He looked at Branch and narrowed his eyes. "For now." Then he nodded.

Branch closed the small distance between us before I could meet his eyes. He put his arm around my waist, his hand on the back of my neck, and pulled me in close. It was like he knew exactly where my body fit in his—it was familiar, safe. And for a moment, the dark room, the twisted game, Mr. Dabir himself, were all gone. When he pulled away, I saw Nash, standing behind Branch. There was something on his face—something I couldn't read.

I just stood there. I couldn't move.

"Blakely." One word from Mr. Dabir, and the door opened, the girl walked quickly through the door. She held a machine out, and Mr. Dabir looked at it for a few long seconds. Then he looked up.

"But that's not—that's—" His eyes were wider than I had ever seen. "Impossible."

My head felt light, my chest too heavy. I took a step back.

"I knew you would be of use to me, Laney." Mr. Dabir was shaking his head now, his voice quiet. "I knew I chose right."

Chose right?

Mr. Dabir handed the device back to Emily, a look on his face I had never seen before. It was like he was at a loss for words for once.

"What's wrong?" Blakely looked at the machine herself. "Did we get it?"

"Yes. Twice." Mr. Dabir shook his head. He breathed in slowly, touched his fingertips to his cheek. He was staring at me. Something was wrong. Something was very wrong.

He blinked. "She loves them both."

35

THEN

I'm three hallways away from the door to the outside when a sound splits through the air.

The two fake-black-eyed men behind me stop for a second, and I turn on instinct, every muscle in my body tense.

I've heard that sound before. The alarm that went off during the fake end of the world.

The two guys look at each other, and one shakes his head to the other. Both their eyes widen.

"What's happening? Another test?" I have to yell to be heard over the siren. It pounds against the air and echoes off the walls—it feels like the whole building is shaking.

One of the guys looks at me, and I can see a purple vein sticking out in his neck. "Good luck, kid."

Then they turn down the hallway and run.

Good luck? I stand there for a second, watch them disappear around a corner. A prickling feeling spreads across my skin, makes my head light.

It can't be.

"—is not a test! Everyone get to the Dome, now!" Pimples's voice comes from the hallway next to mine, his voice muffled. It sounds like he's running. "Bring as many people as you can along the way!"

I duck around the corner, my heart pounding. A blur of clothing rushes past, then another, and another. A few seconds later, I hear the large gray door bang shut once in the distance, twice, three times.

I breathe in sharply. It is.

The end of the world.

I press my hands against the wall, a dozen thoughts filling my head at the same time. I pluck one out, and I know without a doubt that it's the right one. The only one.

I need to get to the Dome.

I push myself off the wall and run the opposite way of the others, deeper into the building, toward the largest room, praying that Pimples already knew the way so he hadn't grabbed the last one.

I run around the final corner and barrel through the doors, stop for a second, take a breath. The table against the wall still has the platter of empty cake, a few crumbs on its sticky surface. But aside from that, the table is empty.

No.

All the folders with the directions to the real Dome are gone.

Heat rises in my chest, and I grab the edge of the table, heave it on its side. The plastic cake pan slides halfway across the room and stops. The alarm is screaming now; I swear it's gotten louder in the last few seconds. I close my eyes, try to push back the sound, to order my thoughts. My eyes snap open.

I can follow the others. They didn't leave that long ago, and they all have directions to the Dome, and I can—I can catch up.

I whirl around and push through the door, run back the way I came. The gray walls rush past, and I clench my fists, run faster.

It's like the alarm jolted me awake, reminded me of a simple fact that had slipped when I let the others get in my head.

The Dome is mine.

It's always been mine, from the moment I stepped through this door. I passed the tests, fought my way to the

229

top. I'm the leader of the future of humanity. *Me.* And no one is going to take that away—especially not some psychotic nerd.

When I push open the door and sunlight hits me like a wall, I hear footsteps behind me. I whirl around as someone else crashes through the door, blond hair spilling in the wind.

"Jonathan?"

I drop my arms. Hope? And then something happens, something I don't expect—her mouth lights up in a smile.

"I'm so glad I ran into you! I was afraid they kicked you out already."

I try to make sense of her words with the alarm pounding in my head.

"They did." I blink, look at her. The smile—it doesn't make sense. Then something inside me shifts. I open my mouth, unsure if I believe it myself. "You believed me. Didn't you?"

Her eyebrows crease, surprised I would even ask. "Of course. But I knew they would vote against you. That man—there's something wrong with him. He killed them, didn't he?" She shakes her head, her face dark.

And I can't move for a moment. The thought rushes through my mind, bigger and bolder than all the others: *she believes me.*

I don't know why I think it, don't know why it means so much. But it does. And the feeling—that unnamed feeling—rushes through me again, stronger than it ever has before.

Hope looks up, her eyes wide, like she can see the alarm screaming through the Oval.

I look at her, that goal suddenly vital, overwhelming. "We need to get to the Dome!"

Together.

She looks at me for a second too long and then nods, takes off a black backpack and plants it on the ground, reaches into it. She pulls out the folder, pushes it into my hands.

"The directions!" I let out a breath of relief, flip it open quickly, and scan the six sentences on the page. It seems too short, anticlimactic. But that's it. The directions to the Dome.

I look gratefully at Hope, push the folder back in the pack. When I do, my hand brushes against something small, hard. It's not a book. I pull it halfway out and recognize it immediately.

A plastic head device.

I pull the top of the pack open further and see dozens of them clustered together, a mess of wires and hollow, head-sized circles. I look up.

"They can detect feelings and what parts of the brain they come from." Hope watches me, unsure what I'll think. "It's a last resort. But if it comes down to it, and there's no other way...these devices can find love again."

I hesitate, look back in the pack. The alarm is loud—so loud. The men with black eyes have to be close.

And she believed me.

I zip it shut, swing the pack on my back. "We need to go. Now!"

Before the world ends. Before they shut the door.

Hope nods, and her eyes shift from the pack to me. "I'm right behind you."

I nod, tighten the pack, look at her once more. And then I run. I hear her footsteps behind me, padding against the grass, as I head toward the place we watched the sun turn from yellow to red to black.

Directions to the Dome, number one: A small space of wall will be opened behind the large cluster of trees when the alarm sounds. Exit through this space.

We run into the trees, the air instantly cooler, then burst into the sunlight again. And I see it. A small space in the wall, cracked open just barely, enough for one person to fit through.

I reach it and duck, push into the hole in the wall and come out the other side with only a few inches between my arms and the stone next to me. They had to make this difficult, didn't they?

Hope comes through a few seconds later and she stops next to me, sucks in a breath. I realize I haven't even looked in front of me yet, haven't taken my eyes off the wall that surrounded us for so long. I follow her gaze, try to start running again. But I can't.

A few hundred feet in front of us are houses, neighborhoods—a small town. It's dry, the ground cracked and dirty. But the sky above the town is black.

Smoke pours from dozens of houses, reaching in the air like a hand and choking out the blue. One building collapses to the ground in a crackling heap. And I didn't hear it in the walls, because the alarm drowned out every other noise, but I hear it now.

The screaming.

Hope's fingers tighten on mine, and the electricity from her touch makes me tear my eyes away, my head still pounding from what I just saw.

"Promise me, Jonathan." Hope's eyes are filled with fear, and I realize it's the first time I've ever seen her scared— really scared. "Promise me you'll do whatever you can to find love again."

I feel paralyzed, like I'm being tested again. This can't be real.

I realize Hope's green eyes are still on me, waiting for my answer. I shake my head firmly, try to convince myself.

"We can make it. This is what we trained for."

"Promise me." Her voice is a whisper now, and suddenly my mind goes back to the fact that she believed me. Trusts me. The others may have betrayed me, but she didn't. Someone out there still thinks I deserve to be the leader. This crazy girl named Hope that challenged me and showed me things I've never seen before and touched her hand to my cheek—she may not be so crazy after all. I didn't realize how much I needed that one person, the person who never gave up on me.

The feelings I pushed back when the others voted against me, the feelings I crushed—I pull them out again. One by one. Everything I've ever been told and everything I've ever believed in seems to hang in the air, hover next to us, wait for me to grab it, like I've always done.

But I don't.

That crazy, unknown feeling reaches inside me and overwhelms me and makes me feel like I'm back in the trees again, when we watched the sunset, and I told her to stop. I wanted her to turn around.

Why? Why did I want that?

The siren is a dull ringing in my ears now, and everything around me seems to blur together in one giant watery picture. Everything except her.

I'm not crazy. I know I'm not crazy.

Or maybe I am.

I bring my hand up to Hope's face, look into her eyes. I don't move, for a moment. And then I touch her cheek, just barely. The warmth runs through me, and I suck in my breath.

One second.

Two seconds.

I lean in, and I touch my lips to hers.

I don't know why I see sunlight touching the tops of trees. I don't know why I see red skies and feet running along grass and curved lips and blond hair, the way it spreads out in water, weightless. But I do.

I pull away.

I can't explain it. I can't explain the feeling that rushed through me like laughter, like water, like stone when my lips touched hers. But maybe that's the point. There are no words to describe what is created when two people with different lives and different personalities and opinions abandon all of that, abandon all of them, for a moment like this. So instead, I look into her eyes, and I take a breath. And I mean it.

"I promise."

I'm shaking. Touch was banned from society, along with love. I just broke the law. So why don't I feel guilty?

Hope reaches up, touches her lips. And I see it then, her

expression. Her lips tremble, and her eyes are round. She's not smiling anymore.

"Hope?"

She shakes her head, reaches into her pocket and presses something in my hand. I turn my palm, open my fingers, and I see the photograph. The picture of Hope with her grandfather.

I look up, confused, and her face has shifted slightly. The fear in her eyes isn't just fear now. It's pain.

"I need to try and save him, Jonathan. I can't just let him die. Please understand."

I look back at her, my mind slowly putting together all the missing pieces.

"I'm going to do everything I can to reach the Dome in time." She nods, like she's trying to convince herself. "But if I don't make it." She looks at the photograph. She wants me to have it.

Something inside me drops.

"No. Hope, it's too dangerous! Just come with me. You can still make it. We can make it. I—I've never felt this way before. Ever." The words are coming out of me so fast, it's like I can't control it.

Hope squeezes my hand once, then drops it. "I have to do this." Her eyes are so wide, so green. "I'm sorry."

She looks at me a second longer. And then she turns, away from the path to the Dome, away from direction number two on the piece of paper. Away from me.

36

NOW

I didn't know why I stood there, staring at the man in front of me when he spoke those four words. But I did.

Mr. Dabir cleared his throat, dusted off his hands, and found his voice.

"Find Arsen and have him kill them all." He looked at me, and his eyes dropped slightly, but he caught himself. He turned to Blakely. "They are of no use to me anymore."

"No." Nash's voice cracked, and he lunged at Mr. Dabir. Mr. Dabir whirled around and grabbed his arm, threw him on the ground.

Then he dusted off his shirt, once. "Thank you for your participation. You have all been most helpful." His eyes twitched to me once more. "It's kind of sad our rivalry is finally coming to an end, isn't it?" A few seconds passed, and he shrugged. "Oh well."

Blakely pulled open the door, Mr. Dabir walked through first, and she followed. I heard the *click* of the lock before their footsteps echoed down the hall.

I let out a breath. Didn't know what to say. What to do.

I heard a grunt. Nash was picking himself off the floor. He wiped his hands on his pants. "We have to do something. Get out of here. Save them."

Branch was standing motionless, still staring at the door.

The test.

My heart fell.

Branch turned to me, stepped over, and put his arms around me. "Are you okay?"

I nodded, stunned. It was just a test, right? It meant nothing. Maybe they understood that. I looked over Branch's shoulder at Nash. He was by the door now, trying to pull it open.

It *was* just a test. Right? I swallowed.

You couldn't love two people. It was impossible. Like Mr. Dabir had said.

The air down here was so thin. I released my arms from around Branch's neck, stepped back into the wall, and sank to the floor. Tried to breathe. Branch lowered himself beside me.

Nash took a step back, sucked in a breath, and slammed into the door. It didn't move. He backed up, braced himself to do it again.

"You're just going to hurt yourself." Branch was watching Nash now, amused.

Nash turned, breathless from colliding with the door. "Okay. What's the plan, then?"

I turned to Branch, waited for his answer. Branch didn't say anything for a long moment, and then he opened his lips, his eyes still on Nash. "We wait."

Nash let out a breath, stared back at Branch in disbelief. "For what? Arsen to come in and kill us?" He lunged at the door again.

Branch took my hand in his, and I turned, met eyes with him. "Branch, we need to get out of here. Arsen will be here any second. We need to save everyone."

"Laney's right." Nash banged on the door with his hands, the sound too loud in the small room. "Help us! Anyone— help us. Please!"

"The people with gray eyes are not going to help you, Nash."

"At least I'm trying!" Nash stopped banging, turned around suddenly. "Are you seriously just going to give up?"

I tried to swallow, but it caught in my throat.

Branch kept his lips closed. Nash's eyes dropped to our hands, saw Branch's fingers threaded through mine. His breathing slowed, and his eyes softened. He looked back up, and I could see them—deep brown, like the canyon walls.

"This is about the test, isn't it?" Silence. Nash didn't move. "I'm not going to fight you, Branch. She chose you." He nodded slowly. "I respect that."

I could feel Branch's hand tighten slightly in mine, and Nash turned to the door again. "I'm just sorry we got into this situation in the first place. I can't understand how Mr. Dabir knew you were here. It's like someone told him or something."

Nash ran his hands along the surface of the door, looking for cracks or weak spots. Branch shifted next to me.

"Emily told him."

Nash froze. My throat tightened.

"What? Why would she—?"

"Because I told her to." A small smile formed on Branch's lips, and something cold ran over my skin. I released my fingers.

Nash turned, his eyes wide, confused. He opened his mouth, but then the footsteps came from the end of the hall, soft at first. Every step grew louder, and I sat there, my back pressed against the wall, wondering if the last moments of my life would be this—two boys, a cell, and more confusion than I thought was possible to feel.

The footsteps stopped right outside the door.

I was paralyzed.

Click.

Nash stood against the wall, his arms braced, ready to attack.

The person stepped in from the shadows of the hallway— short red hair, emerald-green eyes.

"Anyone up for one more Collaboration before we leave this place forever?" Theodore grinned.

37

THEN

I take a step back. Press my back against the wall.

The world is screaming and crying and running and fighting, but I'm not.

I can't.

I watch her run across the grassless field, watch her pull her hair up on her head as she runs. I watch her reach the nearest house and I watch her disappear behind it.

She doesn't look back.

I almost suffocated once, in my pond, the water so cold and so heavy I couldn't even scream. I watched a man die once. Just watched. I've been beaten and bullied and used and broken and betrayed.

But I've never been paralyzed.

When I was a kid, I pretended once. I lay on the yard outside my house, waiting for my mother to come home. I thought it was the greatest trick in the world—I was going to scare her into thinking I was hurt, that I couldn't move. But as I waited, as I watched birds flying in the air and cars moving down the street and trees swaying back and forth with the wind, I placed my hands on the grass and stood. I couldn't stand the fact that even though I wasn't moving, the rest of the world still was. It just went on without me, like I was nothing.

Like this. Like now.

Except then, there was no pain.

I try to breathe, but my breath gets caught in my throat. The black clouds are above my head now, heavy and growing. The alarm fades to a dull pulsing in my mind, and the corners of the world blur slightly.

She left. She just left.

Green. All I see now is green. My mother's voice fills my thoughts, screams at me.

Every step has a purpose, Jonathan Dabir.

I kissed her. I kissed her, and she left.

Every step has a purpose. Do not sway from your path. Otherwise, you will end up—

"—you hear me? Run!"

I heave in a breath, and the world rushes at me in browns and grays and blacks.

I blink. A man is sprinting across the ground in between the wall and the houses. He's yelling at me, a hundred yards still between us. He looks frantic, like he's trying to get somewhere. The wall? I watch him, confused.

Others suddenly appear from behind a house—three, four, five. More keep coming, and they're dirty, with torn clothes and wild hair. I swallow.

The man isn't trying to get *to* something. He's trying to get away.

The world is suddenly sharp pieces and jagged edges thrown together into one. The people with black eyes, they're here. They're real. And they're coming right at me.

I push myself off the wall, run as fast as I know how. I swallow down the pain, try to focus on what's in front of me, what's real. But where do I go?

I see two of the men break from the group and run after me, and I clutch the pack on my back tighter, run even faster.

Direction number two—what was it? I sift through my thoughts frantically, my mind all but taken by the pain of what happened.

Go to— Find the— *What was it?* I shake my head, frustrated. Think, Jonathan Dabir. Just think!

The men are gaining on me slightly, and I wonder how that's possible when I've been running for months and they probably just started today.

I reach the closest house, run past the crumbling walls and into a neighborhood. I stop, heaving, fear rushing through my veins like blood.

I can't do this right now.

I whirl around, looking for somewhere to hide. I just need to gather my thoughts. I just need to bury this pain. And then I'll run, and I won't stop until I get there.

Something yellow catches my eye, and I freeze. A field spreads out behind a house to my left, filled with hundreds of sunflowers, their heads bobbing a few feet from the ground. For a second I think of her hair, but I can't. I push away the thought, and I run.

When I reach the edge of the flowers, I keep running. I run until I'm a dozen feet in, two dozen. I look back, sucking in breaths, and I see the men with black eyes rounding the wall of the house, squinting their eyes to see where I went. I dive in the flowers, lie on my stomach, push my fingers into the dirt. I don't move. Everything I have ever learned about silence has come to this moment.

I wait. Ten seconds. Twenty seconds. The stems of the flowers sway beside me, their large heads like a canopy above me, and for a moment, I hear nothing. No screaming, no houses crumbling to the ground. Forty-five seconds. Maybe they're gone.

The pain pulses through me again, and I shake my head. Empty. I've never felt so empty. I don't know what this pain is, but it squeezes my lungs over and over again, leaves me breathless. What did you do to me, Hope?

No.

What did I do to myself?

I was stupid. I should never have abandoned my knowledge, should never have allowed that crazy feeling in my mind. It twists my thoughts, pulls them until I can't think anymore. And I need to think. Right now, I need to think more than anything.

I focus back on the dirt beneath me, on the flowers. Two minutes. It's been two minutes of silence.

I start to lift my head, to push myself up, but then a sound, soft, reaches my ears. It's a woman. I freeze, listen again. She's saying a single word, saying it frantically. But what is it?

The wind pauses for a moment, and I hear it, loud and clear.

Laney.

I don't know what that is. Some code? Are they after me again?

I lift my head slowly, level with the bobbing heads, and I see the woman. She has brown hair that falls over her shoulders, and her eyes are wide. She doesn't see me. And she doesn't look crazy. She continues to call out the word, continues to sift through the flowers. She's looking for something, I can tell.

I move my eyes from the flowers back to her, and heat rushes through me. The men with black eyes round the corner of the house and their eyes fall on the woman. How did they find me?

I panic. I should call out to her. I should tell her they're behind her.

The woman keeps calling out that word, and I see the mouths of the men twist, see the darkness in their eyes.

My breath catches in my throat. Scars. Dozens of them, scratched into the cheeks and foreheads of the men with black eyes. Who are these people? What happened to them?

One of the men lifts a gun, and my eyes snap back to the woman.

"Wait—!"

Bang.

The woman blinks once, twice. Her eyes widen, she clutches her chest. And then she falls, her hair catching in the wind as she does, then settling on her lifeless body in the flowers.

A scream splits through the air, and I whirl around, my heart pounding.

A girl, just a dozen feet behind me, in the flowers. The petals reach just above her head—she can't be more than five years old. And the pieces suddenly come together like glass.

That woman was her mother. And this girl—this girl must be who the woman was looking for. Laney.

It's a name.

I swallow, my throat hot, and whirl around, turn back to the men with black eyes. They're grinning now, their mouths twisted and ugly cheeks unnaturally wide. The man with his gun still raised in the air moves it slightly, points it at the girl.

A dozen thoughts rush through my mind, but it feels like my feet are rooted to the ground and my arms are lead.

I'm paralyzed.

Suddenly the house next to the field bursts in flames, white-hot, and the other man nudges the one with the gun, the smile still on his face. He picks up something, a burning piece of wood from the walls of the house, and he throws it into the field.

I hear a woman scream somewhere in the neighborhood, and the men turn, disappear behind the fire.

Dozens of flowers go up in flame before I realize what's happening. The fire licks through the field, easily catching flower after flower, the dry ground the perfect meal.

The field is on fire. I need to get out.

I start to turn, to run the other way, and then the pain pushes through me again and I gasp. When I open my eyes, I'm looking at the girl, trembling in the stems of the flowers. Tears are streaked across her face. But why? No one cries for anyone else, not even a child. I swallow. Unless she—unless she loved her mother.

Promise me. Hope's voice fills my thoughts. *Promise me you'll do whatever you can to find love again.*

I take a breath, push through the flowers between us, and stop in front of the girl.

She's smaller than I thought, her head buried in her hands,

a blue bow crooked on her brown hair. She's sobbing.

I don't know what to say. But the fire is burning, quickly. I can feel the heat on my skin. What would a child want to hear right now?

"Everything is going to be okay." I say the words calmly, swallow down the lie. "Shhh. Everything is going to be okay."

The girl stops crying. She looks up at me, and she doesn't seem surprised that I'm there. Did she see me, in the flowers?

She wipes a tear from her face, doesn't move for a moment. A small, yellow flower is clutched in her fingertips.

I look at the fire, then back at her.

She takes a deep, shaky breath. And she nods.

Okay. I breathe in, can't believe this is happing. Don't know what I'm doing.

And there, in the field, in front of the girl, they come back to me suddenly. The directions to the Dome. I blink, ordering my thoughts, mapping it out in my head quickly.

We need to go, *now*.

I run out of the flowers and I hear the soft padding of feet as the girl follows.

The next few minutes are a blur as we run past buildings crushed into the ground, flowers and trees heaped into burning mounds on the side of the road, and people, screaming, with arms in front of their faces and children cowering behind them. Shrieks of laughter ring from the shadows, creating a disturbing harmony to it all.

I'm a dozen feet ahead of the girl when I realize her footsteps have stopped. She's standing in the middle of the road, her eyes on a barred window in a house to our right. The window is empty.

The girl turns to me again suddenly, runs to catch up. But in that moment, I see something on her face that makes me pause. It's small, her lips barely turned up.

She's smiling.

I shake my head, push away the chill that runs down my spine. And we run, the boy who gave up everything he ever knew for love, only to be broken apart. And the girl who smiled during the end of the world.

38

NOW

In a single moment, the world seemed to come together again in grays and blacks and reds.

"Theodore!" Something rushed into my chest, and it took everything in me not to cry.

Still grinning, he stepped into the room, and I pulled him into a hug.

"We missed you so much, Laney!" He pulled away, looked at me. He seemed older, somehow. Wiser. "Are you okay? Did he hurt you?"

I shook my head. Just seeing his face, seeing Theodore, made it okay—he was everything that was innocent and good in this world.

"How are you here?" I choked out the words, overcome with an emotion I couldn't explain.

Theodore looked at Branch. "It's all part of the plan."

Branch stood. "Did it work?"

"Yes, we got them!" Theodore nodded, breathless. "You were the perfect distraction."

Distraction. I whirled around. "So you told Emily to tell Mr. Dabir you were here because—"

Branch smiled. "Because I knew it would gain his *full* attention, at least for a little while."

Theodore smiled too. His eyes fell on Nash in the corner, and his smile faltered.

Branch followed his gaze. "He's okay, Theodore." He met eyes with Nash. "He's on our side."

Theodore nodded, and his smile grew again. He stepped forward and threw his arms around Nash. "Sorry, I just had to make sure."

Nash chuckled. "It's good to see you, Theodore."

Theodore pulled away, his eyes still on Nash, a solemn look on his face. "Thanks for keeping her safe."

Nash's gaze moved slowly from Theodore to me.

"I hate to break up the reunion." Branch stood there, that crooked smile on his face. "But we don't have much time."

Theodore nodded again, like he suddenly remembered what he was here for. "Right. Follow me, please." He gestured to the door, so sure of himself, so determined, and I couldn't help but smile.

Nash followed Theodore into the hallway, and I fell into step beside Branch.

"What's going on? We need to get everyone out of here, Branch. We should be saving them first."

Branch took my hand in his and looked at me, his eyes brighter than I had ever seen them. "We did, Laney. While Mr. Dabir was in the room with us, Gavin, Dalia, Alese, and Emily let everyone free. They saved everyone who wanted to be saved."

I stopped. "What?"

Branch stopped too, took both my hands in his. "All the gray-eyed people are up there in the world with Emily right now. Like Theodore said—we were the perfect distraction."

I felt like my breath was pulled from my chest. It couldn't be true. Everyone was—free? Up there, in the world?

"Then what are we doing down here?" My words came quickly, and I tried to make sense of them.

Branch's smile, the brightness of his eyes, faded slightly. "We have one more order of business to take care of before we join them."

I looked at him, waited for more. He looked down the hall—empty now, Theodore and Nash gone.

"We don't have much time. You said you trusted me. Right?"

I hesitated. Nodded.

My fingers still in his, Branch turned and led me down the hall quickly, deeper into the Dome, until we turned in front of the sets of double doors that I knew like the back of my hand.

The room for Collaboration.

When we pushed through the doors, the first thing I saw was three people standing with their backs to me, dozens of empty chairs spread out in front of them.

Alese turned first.

I let go of Branch's hand and broke into a run, and we swept each other up into a hug.

"Laney, we did it! We got as many people out as we could. They were so scared, so hurt from everything Mr. Dabir had done to them—most of them came with us, no hesitation at all. They just wanted out." Alese's eyes were as brown as ever, and I could hear the emotion in her voice—deep, thick emotion. She hugged me tighter. "Are you okay? I can't believe Mr. Dabir did that to you. We knew it couldn't be true. That you would never betray us."

I smiled, her words coming so fast, so apologetic.

"I'm okay." I looked into her eyes, nodded. "I'm so glad you guys are okay too."

Relief fell across her face, and she pulled me in again. After a few seconds, I felt someone wrap their arms around me from behind, and I turned as much as I could, caught in the middle of a hug.

"It has been *way* too long since we've had one of these." Dalia's voice. I laughed and pulled her in too.

"Don't forget me!" Theodore walked up and threw his arms around us all.

Something was bubbling up inside me like oxygen, like air. There were so many feelings running through me, and it made my head light. They were okay. We were all okay.

"Sorry, guys, but we don't have much time."

I looked up. Gavin was watching us, and his eyes met mine. He looked different—tan, like he spent every day under the sun. He mouthed, *Are you okay?* and I nodded, smiled. He nodded back, some deep emotion filling his eyes too. I stepped back from Alese and Dalia, their hands in mine, and Gavin took a breath, looked behind me.

"Branch. It's all you."

I turned, saw Branch looking at something in the middle of the room. And then a voice stabbed the air, one that was all too familiar.

"*Finally*. I can't stand to watch a second more of this."

I whirled around, my hands clenching into fists involuntarily.

Mr. Dabir was here.

He sat smugly on one of the chairs on the stage, his hands and feet tied tightly together with rope. Arsen was next to him, tied up too. He looked less smug, though. I could see that he was trying to hide it, but there was fear in his eyes.

I felt a hand on my shoulder, saw Gavin next to me.

"It's okay. We've been preparing for this."

I swallowed back the heat, swallowed back the sleepless nights and the endless tricks and games, swallowed back the constant darkness and the pain of everything Mr. Dabir had done to me. His eyes fell on me, and he shrugged.

"Mr. Dabir. Arsen." Branch walked up to the front of the chairs slowly. "We're going to hold one last Collaboration before we all leave this place forever. But we're going to switch it up." He stopped next to the very first row of empty chairs.

Mr. Dabir raised his eyebrows dramatically, but Arsen just stared straight ahead, at Branch.

"Instead of us voting, like Collaboration is normally done, you two will have the only votes." Branch's voice was soft, but firm. "Your answer has to be unanimous, or neither of you wins. And your choice is this." Branch paused. "You can come with us, leave this Dome forever, and we give you a second chance. Or you can stay down here and die."

Silence. Something cold washed over me, and I looked at Nash. He looked back at me, and I fought back the urge to walk over to him, take his hand.

Branch looked at a watch on his wrist. "You have thirty seconds."

Arsen shifted, and I realized his face had never looked so pale. "Come—come with you. We'll take the second chance."

He was shaking, I could see it from here. Something in Arsen had finally broken.

"Speak for yourself." Mr. Dabir's voice was loud, confident. "I'm staying here."

Arsen breathed in deeply, looked sideways at Mr. Dabir from his chair. "But—didn't you hear him? You'll die if you stay here."

Mr. Dabir didn't move. "How many times must I say this? *I'm. Staying. Here.*"

"That's not how it works." Branch broke in, his voice calm. "You've been working together since the start— plotting, torturing, lying. You framed Laney for something she didn't do and locked her down here for weeks. No. It's both of you, or neither of you. Your vote has to be unanimous. Five seconds."

Arsen looked frantically at Branch, then back at Mr. Dabir. "Please—I don't want to die! Tell them we'll go with them!" He looked at Branch, and he was heaving now, thick breaths. "We'll go with you!"

Annoyance flashed across Mr. Dabir's face, and before I knew what was happening, he pulled his hands free from the rope, reached over to the chair beside him, and grabbed Arsen's neck.

The world was still moving, but I couldn't. I was paralyzed.

Dalia gasped, and I heard Alese scream, "Branch!"

The touch on my shoulder disappeared as Gavin sprinted to the stage just as Branch must have realized what happened. Arsen was choking, gasping for air, and I felt a strange warmth as a hand grabbed my own.

249

Branch reached for Mr. Dabir's arm, tried to pull it free, but Mr. Dabir was too strong. Mr. Dabir lunged out of the way, the ropes on his ankles straining, and climbed on top of Arsen, their heads inches apart as he clutched his neck.

Arsen screamed, lunged at Mr. Dabir's side with the only thing that wasn't tied up—his mouth. He dug his teeth into Mr. Dabir's skin and the yell that escaped Mr. Dabir's mouth made the world freeze for a moment. But it only made Mr. Dabir more upset.

He pushed harder, slammed Arsen's head back against the chair, forward, back again. Arsen gasped, and I could see his eyes from where I stood—so wide they looked white. Gavin jumped on Mr. Dabir, but he pushed him to the ground.

Arsen was slowing now, and his hand dropped to his side like lead. He tried to shake his head, but Mr. Dabir wouldn't move. Didn't move.

Then everything was silent.

I clutched the hand tightly, frozen. Tried to look away, at anything but Arsen's lifeless eyes and pale face. I turned, saw Nash standing next to me, his face white. I clutched his hand tighter.

Gavin was lying on the ground next to the chair, staring up at them in disbelief. Branch was standing at the edge of the stage, his back to me.

Mr. Dabir pushed himself off Arsen's lap, settled back into his chair. He looked up at all of us and smiled. "Decision made. I'm staying."

No one moved. Finally, Branch spoke, his voice shaking. "We're done with you."

He turned and started walking up the aisle, and his eyes were darker than I had ever seen them.

Branch walked past us, to the door. Gavin stood up, brushed his hands on his pants, and after one more look at Arsen's lifeless body, followed. Alese looked at me. There were tears in her eyes. Then she, Dalia, Gavin, and Theodore followed too.

Something crossed my mind then, suddenly, and I looked

back at the man who had just killed Arsen. I couldn't leave without knowing. Couldn't let this monster get away with everything and give nothing in return.

"Wait." I took a breath, pushed the word out of my throat. I saw the others turn, saw Nash look at me from the corner of my eye. "Who was the girl in the photograph?"

Mr. Dabir froze in his chair, his smile turning unnatural until it disappeared from his face. He blinked, and for a moment it looked like the air was kicked from his chest.

"I was right, Laney." Mr. Dabir breathed in slowly, straightened in his chair. "And to think, all those years ago, I brought you down here because I thought a child could find love again." He chuckled. "I was crazy then. Not thinking straight. But I was right."

I blinked. He was feeding me things again, ridiculous things, like he always did. But I was done falling for his games.

"Who was she?" I heard my voice, loud and strong, and it didn't sound like me—the girl who lived underground in darkness. The girl who had to be saved.

Mr. Dabir's mouth closed, his eyes on mine.

"Laney, we need to go." Branch's voice, but I shook my head. Waited.

Mr. Dabir watched me for a second longer. He swallowed. "Her name was...Hope."

I thought I saw something in his eyes then—a flicker of emotion, a touch of sadness. But it was the darkness, the shadows. It was the torches burning slowly on the walls. He wasn't capable of feeling.

I looked at him one last time, then I turned to the others, ready to get out of this Dome forever. But something wasn't right. I blinked. Water was trickling under the doors, spilling into the room. It reached Branch first, soaked his shoes, and he looked down.

"No. It's too soon." He looked at his watch, and when he looked up, his eyes were wide with alarm.

Gavin's eyes were on the water too now, and he took

Dalia's hand in his. "We need to get out of here. *Right now.*"

"Branch?" I could feel panic rising in my chest. "What's happening?"

Branch flung open the doors and looked back at me with an urgency I had never seen before. "The Dome." He yelled the words as Dalia, Gavin, and Alese ran through. "It's flooding!"

39

THEN

I don't know what I imagined the Dome to be.

Something huge, with fortified walls and an impenetrable weapons system built into the side of a mountain. Something obvious, and terrifying, and visible.

I look down at the piece of paper again, pulling in breaths, and wipe the dirt from my hands.

The last direction is there, as clear as day: *You will see the entrance to the Dome in the canyon.* I look up.

There's an opening in the far canyon wall.

A large, gray, square-shaped opening.

That's it?

The little girl next to me—Laney—is breathing hard, and she pushes her hair behind her head and looks up at me. I nod. She looks at me for a second longer, and it makes me uncomfortable. I turn and head into the canyon, knowing she'll follow. It's empty here, but not surprisingly. We ran through fields, over hills, across valleys. There are no towns near here. No men with black eyes for miles.

Smart, to put a hidden survival Dome in the middle of nowhere. Not smart, to forget to bring water in my pack.

When we reach the opening, I stop. It's black inside, like the door to another world. But this has to be it—the directions wouldn't lie. And it's open.

That means we made it.

We step inside, and it's immediately ten degrees cooler. The girl hesitates, looks back at the sunlight, the canyon walls.

But she sees me step in, so she steps in too.

We walk down a long staircase that winds deeper into the ground, and my eyes adjust slowly to the pulsing of a few hundred torches on the walls.

Goose bumps prick my skin.

This is it. This is what I've been waiting for.

After the stairs are hallways, dozens of them. We keep walking, and I wonder where we're going, but I don't stop. We pass a furnace on our left, its fire orange behind a glass cover, but we keep walking. It's completely silent in here. There is no wind, no rustling of leaves in trees, no sound of cars or water or air. There are only our footsteps echoing on the cold gray walls.

Where is everyone?

Hope flashes across my mind, but I push it back. I push her back. Not here, not now.

A set of doors stands firm at the end of the hallways, and I can't help but feel relieved. Finally. I step up to it, push it open. I blink against the darkness, the shadows. And I see them. Dozens of them, people standing and sitting in this huge room with stone walls. I stare, wondering how the other leaders managed to bring so many people here safely.

The little girl next to me lets out a breath. She's still holding the flower, after everything, clutching it like it's the last thing she has. And I almost feel bad for her. But not now. Not here.

I need to find him.

"This will be your home now." I turn to the girl, but she doesn't look up. She's staring at the people in the room. "You're safe here. Until it's done."

This time, I believe every word I say.

I leave the girl standing on the side of the room and walk into the people, look at the faces. I pass dozens of them, and most don't even look at me. No. No. No again. None of the leaders, actually. I start to think even Pimples might not have made it.

A door behind me opens and shuts as another person files into the room, and in the space between the hallway and the open door, I see him.

Pimples.

I would recognize that face anywhere. The man who framed me for murder. The man who made others betray me. The man who tried to steal the Dome from me.

Heat washes over my neck, and I push through the doors, whirl around.

Pimples is walking to the end of the hallway, but he turns around, blinks.

"How in the world did you—?"

"Make it to my Dome?" I cut in, can feel the anger rising in my chest suddenly, like fire. "Because it *is* mine, you know."

Pimples falls silent, looks at me. His face slowly turns from pale to paler. I notice he has scrapes on his arms, tears in his shirt. He must have lost his gun out there, in the fight, otherwise he would have pulled it on me by now. I can feel my lips turning up slightly at the corners—the closest I've ever been to smiling.

Pimples takes a step back. "We can lead together. I'll tell the other leaders that you and I—"

A laugh escapes my lips, hot and short. "There is no you and I."

I don't know how to explain it, this burning inside my chest. But it builds by the second, adds on layer after layer of anger and annoyance and disgust. And I let it.

I take a step toward him, then another. Hope is gone. My life in the world is gone. This Dome is the only thing I have left.

Pimples's face twists and his eyes almost bulge from his head. He turns frantically, but he's not fast enough.

I lunge on him, take him to the ground easily, hear his head crack on the stone floor. He cries out in pain, heaving in air, trying to push me off him but not succeeding.

Small, stupid Pimples. You're nothing without a gun, are you?

"Please!" Pimples gasps, and I can hear real fear in his voice. A rush of pleasure floods my chest.

The last bit of pain pricks my mind, a dull reminder of the mistake I made when I cared for someone. I push it back, crush it, kill it. I will never make that mistake again. I will never allow myself to feel again, and I will never allow anyone else to feel either.

Love was banned for a reason—because it makes people stupid.

I wrap my fingers around Pimples's neck and push his head into the ground, over and over again. The first time he gasps, the second he tries to speak. The third time he's silent, and his eyes roll back into his head. But I keep going.

Four.

Five.

Six.

Seven.

I stop, sweat trickling down my face to his dead body. I take a breath. And then I stand, drag him through hallways until I reach the furnace. I heave him up, and I push him into it.

I feel nothing as I watch his body burn in the flames.

When the last trace of him burns to ashes, I turn. I walk down the hallway and press open the door. The other nine leaders are standing in the center of the room now, and they all look up. Scar Boy looks confused. Geena looks amazed.

But I don't care anymore. I don't care about any of them.

I walk up to them, passing dozens of silent, white-faced people as I do. When I reach them, I stop. I meet all their eyes, one by one.

"I am the leader of the Dome." I look at them calmly, like it's just a normal day in a normal world. "Does anyone want to question that?"

No one moves. Geena's eyes are so round, so nervous.

"Good."

One day I'll get them all back for betraying me. One day I'll pick new leaders in their place. One day I'll lie to them, torture them, and destroy them all.

But not yet.

Geena shifts, her eyes on the blood on my hands. "Jonathan Dabir...what happened?"

I lift my hands, shrug. But before I walk away, before I take my rightful position as leader of humanity, I turn back. "Oh, and one more thing. Don't ever call me Jonathan Dabir again. It's Mr. Dabir now."

I smile.

I turn, start to walk away. At the end of the room, the door opens and an old man walks in. His face is wrinkled, his back stooped slightly, and I swallow back disgust. We're bringing old people into the Dome now? He'll be dead in a few years, anyway. He's just taking up space.

I start to walk over to him, to tell him to leave, but then a girl steps in behind him. Blond hair, the greenest eyes I've ever seen.

Hope.

She looks up, and her eyes meet mine. A smile spreads across her face, and she starts to walk over to me, pulling her grandfather with her.

Something in me reaches for the feeling, searches for it.

But it's too late.

I almost suffocated once in my pond, the water so cold and so heavy I couldn't even scream. I watched a man die once. Just watched. I've been beaten and bullied and used and broken and betrayed.

But I've never loved. And I never will.

257

40

NOW

I didn't know what I imagined Branch's plan to be.

That they would all come in the Dome with arms up, surprise everyone, and save us all. That they would hide in the Dome until the right moment, sneak everyone out one by one until Mr. Dabir realized there was no one left. Something amazing, and daring, and foolproof.

But I never imagined this: water pouring through hallways, sloshing into rooms and lifting beds and tables off the ground. A wall of blue soaking my hair and clothes and splashing into cold stone walls. Nash's hand in mine as we ran, tore through hallways and doorways against the strong current.

I never imagined we would be racing against a flood.

They had made a dam, Branch said as we rushed out of the room. In the past few weeks, they had made a dam in the river above the canyon, and at a specific time they had all planned on, Emily was supposed to release it. They had timed everything to the second, so Mr. Dabir couldn't get away. And so no one could ever go back.

Arsen's death had distracted them, had thrown off the timing. We were supposed to be out by now. But we weren't.

The Dome was flooding, with us in it.

I splashed through the water, tried to run as fast as I could with currents pulling at me from the opposite direction. It was up to my knees now. I saw Theodore right in front of me, pushing hard against the water, and Dalia, Gavin, and Alese in front of him. Branch was leading, said he knew the quickest way out.

"You can do this, Laney." Nash was next to me, pulling me through the icy wall.

I breathed in, breathed in again. I tried to focus, tried to watch the backs in front of me. But the water was coming so fast, and we were still so far underground. Panic pricked my chest, made every nerve in my body stand up.

A desk suddenly came crashing into the hallway from the room next to me, flipped over by the rushing water. I stopped, gasped. Nash turned quickly, pushed it hard into the wall beside me.

"Keep going!"

I swallowed, tried to push back the feeling of dread. The water was so loud, so *not* silent. I saw the gray walls rush past the doors to the indents that belonged to the gray-eyed people who lived here for so long.

I walked these hallways for the first time, so many years ago. A five-year-old girl who had just lost her mother, who knew nothing about the world or the seething hate that lived inside so many people. A girl who had no idea that the search for love would be so long, so hard.

I was just a five-year-old girl who thought she was saved the moment she stepped through the Dome's door.

I bit back pain as my foot hit something that felt like stone. My eyes snapped back to reality, and I saw them: the others, going *up*.

We had reached the stairs.

I wiped the water from my face and gripped Nash's fingers as I started to climb, but I slipped backward. The water was rushing quickly here, much stronger than the hallways. It was pouring down, knee-deep, and I couldn't see where my feet were stepping. It was like a waterfall inside the Dome.

Nash pulled me up, but I couldn't tell if he was struggling

too. I looked back. The water in the hallways was halfway up the doors in the walls and rising quickly.

Every feeling in my body was filling my chest, making my lungs ache. We weren't fast enough.

Nash was looking back at me, and the pain in his eyes made me catch my breath. He just nodded. *We're going to make it. There is no other option.*

I took a breath and pushed, keeping one hand on the wall, just in case. Theodore looked back, his face red.

"We're almost there guys! Just a little farther!"

Theodore, always the optimist.

I picked one foot up after the other, shoved them through the water, bit back the pain in my legs and feet. The Dome looked so different now. The walls were black against the water, and the ceiling was the deepest gray I had ever seen.

I remembered climbing up these stairs the first time we stepped into the world after thirteen years. I was excited and terrified all at once. The stairs took too long, but not long enough.

We were going to make it. There was no other option.

I pushed, stepped up over and over again, the water reaching my thighs now. We had to be getting close. The others had to be near the top.

I didn't realize what was happening until after I slipped, plunged into the water below me. For one brief moment fear consumed me, and all I saw was black. All I heard was the pounding of something faraway, like I was in another world.

I felt a hand grab my shirt, and I broke through the surface, gasping for air.

"Go ahead of me!" Nash pushed me forward, wiped the sweat from his eyes.

I coughed up liquid and stood there for a moment, reality pulling me back in. The water was up to Nash's chest. I turned, the hallway spinning, and stepped up.

And I saw it. The doorway at the top of the stairs. I saw Theodore grab the sides of it, pull himself through into the room at the top.

I blinked back an icy spray and pushed harder, stronger. It felt like I was walking through mud, but I was almost there. Almost to the top of the stairs.

Then something happened. The water seemed to pause, take a breath. And it started to lower.

I looked back at Nash. The water behind him was to his thighs now, then his knees, in just a few seconds. The rushing of the blue seemed to have stopped, and now it was just trickling back down into the Dome. It's like it was drinking it, tipping its head back and downing it all.

The Dome was un-flooding itself.

"I don't know what's happening." Nash was looking around, as confused as I was. "Keep going."

I nodded, forced myself to turn away from the disappearing water. It barely covered my shoes now, and it was sliding down the stairs easily, calmly. I took the last few steps to the top. The water was puddles at the top of the stairs; it didn't even cover the whole floor.

Goose bumps pricked my arms. I knew I should be happy, that we didn't have to worry about drowning. But where did it all go?

I stepped into the room at the top of the stairs, and I blinked to adjust them to the sudden light—blinding, yellow. The door to the world was wide-open, and water was still rushing in, covering the floor and the shoes of Theodore, who was standing just inside. His hands were grasping one side of the open doorway, and he turned back.

"Come on, Laney! Almost there!"

Maybe I was just imagining things—like one of Mr. Dabir's games, where reality was distorted. Maybe the water wasn't receding after all. But one thing still hadn't changed: I needed to get out.

I took a breath, waded through the water that was disappearing down the stairs. I saw Theodore step though—first his body, then a shadow, then nothing, as the light from the world swallowed him.

Light. There was so much warm, invigorating, beautiful

light. I clutched the side of the door, as Theodore had. And then I pushed myself through, into the world.

The first thing I saw was the canyon—brown walls with water trickling down the sides because of the upset from the river above. It looked strange, like something that didn't belong in this world. The second thing I saw was Theodore's back walking toward a blob of peach and gray on the side of the canyon, away from the path of the water.

Alese, Gavin, and Dalia.

"Are you okay?" Branch rushed to my side, took my hand in his. I started to look up at him, to nod. But then I noticed something else, another blob of peaches and grays a few hundred feet away, standing in the mouth of the canyon.

The people. All of them. Standing out here in the open, in the color, in the world.

I saw Emily standing in front of them, her hand above her eyes, squinting into the sun. She waved. To my left, Theodore grinned and waved back.

I felt something break inside of me, felt relief and exhaustion rush into my limbs at once. It was over. It was finally over.

I turned around, wanted to see Nash's expression when he saw all of this, but the doorway was empty. I waited, the breeze making my skin tingle. The water coming down the canyon walls was barely a trickle now.

A hand grabbed the doorway, two feet stepped forward into the light. I started to smile. But Nash's face was all wrong—his mouth was a line, as straight as the canyon's walls. And his eyes were deep, pained. Like he had done something he regretted. But it wasn't his face that made me stop. It was the voice.

"Did you honestly think that after thirteen years of living here, I wouldn't make the Dome flood-proof?"

Something trickled up my chest like ice.

And I saw it—the shadow behind Nash, clothes dripping wet and eyes dark. Mr. Dabir pushed Nash slightly and walked behind him, just into the doorway. His face lit up from the sun, casting shadows in all the wrong places.

I tried to swallow, tried to blink and make the distorted reality disappear, but it didn't.

And this reality had a gun to Nash's head.

"You want to live out here in this world, fine! All of you will die!" Mr. Dabir spat the words, his eyes wild. Alese whimpered, and Branch took a step forward, only to be met with a frantically waving gun. Mr. Dabir laughed. "I don't need you anymore! I have the Dome, I have everything I need. It's mine. It has always been mine." Words were rushing from Mr. Dabir's lips, faster and louder than before. He sucked in a breath suddenly, grimaced and pressed a hand to his side. His shirt was red. Why was it red?

I blinked, looked at Mr. Dabir's hand as he pulled it away. Blood. And then it rushed back at me, like water.

The wound Arsen gave Mr. Dabir before he was killed. It was larger, pooling into Mr. Dabir's shirt slowly.

The pain was suddenly real, and it was making him delirious.

"The Dome will always have a leader. Always. It can't be over. It's not." Mr. Dabir's face twisted into a dozen expressions, his breath jagged and thick. "So you can have the people! You can have the stupid, ugly world. But you cannot—" He coughed, bent over slightly, then stood again. The world seemed to slow as his eyes met mine. Chilling. Wild. "You cannot have love."

Something filled my chest, something heavy and light and gray. The world was silent, then. So silent. Nash was watching me, shaking his head. Mr. Dabir's breathing slowed.

"You think I'm stupid? I know Nash brought you out here last night. I know he's been helping you. I can see the way you look at him. I know *everything*, Laney. Why should you get to have love when I never did?"

Every word was a blur, echoing against the door.

"The test may have said you love two people, but I know the truth." Mr. Dabir's lips twisted slightly, like he was trying to smile. "You have always loved one person more."

He paused, and I couldn't move. Couldn't speak. My feet were rooted to the ground, soaked but without a trace of water nearby.

"So here is the deal. You get to keep all of this." He pointed the gun out, at Branch, at me. At the gray-eyed people and the world. "And I get Nash."

Mr. Dabir looked at me once more, the world around me silent and frozen and bright. I could feel my head shaking, could feel my lips tremble. I started to step forward, my head pounding.

"Laney, don't." Nash's voice stopped me. He shook his head, his eyes pleading. "You're finally here. You have everything you ever wanted. Please—I just want you to be okay. I want you to be happy." He nodded then, at someone next to me. I felt a hand slide in my own. Branch.

Something felt all too familiar. A boy willing to die, a hand sliding in mine, preventing me from stopping it.

"Listen to the boy, Laney." Mr. Dabir was wheezing now, his gun trained on Nash's head. His head snapped back at me. "But because I know you won't, I'm going to make sure you can never come in here again."

Mr. Dabir stepped backward, pulling Nash inside with him. He grabbed the lever next to the door and pulled. The slab of gray stone groaned, then started to close, eating up sunlight and air. Then he slammed his gun down on it. I jumped. He pounded it, again and again, until the lever broke off and clattered to the ground.

A door that can be opened only from the inside. A door that weighed more than the strength of a thousand people. A door that would never open again with a broken lever.

"You'll survive, Laney." Mr. Dabir's voice was muffled by the room, the darkness. "We're more alike than you think."

The door was halfway closed now, and the shadows inside disappeared from sight. I whirled around, my breath short, saw Alese and Dalia and the others watching with pained expressions on their faces.

"We'll find a way to get him out, Laney." Branch's voice

came from somewhere on my right. "We'll find a way."

I saw sunlight and air and sky and bodies blur together into one big, watery blob. I saw the last bit of water drip down from the walls and pool on the edges of the canyon floor. I saw a small blob of yellow clinging to the wall a dozen feet away, and I blinked—a flower. A flower that learned to grow on a wall of stone.

And one thought filled my mind, sharp and bold and pounding: Mr. Dabir was right.

I took a breath. I felt my fingers slipping from Branch's.

And I ran.

Before, the choice had always been easy. Sunlight or darkness? Stone floors or grass? Gray ceilings or blue sky?

I heard shouts from behind me, felt my feet hit the uneven ground, watched the door to the gray world—my first world—slowly shut out the last few feet of sunlight and air.

I reached it, touched my hands to the stone.

"Laney, no!" Nash saw me through the door, his eyes round, and at that moment, so did Mr. Dabir. I saw movement, saw a rush of gray clothes and white skin.

Before, the choice had always been easy.

Sunlight or darkness? Stone floors or grass? Gray ceilings or blue sky?

The world outside the door, or love?

I pushed myself through the opening, into the Dome, the door shutting just as a gunshot scattered the silence.

41

EPILOGUE

Laney's Paper Book
Entry 1

A long time ago, eight of us were sent into the world above to search for love.

They thought it was up there—in the trees or the wind or the sky. They thought it was something that can be defined, placed in a box and tied with a string.

I'm back here now, in the Dome. Back where it all started, back where I started. I can't leave. But the darkness doesn't seem so dark anymore, the gray doesn't seem so gray.

I was offered a choice: the world outside the door, or the Dome. I chose the Dome. I chose him.

I chose love.

And the funny thing is this: That journey to the world above? It was pointless. The Dome was never loveless. We never had to journey to love, to search for it in dusty cabins and foggy hills and white pages.

Love may be yellow flowers and red lips and flushed cheeks and golden eyes. But it's also in the soundless walls, in the starless air, in the watery shadows and the space between hands.

Love may be red. But it's also gray.

We just weren't looking hard enough.

ACKNOWLEDGEMENTS
Everyone who believed that I was worth fighting for

This is my very first acknowledgements section, of this series and of my career, and because of that, these next few pages are something of a miracle to me, something I will always hold close. But to understand why, I want you to know a little bit of my story.

I wrote Loveless because of a lifelong dream I had that began when I was just five years old and my younger sister handed me a little white book with blank pages that she had chosen as a prize in her preschool class. "Use this to write your first book," she said. That day, she gave me so much more than just a book. She gave me hope. She gave me possibility. She gave me the idea that this crazy dream I had could maybe, one day, become a reality.

And it did. But in every way that I did not expect.

I wrote Loveless in two and a half months, and I loved every minute of it. I sent out queries and pitches just as quickly, and after a few months, I signed with the first publishing company that showed interest in my book. It wasn't exactly what I was hoping for, but they were interested, and I was excited and hopeful.

When that publishing company went bankrupt just a few months afterward, I was stunned. The release date of Loveless was just a few weeks away and I had already set up book signings, ordered books, contacted friends and family and newspapers and told everyone I knew. So in that moment, I was faced with a choice: give up, cancel it all. Or self-publish, and hope we could make it happen in time for the release date.

That was one of the worst and best moments of my life.

Because of hope, because of my husband, because of family and friends and unexpected strangers, we published Loveless on the very same release date. We published it despite this plan in my mind getting crushed in a single moment and not having a plan for what I was going to do next. We learned the art of self-publishing in less than a week, and Fearless and Pointless were released the same way.

I say *we* because in the bindings and pages of these three books is the hands of friends, the encouraging words of family, the lost sleep of late nights, the frustrations of trial and error, the little victories, endless cups of coffee, and invaluable, tireless support. This series wouldn't exist if so many people in my life hadn't believed that it could. It wouldn't. It's as simple as that. The Loveless series is not mine—it's everything but mine.

It's my little sister Mel's—the first to believe in me, the first to see my passion, and even to this day, comes to every book signing and cheers me on through every moment and every sentence. I based Alese on her, and though Alese is a friend to all with a contagious spark that lights up every page, she does not even scratch the surface of who Mel is.

This series is my husband's—my unbreakable support system, ever-present cheer team, my tireless encourager, and the guy who picked me up during the frustrations and in the high points, raised me even higher. The guy who stayed up late to add a final touch or ensure an order was placed or make sure a deadline was reached. The guy who was with me every step during the publishing process and eventually became my publishing company itself. And the guy who believes in me with his whole heart, even when I don't believe in myself.

It belongs to my mom and dad—who told me I could do anything, and believed those words. Who have constantly supported me, encouraged me, and in doing so placed a determination inside me that I carry with me to this day, and will for the rest of my life.

It's my dad-and-mom-in-laws'—who still carry my books in their bags, sticking out at the top, in the hopes that a passerby will see. Who ordered one hundred copies of Loveless to give to friends before they had even read it yet, because they believed in me so much. Who never fail to show their pride, and always take time to celebrate me at the same white sand beach I spent days filling pages and writing these books.

It's Leanne's—a stranger when I wrote Loveless and now one of my dearest, fiercest author friends who now goes by the name L.A. Tavares. When we met, being authors was a dream for us. She is so much of the reason I kept fighting, and I will fight alongside her for the rest of my life.

This series belongs to Ava, one of my first real and favorite fans, who sends me the sweetest and most enthusiastic emails and makes me remember why I do what I do.

It belongs to Main Street Books, the place of my very first book signing, and to all of my Minot, North Dakota friends who showed up in negative temperatures and four feet of snow, and made a line that went out the door.

It belongs to my Aunt Mary, who shares every Facebook post I write and shouts to the world every chance she gets about how proud she is, which means more to me than she will ever know.

It belongs to Jenkins Middle School and all the amazing, inspiring students who sit in the same desks I sat in and have the same crazy, possible dreams I had. It belongs to my English teacher Mr. Mandabach, and that teacher in college who said my writing is too happy—those journal entries in Fearless are for you.

It belongs to my fellow Air Force wives—friends and strong women who truly understand and have my back in ways I know a person can only hope for.

It belongs to Lana Barnes, the most dedicated freelance editor who jumped on my series, owned it, and went above and beyond in every way.

It belongs to my favorite authors—Lauren Oliver, Ally Condie, Suzanne Collins—who pulled me into stunning stories and worlds and made me want to create my own.

It belongs to my pups, Boomer and Bentley, who sat

faithfully by my side through every word, sentence, and page and kept me sane with endless kisses.

I could go on and on—this series belongs to my whole family, every friend who has cheered me on and laughed and cried with me, every store owner who gave me a chance, every person who picked up one of these books and took the time out of their busy lives to read them.

The journey for this series was everything I didn't expect, and I'm so grateful for that, because it showed me a dream I didn't know I had—a group of friends and families and strangers who gathered at my side, rallied for me, fought for me, went above and beyond for me, and showed me a love that defies odds and glues together broken pieces and publishes books.

That's why this series isn't mine. That's why I can write of a love so simple yet so powerful, a love that exists in the yellow flowers and the red lips and the flushed cheeks, but also in the gray walls, the silence, and the space between hands.

A love that exists in the good, but also in the unexpected.

And that's the love this world needs.

A line from this series that I will always hold close is, "Love is worth the fight." So I hope you, my dear reader, never stop fighting. I hope you believe you can be fearless. And I hope you know that your life is everything but pointless.

Because when people stand up, rally together, and fight for each other, when people clutch hands and hold them up high, together, anything is possible—and this world will be anything but loveless.

Marissa

www.marissahowardbooks.com

Follow me on Instagram and Facebook

[Keep an eye out—more books are coming soon!]